"Do you remember all the wicked things we used to do, Evie?" Jack murmured, his breath brushing across her neck.

"All the hours we spent naked and hot and sweaty? All the times I made you explode?"

Evie tried to control her body's responses, but they were too immediate, too strong. A shudder rippled through her, and before she could stop herself, she leaned back against him, pressed herself against him.

He stepped away, his smile cold and hateful and mocking. "You're so easy, Evie."

Then the smile disappeared, and his features settled into a mask so forbidding that it chilled her blood. The intensity of his hostility was breathtaking. Once he had loved her with that intensity. Now he hated her. She could never let herself forget that.

Jack Murphy hated her.

And he just might get her killed.

Dear Reader,

Happy New Year! And welcome to another month of great reading from Silhouette Intimate Moments, just perfect for sitting back after the hectic holidays. You'll love Marilyn Pappano's *Murphy's Law,* a MEN IN BLUE title set in New Orleans, with all that city's trademark steam. You'll remember Jack Murphy and Evie DesJardiens long after you put down this book, I promise you.

We've got some great miniseries titles this month, too. Welcome back to Carla Cassidy's Western town of MUSTANG, MONTANA in *Code Name: Cowboy.* Then pay a visit to Margaret Watson's CAMERON, UTAH in *Cowboy with a Badge.* And of course, don't forget our other titles this month. Look for *Dangerous To Love,* by Sally Tyler Hayes, a book whose title I personally find irresistible. And we've got books from a couple of our newest stars, too. Jill Shalvis checks in with *Long-Lost Mom,* and Virginia Kantra pens our FAMILIES ARE FOREVER title, *The Passion of Patrick MacNeill.*

Enjoy them all—and be sure to come back next month for more of the most exciting romantic reading around, right here in Silhouette Intimate Moments.

Yours,

Leslie J. Wainger
Executive Senior Editor

Please address questions and book requests to:
Silhouette Reader Service
U.S.: 3010 Walden Ave., P.O. Box 1325, Buffalo, NY 14269
Canadian: P.O. Box 609, Fort Erie, Ont. L2A 5X3

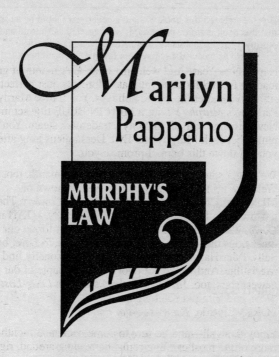

Marilyn Pappano

MURPHY'S LAW

Silhouette® INTIMATE™ MOMENTS®

Published by Silhouette Books

America's Publisher of Contemporary Romance

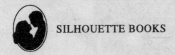 SILHOUETTE BOOKS

ISBN 0-373-07901-X

MURPHY'S LAW

MARILYN PAPPANO

After following her career navy husband around the country for sixteen years, Marilyn Pappano now makes her home high on a hill overlooking her hometown. With acreage, an orchard and the best view in the state, she's not planning on pulling out the moving boxes ever again. When not writing, she makes apple butter from their own apples (when the thieves don't get to them first), putts around the pond in the boat and tends a yard that she thinks would look better as a wildflower field, if the darn things would just grow there. You can write to Marilyn via snail mail at P.O. Box 643, Sapulpa, OK 74067-0643.

Chapter 1

As the air conditioner labored to defeat the heavy New Orleans heat, Evie DesJardien sat back in her chair, blotted the sweat from her forehead and gazed at the heavy drapes that concealed the door to her house. She wished she was back there, stripped down to T-shirt and panties, lying in the middle of her bed underneath the ceiling fan and contemplating someplace cooler than the French Quarter in July.

Instead she was stuck in the tiny back room of her two-room shop with no windows for ventilation and only two dim lamps for illumination. For comfort she wore as little as possible—a flowing print skirt that reached her ankles, a round-necked blouse that kept falling off one shoulder, a wide belt braided with the colors of the rainbow. For effect she wore jewelry, cheap and plentiful. Rings covered seven fingers. Lengths of gold chain circled her neck and caught in her loose dark hair. A matching chain was wrapped around her left ankle.

The clothes were a costume, all part of the setup, like the

dark walls, the dim lights, the massive furniture. The tourists who made up the bulk of her trade wanted the mysterious Evangelina to *look* mysterious. Her regulars didn't care how she looked. They only cared what she knew.

Right now she was dealing with tourists. She had just sent one well-satisfied customer on her way, and there were three more waiting. Her prices were high—twenty dollars for a ten-minute reading, fifty for twenty minutes more—but she had no shortage of customers because she had a reputation for being the best.

The best con artist in the business, according to the New Orleans Police Department.

There was a sound at the door leading to the front, and Evie straightened in her chair. Anna Maria—her assistant, cousin and best friend—liked to play out the moment before opening the door and escorting the next client inside. She would seat the client across the table, gesture grandly and intone, "May I present…Evangelina," and Evie would lean forward, out of the shadows and into the light. It was great drama.

Great theater.

More sounds came from the door before it was pushed open. Anna Maria's voice, taut and angry, filtered through the opening. "Wait a minute— You can't— Stop!"

Evie rose from her seat, took three steps toward the door, then stopped abruptly. The man standing in the doorway blocked the light from outside and stood out of reach of the dim illumination in the reading room, but she recognized him. She knew him from the stiffness that spread through her body. From the sudden chill that made her shiver. From the sickness that made her stomach heave. She knew him in the deepest, darkest shadows of her soul.

Jack Murphy.

She had cried over him, longed for him, damned him. She had begged to see him again, had prayed to never see him again.

Jack Murphy. Skeptic. Cop. Hated enemy. And the first—
and last—man she had ever loved.

His dark suit blended with the dark walls, and his dark
presence blended with an aura that was quickly becoming oppressive. If the room had felt small earlier, it was claustro-
phobic now. If the air had been heavy, now it had become
unbreathable. Her lungs were tight, her muscles tighter, and
the panic hovering at the edges of the room crept ever closer.

He watched her without moving for one long, paralyzing
moment, then came into the room. Behind him Anna Maria
appeared in the doorway, looking as distressed as Evie felt.
"Evie, I'm sorry. I tried to stop him. I—"

He closed the door in her face, clicked the lock into position. Still watching Evie, he picked up the glass ball that rested
in the middle of the table. It was a theatrical prop for the
tourists, a sentimental one for her. The handblown crystal
sphere had been a gift from a client of whom she had grown
fond, a woman who had taught Evie to trust herself.

She wished someone had taught her to not trust Jack, because she had, and he had nearly destroyed her.

She hadn't seen him since the night their affair had ended—
the night he had hauled her off to jail in handcuffs. He'd
grown a year older, a year harder. He'd lost a few pounds that
he hadn't needed to lose and had gained a few lines that should
have made him look older and troubled but simply added character to what was already an interesting face. He looked like
her best dreams and her worst nightmares, all rolled up in one.

Wanting very much to remove her treasured crystal sphere
from his hands but wanting even more to keep her distance,
she folded her arms across her chest and tucked her hands
underneath. "What do you want?"

After a moment, he returned the sphere to its marble rest,
slid his hands into his pockets, then looked at her. She was
grateful that, in the shadows, there wasn't much to see.
"Hello, Evie."

Such a casual opening from such an intense man. It made
the hairs on the back of her neck stand up, made the panic
turn her stomach queasy. She made no effort to duplicate his
easy greeting, made no effort to be civil or anything beyond
what she truly was: antagonistic. Hostile. Full of hate. "What
do you want, Jack?"

"To talk."

"The time for talking is long since over. If you'll excuse
me, I have clients waiting."

He showed no intention of leaving but stood there, hands
in his trouser pockets, as if his feet had taken root. "I just
need a little of your time. Please."

In the months they'd been together, Jack Murphy had never
said please except when they were in bed, when she was teasing him, making him suffer before bringing him relief. That
last night he'd said plenty, but none of those enraged words
had included please. The ones she remembered best were
bitch, liar, whore.

"I'll pay you for your time, Evie." He pulled a twenty-
dollar bill from his pocket and slapped it on the table.

She stared at the bill, remembering other talk about money
and payments, about how much she had cost him and how
little she was worth, then she ducked behind the drapes and
went into her house. She knew he would follow—felt the
change in the air the very second he stepped into the hallway—but she didn't look at him, didn't speak to him. She
turned into the kitchen, took a cold beer from the refrigerator
and drank deeply before finally gazing toward him. Not actually at him. Not where she could see anything beyond a blur.

"Twenty bucks gets you ten minutes, and the clock's already running. What do you want?"

He didn't get down to business right away, but then, that
wasn't the way he worked. He took his time, was dogged,
slow and methodical—and good. He was so damn good, and
she wasn't good enough.

He took a soda from the refrigerator and drained half before gesturing toward her with the can. "You look like a damn gypsy in that getup. Do the tourists really buy this crap?"

"It meets their expectations. Eight minutes."

He leaned back against the cabinet and crossed his ankles. He looked perfectly at home, perfectly relaxed, as if she'd never meant a damn thing to him. Maybe she hadn't. Maybe all he'd really wanted from her was sex, and when it had become complicated, he had moved on to the next willing woman. In a city like New Orleans, for a man like Jack Murphy, there was always another willing woman.

"I need your help."

She mimicked his stance against the opposite counter. There were many things she knew as hard, cold fact: life wasn't fair. Being different wasn't easy. Happiness was never guaranteed. And the hardest, coldest fact of all: Jack Murphy was a world-class nonbeliever, and what he didn't believe in most was Evie. Not her powers, not her loyalty, not her decency or her integrity and certainly not her love.

Yet here he was, standing in her kitchen, asking for her help, waiting for her to agree or walk away. There was no way on God's earth she was going to agree, but she wasn't walking away, either. Not yet. "Exactly what kind of help is it you want?"

For the first time since he'd strolled through the door, he looked less than confident. With an awkward shrug, he gave an answer he clearly didn't want to give. "Your kind. Your voodoo, hoodoo, psychic, mystic bull."

"I don't play around with voodoo," she said flatly. "Voodoo is a religion. Psychic ability is—"

"A gift," he said sarcastically.

Or a curse. "You don't believe in such gifts."

"No, I don't, but…"

She waited, made him say it again.

"I need your help, Evie."

A year ago she would have been thrilled to hear him say he needed *anything*—her powers, her time, her body. A year ago she would have danced the dance of joy if he'd even hinted at the slightest acceptance of her ability, of her self. Today it brought her no satisfaction.

"Time's up," she said flippantly as she started toward the hall. "And the answer is no."

He grabbed her arm and pulled her back. The contact was jarring, sending heat and lust and hatred exploding through her. In the space of a heartbeat, an instant of touching, her body was tingling, her blood hot, her nerve endings alive. *He* looked unaffected. "Damn it, Evie—"

Cold anger surged through her. She drew on it to keep her voice steady, to free herself from his grip, to keep the panic and heartache at bay. "There are other psychics in town. I'm sure you can find at least one willing to work with you, but I'm not the one. Now, if you'll excuse me, I have clients waiting. You can let yourself out the back. Into the alley. Where you belong."

She didn't wait to see if he followed the command, but went back the way she came. She had no doubt he would leave. If there was one thing Jack Murphy excelled at, it was leaving.

Jack stood in the kitchen a long time, listening to the ticking of a clock somewhere, feeling the faint currents left behind from Evie's passing, and wondered what the hell he was doing. He'd known better than to come here, had known Evie wouldn't be happy to see him. Hell, the last time he'd seen her, she'd been on the wrong side of a cell door, put there by him. It hadn't been a good omen for their relationship.

There were other psychics in town, as she'd pointed out, some rumored to be legit, but none supposedly as good as the great Evangelina. Hell, her reputation was such that she needed only one name. Even he hadn't learned her last name until well into their affair. They had been upstairs, naked in her bed, and he had been buried deep inside her when she'd spoken so matter-of-factly. "My name is Evangelina Des-Jardien, and if you do that one more time, I'm going to explode."

"Do what?" he had asked. "That?" And he had stroked her, and she had been true to her word. Only later, hours later, had he realized that he now knew more about her than virtually anyone else in New Orleans.

Only weeks later did he discover that he didn't know her at all. He hadn't known she lied as easily as she breathed, hadn't known that the same sweet mouth that promised him love could also betray him so completely. She had almost destroyed his career, had almost destroyed *him*.

And here he was back again.

He was a fool.

Leaving the kitchen, he walked down the broad hall to the living room where French doors looked out on a courtyard. A fountain gurgled in the center, and flowers bloomed everywhere. High brick walls enclosed the property, providing security from prying neighbors. They'd had sex a hundred times within those walls—indoors or out, daytime or night. Evie was the least inhibited person he'd ever known, and his desire for her—pure, raw, primal lust—had outstripped his own modesty every time.

He had never in his life wanted anything the way he'd wanted her. He had craved her, had felt an actual, physical hunger when she wasn't around, and sex had been only a small part of it. He had needed *her*—the woman. She had become vital to his well-being, to his very existence.

Until she betrayed him.

He wandered around the living room, through the dining room and up the stairs. There was a large, open room at the top, used by Evie as her own private art gallery. She collected local artists, people with talent and little to no following. She had even posed for one of them—six months of free psychic readings in exchange for a portrait. She'd sworn that her friendship with the artist was simply that, and Jack believed that was what she believed. But the painting—soft, hazy, erotic—had told a different story. Maybe she had felt nothing but friendship, but the portrait had been painted by a man with a case of serious, all-the-way-through-his-soul lust. Being similarly afflicted, Jack recognized it in others.

He walked past the paintings, the sculptures and the weavings, past two empty bedrooms and a yellow and green bathroom and stopped at her bedroom door.

They had met at a blues club four blocks away, had shared a dance and a few beers and had been here in bed within the hour. He had never experienced such lust, not even as a teenager. He had never been so aroused, so hot and ready, as he'd always been around Evie. Not before, not since.

The room was exactly the way he remembered it—almost as big as his entire apartment, with a twelve-foot ceiling and two walls of French doors that opened onto a balcony. The floor was wood, the walls deep silvery blue. The curtains on the doors were thin and white, hanging loose at the bottom so they fluttered in the breeze. The bedcovers were also white— lace-edged sheets, pillows, a comforter. In the wicker table on this side he would find a box of condoms. Evie was always prepared.

Too bad he couldn't say the same about himself. If he'd been prepared, maybe he could have used her the way she had used him. Maybe he could have stopped himself from falling head over heels for her. Maybe her betrayal wouldn't have damn near killed him.

The bedroom had her smell, her feel, more than any other room in the house. This was where she spent most of her time, where she worked her magic, told her lies, betrayed her lovers. It was here that she'd posed for the painting—standing in front of the cheval mirror in the corner, wearing a white gown that was little more than a drape of sheer fabric, that revealed the shape of her breasts, the narrowness of her waist, the womanly curve of her hips. She couldn't have looked more enticing or innocent. She couldn't be more deadly.

He was a fool to come here. Any halfway decent con artist could help in his investigation. He didn't have to have the best. It was simply a matter of buying someone's cooperation.

Of course, he knew from past experience that Evie could be bought, and fairly reasonably. She'd sold out last time for only five thousand dollars.

Five grand. A few months' living expenses. A luxurious vacation. A rattletrap of an old car.

The price of a man's honor. The worth of a woman's life.

He wondered if Celeste Dardanelle's death weighed on Evie's conscience. For months after watching the divers fish her body out of Lake Pontchartrain, he had dreamed of her damn near every night. He had lived her fear, heard her screams, felt her struggles and awakened every time in a cold sweat. Drinking hadn't helped. Neither had the sedatives the doc had given him.

The dreams continued to haunt him, and the need for justice continued to consume him. That was what had brought him here. Foolish or not, he needed Evie. Whether he could trust her or not, there was no one else who would do. She was the best con artist around, and he needed the best. She had a history with William MacDougal, had made it possible for him to order Celeste's death a year ago. He would never suspect her of working for a cop, especially the one she'd already betrayed. He would never suspect that she might betray *him*, not when she knew too well the consequences of crossing him.

Jack just had to make sure that she understood the consequences of crossing *him*.

He opened one French door, then another and another before stepping out on the balcony. The sun was still blazing as it slipped into its daily downhill slide, but the giant live oak in the courtyard shaded and cooled the balcony. It kept the temperatures inside tolerable for midafternoon distractions. The shadows lowered his own temperature by a few steamy degrees, but the mere sight or the wrong thought of Evie would make him burn again. In their few months together, she had crawled under his skin and into his soul. Sometimes he was afraid he would never be free of her. Sometimes he was afraid he would, and then what would keep him going? What would make this miserable life worth living if he no longer hated Evie?

Getting MacDougal. Bringing down the bastard and making him pay for all his sins, for Evie's sins, even for Jack's own sins. *That* would make life worthwhile.

He was contemplating leaving when, soft through the distance, he heard the downstairs door close, then footsteps—bare feet—on the wood and tile floors. From his position at the balcony rail, he followed Evie's progress—down the hall, a detour to check the answering machine for messages, up the stairs, slowing as she approached the room.

She was removing jewelry as she came in, pulling necklaces over her head, rings from her fingers. The half-dozen gold bangles didn't come off, though, and neither did the row of diamond studs that curved from the lobe to the top of her left ear. The chain around her ankle remained, too, though for effect rather than sentimentality. He wondered if she even remembered that he had bought it on their first full day together. He had secured it around her ankle, then made love to her—

No. He wouldn't think about that. He wouldn't remember.

She first realized that the doors were open, that the curtains were shifting in the breeze. Slowly she laid the jewelry on the dresser, took a few steps, then saw him. Some emotion flitted through her eyes—something vulnerable, gone too quickly for him to identify—then resignation underlaid with hostility settled over her features.

Even so, God help him, she was beautiful. Her hair was dark, thick, reaching down her back. Her eyes were almond shaped, giving her an exotic look, and the color was so brown that it was almost black. And her mouth... Lush, full curves, sensual, it put a man in mind of wicked, hot, powerful sex. It was a mouth made for kisses of the most intimate variety, for whispering promises of love and forever, for shattering those promises with lies and deceit.

She unfastened the wide belt, dropped it on the bed and came to stand in the nearest doorway. ''You were supposed to leave a half hour ago.''

''I didn't finish what I came to say.''

''You mean, you didn't get the answer you wanted.''

He shrugged.

She gazed past him for a time as if there were something of great interest in the branches of the live oak, then quietly asked, ''Have you suddenly developed a belief in my powers?''

Oh, he'd known from the very first instant he'd seen her that she had powers. She'd had the power to turn him inside out and upside down with no more than a look. She'd made him weak and given him strength, had brought him to his knees and made him glad to be there, had made him beg, then given him his own power. She'd had the power of life and death, and she had exercised it to her own advantage.

To Celeste Dardanelle's great disadvantage.

''Do I believe in your mumbo jumbo? No.''

''Then why are you here?''

''What I believe doesn't matter. What matters is what a woman named Irina believes.''

A look of sadness crossed Evie's face, changing her for those brief seconds from beautiful to exquisite. It was enough to spark a pain deep in his belly that didn't go away when the look did. ''You're wrong, Jack. What you believed was all that mattered. Not the truth. Not trust. Not love.''

The pain intensified, and he pressed his hand to the place.

Maybe he was getting an ulcer. It wouldn't surprise him in the least. "We both know what you love, don't we, Evie?"

"And we both know what you trust."

He trusted what he could see, what he could believe in. He trusted himself and a few—very few—of the cops he worked with. He trusted that the sun would come up tomorrow, that life in New Orleans would continue and that sons of bitches like William MacDougal eventually got what was due them.

He *didn't* trust Evie. He never would.

"Who is Irina?"

He braced his hands on the railing where he leaned. "She's the sort of person you people prey on. She came here three months ago from someplace in the Caribbean. She's into tarot cards, fortune telling, palm reading, astrology—all the scams. She's one of the faithful."

If the sarcasm in his voice on that last word bothered her— and he knew it did—she didn't let it show. Her expression was as hard as the cypress beneath his feet and impossible to read. That was one way she had changed. Before, she'd worn her emotions on the surface. He'd been able to read her with one glance.

Until she'd decided to sell the information he'd told her in confidence to William MacDougal, owner of the *Scotsman's Queen* riverboat casino and comptroller of the biggest money-laundering operation in the state. MacDougal had paid with five thousand dollars. Celeste had paid with her life. Jack had paid with the damage to his career, the threat to his sanity, the near-loss of his sobriety. And Evie… There'd been enough evidence to damn her, but never enough to charge her. She'd paid with one lousy night in jail, and then life had gone on as usual. But without him.

He wondered if she'd missed him.

"What is your interest in Irina?"

"She's a way for us to get close to her husband."

"And who is her husband?"

He moved toward her, stopping just out of reach, and answered in deliberately even tones. "William MacDougal."

Evie drew back involuntarily. An honest reaction. She didn't have too many of those. "You want to use me to get close to MacDougal. You're still trying to make a case against him."

"Yeah, but this time I'm trying to level the playing field by buying you first."

"I'm not for sale."

When she whirled around, he caught her arm and pulled her back. "Since when?"

She didn't dignify his question with an answer, nor did she try to pull away. For that reason, he released her. Not because her skin was even softer than he remembered. Not because the temptation to do more than hold her was great. Not because it had been a hell of a long time since he'd touched a woman— any woman.

She backed away a half-dozen feet, then folded her arms protectively across her chest. "If you don't leave now, I'm going to call the police."

"That'd be a change of pace, wouldn't it? The con artist requesting the cops' attention instead of hiding from it."

She went to the night table, picked up the phone there. He didn't believe she would call, but the risk, no matter how small, was one he couldn't take. He crossed the room to the hallway, then turned back. "It's not over this easily, Evie. I'll be back."

With that parting shot, he left.

Though the shop didn't open until ten o'clock, Evie had been up since six, pacing the floor, seeking a place in the house where she felt safe, where she wasn't assaulted by memories best left in the past. Finally she'd settled in the reading room, curled up in the great, thronelike chair, her hands clasped around her ankles, her chin resting on her knees. That was where Anna Maria found her when she arrived a few minutes before ten.

"Girl, you look like you haven't slept at all. Here. I think you need this more than me." Anna Maria set a cup of fast-food cappuccino on the table in front of her, then plopped a bag of beignets from the Café du Monde between them. "Have a beignet, tell Mama Anna all about it, and you'll feel better in no time."

Evie pried the lid off the coffee and sniffed. French vanilla, her favorite. "Grab a cup, and we'll share."

Her cousin waved the offer away, then broke out the beignets. "I've already had two cups of coffee today. I don't need the caffeine or the calories in that one. So tell me what has you curled up in here like you're back in the womb."

The smile that touched Evie's lips was brittle. She was quite sure that her mother's womb hadn't been nearly as hospitable as this dark, warm room. Antoinette DesJardien hadn't liked being pregnant any more than she'd liked being a mother. Being mother to a "special" child had been her greatest nightmare. Sometimes Evie believed Antoinette simply didn't like her. Other times she was convinced that her mother was afraid of her—afraid of her own daughter—because she was different.

"It's him, isn't it?"

Evie sipped the coffee and burned her tongue. Her cousin had watched from the sidelines as Evie fell in love, and she'd been there to pick up the pieces when everything fell apart. Without her, Evie couldn't have recovered from Jack. She would have lost herself and not even been able to regret it.

"I tried to stop him from coming in here yesterday, but…"

But nobody told Jack Murphy where he could or couldn't go. He did what he wanted, and damn anyone who got in his way. "It's not your fault. Don't worry about it."

"What did he want?"

She had spent most of the night trying to make sense of his

visit. Distrusting her the way he did, why in the world would he come to her for help? He didn't believe in her psychic abilities. He didn't believe in her, period. If she told him it was raining, he would have to feel the drops on his face and make sure they were falling from the sky before he would believe her. Plus, considering her peripheral involvement in his last go-round with MacDougal—her totally *innocent* involvement—and the tragic results, it didn't seem logical that the police department would want her anywhere around this time.

Absolute desperation. It was the only answer she could come up with.

Anna Maria insisted that all the unusual talents in the family were Evie's, but as accurately as if she could read minds, she asked, "Does he still blame you for that woman's death?"

"It didn't come up." But the answer was a resounding yes. It had been in his eyes when he looked at her, in the revulsion, sometimes subtle, sometimes blatant, that colored everything he'd said. This man whom she had loved, who had claimed to love her, this man who had shared her meals, her bed and her life, who had turned his back to her a hundred times, who had made himself vulnerable to her a thousand times, honestly believed that she'd played a role in his informant's death. He believed that she could sacrifice another human being's life for a few thousand dollars. He believed that she had sold him out to the bad guys, with no regret whatsoever for the damage that would be done.

How could they have gotten so intimate without Jack knowing her better than that? How could she have fallen so absolutely in love with a man who understood so little about the person she was? Not once in her life had she ever done anything to cause harm to another person, and she never could. Hell, not even to Jack himself. Not even after all the heartache he'd caused.

"So what did tall, dark and stupid want?"

Evie shrugged. "He asked me to help him on a case."

"Help him how? You mean, with the woo-woo?" Anna
Maria burst into laughter. "So Jack Murphy has seen the light
and become a believer. The end of the world must be nigh."

"He doesn't believe in anything but himself, and he never
has. One of the people in his investigation is a believer."

"And he wants you to manipulate somebody's beliefs to his
advantage. So he doesn't have to recognize that your abilities
exist, but he gets to benefit from them anyway. What did you
tell him?"

"No."

"Good."

"But he'll be back." He had promised, and she expected
as much. He would make her life miserable until he got what
he wanted, unless she found a way to get rid of him once and
for all.

There was a time when she'd believed that what he wanted
was *her*. Now the thought made her unbearably sad.

"It's almost ten." Anna Maria licked the powdered sugar
from her fingers, dusted her blouse and got to her feet. "It
might be good for business if you put some clothes on, honey.
Your clients want to see Evangelina, guide through the great
unknown, not Evie, little girl lost. Go on. I'll get ready out
front."

Reluctantly Evie returned to her bedroom, where tangled
covers reminded her of her restless night. There she dressed
in a tank top of vivid turquoise silk and another long, swirling
print skirt. She did her makeup with a heavy hand, added a
dozen pieces of jewelry and worked her hair into a chignon
at the nape of her neck. All she needed was a thick accent,
and she could pass as the best gypsy any B movie had ever
seen.

Back in the reading room, she pressed the small buzzer to
signal Anna Maria that she was ready for her first customer.
Some days they were lined up waiting when the door opened.

Other days she saw no one before noon. On those days she wandered back into the house or joined Anna Maria out front. Sometimes they sat on the stoop, and Anna Maria enticed passersby into parting with a few twenties. Sometimes they just waited.

She hoped today would be a busy day. She needed the distraction of tourists, one right after the other. She needed to keep so busy that, by the end of the day, her mental exhaustion would match her physical exhaustion. She needed to forget yesterday.

She was meditating, her breathing deep and regular, her entire being focused on a point somewhere inside her, when the door to the waiting room was flung open with enough force to bounce off the wall.

"Make him go away, Evie! I've talked, I've pleaded, I've threatened, and it does no good! I even called the police, and they said the sidewalk is public property. He can stand there if he wants. They don't even care because he is who he is and we are what we are! If we were a restaurant or an antique shop or a damned T-shirt store, you can bet they'd care, but, no, you're just a reader, and who gives a damn about that?"

All the calm Evie had worked for disappeared into thin air as she opened her eyes. It took a moment, coming from that quiet place, to bring Anna Maria into focus. Her cousin's face was flushed, her eyes distressed, and the hand she was waving to punctuate her points was trembling.

"Sit."

Anna Maria obeyed.

"Stop talking and start breathing. I'll be back." She unfolded from her chair and walked into the waiting room, closing the door behind her. Through the plate glass windows, she saw the reason for her cousin's upset: standing on the sidewalk in front of her door, badge in hand and talking earnestly to a middle-aged couple, was Jack Murphy. After a moment of his talk, the people walked on, no doubt on their way to one of her competitors down the street.

Evie stopped in the open doorway and rested one hand casually on the frame. The other was in a tight fist behind her. "You're breaking the law. As long as I'm not doing anything illegal, I have a right to conduct business."

He didn't turn to look at her. "So call a cop."

"Right. Like I could count on the New Orleans Police Department to take action against one of its own. If I could, it wouldn't be one of the most corrupt police departments in the country."

"Did you consider my request?"

"Why would I? I already told you no."

"You're going to have a lot of free time on your hands. You may as well fill it with something productive."

"I have very little free time. You'd be amazed by how good business is."

Finally he turned to face her. "I don't think I would. I've already turned away nearly a dozen potential customers."

Her jaw muscles began tightening, forcing her to consciously relax them before she could speak. "By telling them what?"

"That you're in the middle of a police investigation. That they could come back later, if they really wanted to. You know, it's funny. Most people think that means you're the target of the investigation. I don't imagine that does your reputation much good, does it?"

Evie stared at him. In the morning sun, wearing a snug T-shirt and snugger jeans, with his brown hair carelessly combed and his jaw clean shaven, he looked too handsome for his own good—or anyone else's. He looked decent, honest, like one of the good guys. He looked like someone you would trust if you were a tourist in a place like the French Quarter and he was warning you away from a practitioner of one of their more disreputable enterprises.

He looked like someone who could do her business serious harm.

"I'm going to complain to the police department, to the city, to my lawyer. I'll go to the mayor and the district attorney and the damn governor if it's necessary."

"Go ahead. Complain away. I'll wait here and make sure you aren't disturbed."

"You *can't* do this, Jack."

His hazel eyes were as cold as anything she'd ever seen. "No, legally I can't. But in the time it takes you to stop me, you will have been effectively shut down for at least a week. As an option, though, cooperate with me, and I'll go away right now."

She held his gaze for a moment, then kicked the stop that held the door open, gave it a shove and went to Anna Maria's desk. By the time she got her attorney on the phone, Jack had turned away another group of customers.

The lawyer listened with interest until she told him that it was Jack interfering with her business. First he chuckled, then, as if he felt her displeasure over the phone, he grew serious. "You know Murphy's reputation as well as I do, Evie. He's a good cop. He may cut a few corners, and his methods may be a bit unconventional, but he's honest and dedicated, and he makes damn good cases against his crooks. The department's willing to cut him a little slack because of it. What he's doing may be wrong and unfair to you, but most people—his bosses, their bosses—are going to assume, based on his previous record, that he's got a damn good reason for doing it. They're going to give him the benefit of the doubt."

"So you're saying you won't pursue this for me."

"You're the boss, Evie. You want to accuse one of New Orleans' few honest cops of harassment, I'll help you do it. But be *really* sure that's what you want. Remember, the cops already don't have a great store of goodwill for people in your line of work. If you cause trouble for one of their own..."

"No one cares that he's causing trouble for me. He can deny me the right to do business. He can make this cheap attempt at blackmail, and no one cares. But if I try to make him stop, I'm the pariah here." She heard the bitterness in her voice but didn't care. It wasn't fair. But life wasn't fair. Being different wasn't fair. Being treated the way Jack had treated her was heartachingly unfair.

"What makes you think this is blackmail?"

She told the lawyer as little as possible about Jack's offer while she watched him talk to a cabbie as if he didn't have a care in the world. When she was finished, the lawyer offered an unwelcome suggestion of his own.

"Why not cooperate with him? All he wants you to do is give this woman a few readings, get a little information from her. It's no big deal. You do it in the shop all the time, Evie. And when it's over, you'll have one of New Orleans' finest in your debt. In your line of work, that could come in handy."

"I'd rather be dead," she said flatly. That was exactly how Jack's last informant in the MacDougal case had wound up.

The lawyer gave a long-suffering sigh. "Try to work it out with Murphy, Evie. Help him out or find somebody who will, but don't drag him into court on a nothing charge like this, okay?"

When she didn't answer, the lawyer hung up. Slowly she did the same.

"Well?"

Jack was standing in the doorway, his expression a dead giveaway that he knew her phone call hadn't been encouraging. He knew he could get away with harassing her indefinitely and no one would make a serious effort to stop him. She thought of her expenses and her bank account. It had been healthy only once in her life, and that had been due to an infusion of blood money—money she hadn't earned, that she hadn't known existed until Jack confronted her with the proof. She'd sent the money to Celeste Dardanelle's family, an anonymous donation that couldn't begin to make right what had gone wrong. Nothing could ever make it right.

But sending William MacDougal to prison might be a start.

She slowly swiveled the chair to face him, then stood up, needing to be more on his level. "You know, I really hate you."

He didn't blink or react in any way. He just waited.

"I'll do it. And when we're done..." She let the words trail off, let her voice grow softer, more intimate, before finishing. "You can go straight to hell."

Chapter 2

Jack's car was parked in a red zone down the block. He climbed in, flipped up the visor that displayed his NOPD parking placard and started the engine, switching the air conditioner to high. The Mustang had a lot of years on it—like him—and was showing the effects—again, like him. The air that came from the vents was just barely cool. Muttering a curse, he shut it off and cranked the windows down.

It wasn't far to the station, though tourist traffic made it seem so. He eased the car into a parking place, then went inside and upstairs to the office space he shared with a half-dozen other detectives. All the desks were empty, and his own looked damn near sanitized. Everything had been put on hold, filed or passed around to his fellow cops for their attention. The only thing of importance that was left was the file locked in the bottom drawer. With everything he had at home, that file completed his own personal record of the life and crimes of William MacDougal and Evangelina DesJardien.

He should feel some relief that Evie had agreed to his re-

quest, but there was none. If she hadn't given in, he would
have continued to pressure her. He would have destroyed her
business beyond rebuilding, would have gotten her thrown out
on the street, would have beaten her down to the point that
yes was the only answer she could give. But she hadn't made
any of that necessary. She'd given in easily, and with only
one condition. *You can go straight to hell.*

Thanks to her, he'd been there for a year now.

After unlocking the bottom drawer, he shook out the plastic
grocery bag he carried, slid the folder between a stack of mag-
azines and put them into the bag. From the center drawer he
added a pill bottle that held the last half-dozen pain pills for
the headaches that had plagued him after Celeste's death and,
from underneath the desk, a pair of broken-down running
shoes.

Just as he picked up the stack of envelopes propped beside
the phone, the door across the room swung open and Sonny
Roberts came in, balancing a cup of coffee on top of a stack
of reports. He didn't look surprised to see Jack at his desk.
"Couldn't stay away, could you?" he asked as he shifted his
load to an uncluttered corner of his own desk. "Does the lieutenant know you're here?"

Jack shook his head. "I just came by to pick up a few
things—shoes, bills."

When he held up the stamped envelopes, Sonny's gaze
shifted to them, then dropped lower before sliding back to
Jack's face. "With your badge on?"

"Habit."

"Well, you'd better put it away and get on out of here
before the lieutenant sees you and chews your ass for disre-
garding his orders."

Jack pulled the badge from his belt and looked at it for a
long moment before sliding it into his pocket. A cop was all
he'd ever wanted to be, all he knew how to be. It wasn't an
easy job. The hours were long, the pay poor, and, with cor-

ruption running rampant, many of the good citizens of New Orleans were more fearful of the cops than they were of the crooks. But it was what he did best. It was the most important thing in the world to him and always had been.

Except for one crazy night when he'd let a pair of dark eyes and a sweet body sucker him in. He'd messed up big time, and Celeste had died for it.

If he'd been crazy that night, what was he now? Bringing Evie back into his life, giving her another chance to destroy him—that was more than crazy. It was desperate. Suicidal. He would be lucky to survive her this time.

But as long as he got MacDougal, he didn't care if he survived.

"What are your plans for the next two weeks?"

Jack opened his mouth to give an honest answer, then closed it again. Sonny was the best friend he had. They'd gone through the academy together, had come up through the ranks together. Sonny had watched his back more times than he could count, had saved his life twice that he could count. It had been Sonny who'd warned him against getting involved with Evie, Sonny who'd discovered the evidence connecting her to Celeste's murder and Sonny who'd gotten him through those first hellish weeks afterward.

Now it was Sonny he lied to, for reasons he didn't begin to understand. "Nothing much. Get caught up on my sleep—"

"Get drunk, get lucky, get a woman."

The joking comment set Jack's nerves on edge. He'd stopped drinking nearly eight months ago, when he'd finally realized that the booze was going to kill him as surely as the guilt, and he hadn't been with a woman in more than a year—a year, a month and a week, give or take a day. He hadn't gotten lucky in even longer. Not since before the night he'd approached the most beautiful woman he'd ever seen in a club and asked her to dance. That night had been the start of the worst streak of bad luck he'd ever seen. He wasn't out of it yet.

Saying nothing to Sonny, he started toward the door. The other detective didn't let him go, though. "Hey, Jack, I know you're not happy about this vacation," he began with sympathy in his voice.

Before he could go any further, Jack cut him off. "It's no problem. The lieutenant was right. I do need some time away."

"If anything happens on your cases, we'll let you know. And if you need anything…"

"Yeah, sure. Thanks." Jack left the office and the building, settling into his car again. If he needed anything… He needed a lot, starting with cancelling this vacation. Who gave a damn if he hadn't taken any time off in nearly two years? What was so special about vacations anyway? He had nowhere to go and no one to go with. He lived in a cramped apartment, so there wasn't anything to do at home to keep him busy. He didn't fish, couldn't drink, wouldn't visit his family and had no woman, not since giving them all up for Evie, damn her to hell.

His apartment was a ten-minute drive away. Located on the second floor of a run-down brick building with rusted iron railings, it looked as if it could belong in the low-income section of any city in the country. The rent was reasonable, though—only a little more than it was worth—and it was adequate for his needs. If the walls needed paint and the shag carpet belonged in the dump, what did he care? In good times, he'd only used the place for sleeping. He'd lived his life elsewhere. And in bad times, who cared about things like paint and carpet?

Sunlight streaming through the sliding door reflected off the empty glasses—four of them—on the coffee table and spotlighted the dust that was thick in the air. If he were really on vacation, maybe he'd spend a day or two cleaning up this place—wash the dishes piled in the sink, mop the floor, rent a machine and scrub a few years' living out of the ugly green carpet. If he were *really* on vacation, maybe he'd look for someplace new, someplace with half a claim to decent.

But he didn't need decent. Everything he needed was right in the next room.

The bedroom was as dark as the living room was bright. The drapes at the window were drawn tightly and stayed that way. He turned on the desk lamp, adjusted the shade and, as he did every time he entered the room, took a look around.

Most of the available wall space was covered with notes, reports, newspaper articles, photographs. There were shots of MacDougal, forty-two years old, fair-skinned with reddish blond hair, in a suit here, casual clothes at the country club there, a tuxedo over there. He had come to New Orleans in time to get in on the ground floor of riverboat gambling. He'd started up the *Scotsman's Queen,* the flashiest, most luxurious boat of them all, and he had sailed forth and prospered. He lived like a king off the *Queen's* profits—a little too kingly, some thought, and they were right. A great deal of William MacDougal's money came from enterprises of a shadier nature. A little smuggling here, a little money laundering there... His under-the-table profits by far exceeded the *Queen's* legitimate intake.

On the next wall, as far from MacDougal's photos as possible, was Celeste Dardanelle's picture. Too bad Jack hadn't been able to keep her far away from him in life. If he'd been able to protect her, the way he'd promised he would, she would still be alive today. Instead, he'd been, when all was said and done, responsible for her death.

In the picture, she looked older than twenty-five—working the streets could do that to a woman—and wary of life and the dirty tricks it had played her. She'd had dreams when she was a kid, and they hadn't included working on her back for anyone with the cash to buy her body. Unfortunately, her life *had* included a mother who didn't give a damn and a stepfather who had first forced his way into his eldest stepdaughter's bed when she was twelve. She had run away from home at sixteen and had lived on the streets until she started working them.

Jack had promised her a new start in exchange for her help—a bus ticket to Houston, job training, money to get settled. She'd started dreaming again, making plans, trying on career paths in her mind. Maybe she'd be a hair stylist or a dental hygienist, or maybe she would become a nursing assistant.

Instead she had become just one more victim of New Orleans' increasing homicide rate.

Tacked to the wall next to Celeste's picture was Evie's. He kept it not to remind him of how beautiful she was—he would never forget—but as a reminder of how weak he was. He kept it right beside Celeste's so he would never forget to hate Evie, to despise her for what she'd done. He kept it there to keep his rage alive.

In the dim light and from across the room, he couldn't make out the details of the photo. He couldn't see that her hair fell over her shoulders, that her bronzed skin seemed even darker next to her pink blouse. He couldn't see the eight diamond studs or the satisfied smile or the dark eyes. He couldn't recognize the curiously innocent, intensely sexual aura that transcended the limitations of the flat image and grabbed him anyway.

He didn't need to see. Everything about her was burned into his memory, branded into his soul. As long as he lived, he would never be free of her.

Turning his back on the photograph, he sat down at the desk and opened the file he'd brought home. Sonny and the other two detectives assigned to the MacDougal case knew he was consumed by it, but even they would be surprised if they saw this room. They'd seen such places before, usually in the homes of stalkers, usually when the person being stalked had been found dead.

Such obsession wasn't normal, and it wasn't healthy. Jack knew that. He just couldn't do anything about it. He couldn't stop himself from trying to provide Celeste with some justice, to destroy MacDougal and absolve some small part of his own guilt. It was out of his control.

Since meeting Evie, everything had been out of his control.

He emptied the file folder, sorted through its papers and photos, scanned the transcripts of wiretaps. Much of it went onto the wall, covering dirty white paint, overlapping other items. That finished, finally he turned his attention to the rest of the room.

The bed was unmade, and the sheets needed changing. Suits awaiting a trip to the dry cleaner were piled atop the dresser, and dirty laundry overflowed a basket beside the closet door. A couple months' worth of the *Times-Picayune* was stacked alongside the bed, most of them missing an article or two, and empty soda cans crowded both nightstands. The wastebasket in the corner was filled and spilling out on the floor with a collection of pizza boxes and candy bar wrappers.

The place was damn near as filthy as any he'd ever seen— and, in his line of work, he'd seen some real pigsties. When had he stopped giving a damn?

When Celeste died.

When Evie betrayed him.

When MacDougal became the only important thing in his life.

When he damn well wished he had died, too.

When Evie passed through the door into the waiting room, she found the front door locked, the Closed sign up and Anna Maria sitting at her desk counting money into neat stacks of tens and twenties. "Did we have a good day?" she asked, knowing the answer already. Once Jack had left them alone, the tourists had streamed in as if she were the only freak in town. Other than a short break for lunch, she'd worked straight through to six-thirty. Her shoulders ached from sitting so long, and she was tired, but, considering the way it'd started, the day had turned out relatively well. Jack *had* left, and she hadn't experienced one vibe of pure psychic energy all day long.

Anna Maria finished counting, then smiled. "Not bad at all. Want to get some dinner?"

"No, thanks." Evie wasn't counting on having her evening free, not after the foolish agreement she'd made with Jack. In fact, she was surprised that he hadn't returned sometime during the day, tossed her clients out and demanded that she begin working for him immediately. After all, what she was doing here wasn't important. She was just earning a living, and he truly saw no reason why she should be allowed to remain in the land of living. Lucky for her that he was, as her attorney had pointed out, one of the last honest cops in town, or she would have feared for her life the last year.

Taking a broom and dustpan from the tiny corner closet, she swept up, then dusted a soiled rag quickly over the shelves that lined two walls. To supplement her readings, the shop also offered books dealing with various paranormal phenomena and a variety of charms, potions, candles and incense— harmless on their own, but used in one way or another in the voodoo she'd told Jack she didn't play around with.

Anna Maria finished the deposit and slid the money into the zippered bank bag. "Are you meeting him tonight?" Her voice was flat, an effort to hide her disapproval, but Evie heard it anyway. Hell, she *shared* it. She just hadn't known any other way to get rid of Jack, and though she'd thought about it all day in her few free moments, she still hadn't come up with a better solution.

"I don't know. Probably." She turned off all but one light, then opened the door so her cousin could leave.

Anna Maria paused in the doorway. "Lock up behind me."

"I always do."

"Be careful."

"I always am."

"No, you're not. You trust people who don't deserve to be trusted. Because you're good and honest, you think other people are, too, but most of them aren't. You trusted Murphy once. Don't be foolish enough to do it again."

"I'll be careful. I swear."

With a grimace that was meant to be a smile, Anna Maria left, waiting on the sidewalk while Evie locked the door, returning Evie's wave with a worried nod.

Because you're good and honest... Evie appreciated the sentiment, but there were few people in the world who shared it. She'd been deceiving people every day of her life—denying her powers, then manipulating them, manipulating people, ignoring the real thing while using smoke and mirrors to simulate it. She was a fraud, a charlatan. Jack was right about that much.

She went through the reading room into the house, grateful as always for the light, the color, the airy feel of the high-ceilinged rooms. Sometimes the relief was almost overwhelming, similar, she theorized, to what a hostage must feel after being released into the light after hours in absolute darkness. This evening it was comforting. Soothing.

Until she saw Jack.

He was in the courtyard, stretched out on a padded chaise longue in the shade of the live oak. His hands were folded together on his stomach, and it looked from this distance as if he were sleeping. She didn't believe it for a second.

Ignoring him, she checked the machine for messages and found one from her mother, suggesting that they get together sometime. Antoinette and Edward DesJardien lived less than twenty miles away, in the oppressive house where Evie had grown up. Edward worked downtown on Poydras Street and

Antoinette had brunch at Brennan's in the Quarter every other week, but they saw their daughter fewer than a half-dozen times a year. They weren't a close family, and Evie had given up wishing they could be. She wasn't the daughter her parents had wanted, and their disappointment kept them from being the parents she needed. They made do with their friends, and she settled for Anna Maria.

For a long time Evie had longed for a family of her own, and for a while—a year ago—she'd believed she might get it. Jack had been noncommittal on the subject of kids—his upbringing hadn't been much better than hers—but she'd been convinced that she could change his mind once they were married.

But there'd been no marriage, and there might never be any kids.

Refusing to look outside, to acknowledge his presence, she went upstairs, removed her jewelry and scrubbed the makeup from her face. She wished she could rub away her fears and bad memories as easily. Then she could strip off her clothes, crawl into her still-unmade bed for twelve hours of badly needed sleep and awaken to a new and improved world.

But twelve hours' sleep wouldn't get rid of Jack. Not even twelve years could do that. Only giving him what he wanted could, and so she went downstairs and out the French doors, prepared to make a start on doing exactly that.

His eyes were closed when she sat down in the nearest wrought iron chair, but she knew he'd been looking earlier—watching and waiting for her. She didn't speak to him now, didn't look at him or do anything but listen to the fountain in front of her and wait. Like Jack, she had a talent for waiting.

"Nice place for relaxing."

He had forgotten how to relax over the last year, she would bet. He had too much negative energy inside him, filling him with hatred, driving him to seek vengeance. Even now, as he lay in the chaise longue with his eyes closed, his muscles were

taut with tension, with a hyperawareness of everything around
him.

"You had a busy day."

She wondered how he knew, if he had sat outside all day
and watched people come and go from her shop. She wouldn't
put it past him.

"Can we get on with this?" she asked, careless impatience
coloring her voice. "I'm tired, I'm hungry, and I've got better
things to do." Like curling up in the sanctuary of her bed and
pretending, as she'd done much of her life, that nothing could
get to her there, that nothing could hurt her.

Jack straightened enough to pick up a manila folder from
the grass and hand it across to her. Careful to get no closer
than the twelve inches of the folder, she accepted it, laid it on
her lap and opened it.

On top was a photograph, a glossy black and white of a
young woman. She was in her early twenties, slender, not just
beautiful but striking. Her skin was the color of heavily
creamed coffee, her hair shades darker, long and curly. Her
eyes were dark and pensive, her smile also pensive. She was
maybe half her husband's age, unusually self-possessed, un-
deniably sensual. She was a woman who could make a man's
blood run hot with a look, who could seduce with no more
than half a smile.

She was extraordinary.

Evie wondered if Jack had noticed that Irina MacDougal
was a stunning woman. She wondered if *his* blood ran hot
when he looked at her, if *he* could be seduced by her extraordinarily sensual beauty, then backed away from such thoughts.
There was nothing of that nature between them anymore. He
had destroyed it the night he'd slapped handcuffs on her and
accused her of murder.

She turned the photograph face down and felt it the instant
she broke contact with the woman's eyes. Or had she imagined
it? Was she nervous because Jack was here again? Or had

there truly been some slight connection with the woman in the photo?

She didn't turn it over again to double-check. Some questions were best left unanswered.

The next page contained biographical information in Jack's atrocious handwriting. Irina was twenty-four, though she looked five years younger and ten years more innocent. She had no family back in St. Thomas, where she had supported herself as a waitress before catching MacDougal's attention. With the help of his considerable fortune, the red tape had been shredded, and he had brought his bride home to New Orleans only days after meeting her.

William MacDougal in love at first sight. The idea was laughable.

"Irina's heavy into this paranormal garbage," Jack said at last. "She goes to readers, plays around with voodoo and *gris-gris,* uses psychics, astrologers, channelers. She doesn't make a move without advice from the great beyond and lives her life exactly the way her spiritual advisors tell her to."

If Irina was a true believer, then she was a desperate one, a lost soul seeking something to cling to, to have faith in. She tried a little of this, a little of that, and found no satisfaction.

"Her regular advisor since moving to New Orleans has been a guy named Alexei Romanov." He paused, stroked one finger along his jaw. "He decided to leave town this week in order to avoid another stint in our local jail."

And Jack had been the cop making that recommendation, Evie was sure. The charges might have been real but just as likely were trumped up. Not that Alexei Romanov—born Paul Davis—was any great loss to Irina or his other regulars. He was everything Jack believed Evie to be—a fraud, a scam artist who preyed on the faithful, the vulnerable, the needy. He took more than he ever gave, relying on charm and the force of his personality to carry him through. He played parlor games.

"So Irina's looking for a new guru. With your reputation and her gullibility, you can easily get the job. She'll do anything you tell her to do. She'll give you access to the estate and get you right next to her husband."

Next to William MacDougal was the last place on earth Evie wanted to be. The man was handsome, charming and a cold-blooded killer. Closing the folder, she looked at Jack. "What's happened to make you come to me now?"

His gaze wavered, then slid away, as if the water splashing in the fountain was so much more interesting to look at. She waited, waited, and after a long, awkward time, he looked at her again. "We had an informant—an accountant by the name of Greenley. He's worked for MacDougal ever since the bastard came to town. He was cooperating fully with us."

Had. Was. The past tense gave her a bad feeling in the pit of her stomach. "Until?"

Everything about him screamed that he didn't want to answer, but he offered the information anyway. "Three weeks ago, he left his office for an appointment with MacDougal at the estate, and he hasn't been seen since."

Evie's chest grew tight, making it a struggle to draw the slightest breath. When her lungs threatened to burst, when her vision grew dark around the edges, she forced in oxygen and tamped down the panic. "You want me to use Irina Mac-Dougal to get close to her husband." Her voice trembled, and her palms were damp.

"Yes." There was no hesitance or reluctance to his reply.

Celeste Dardanelle got close to William MacDougal, and she died for her efforts. The accountant got close to him, and he was probably dead, too.

"Do you understand what you're asking me to do?"

"I'm asking you to help put right what you set wrong."

"You're asking me to risk my life for your case."

He didn't deny it.

She stared across the courtyard. There had been times in

the last year when living hurt so bad that she'd wanted to die, or so she'd said, but she'd never been tempted to take that way out. She'd never been that desperate to escape. Now Jack was suggesting that she risk death for the sake of his vendetta against MacDougal. Not for justice, but for vengeance.

"If I do this, someone will die." She said the words as if they were fact—not a hunch, not fear, but cold, hard fact. Somewhere deep inside, she was sure of their truth. "Will you care if it's me?"

His face flushed a deep crimson, and he looked ashamed even as he struggled for distance. "No one has to die. I'll make sure of that."

No one had to die. But if she did… Her life meant nothing to him. She was expendable, a sacrifice worth making for the greater good.

Oh, God, she couldn't bear this.

"Will you do it?" He sounded belligerent now—defensive, because he understood the enormity of what he was asking, and hostile, because he knew that he should care and didn't.

How far she had come—from the love of his life to this.

"Will you let me refuse?"

"No."

"Then I have no choice. But if I die…" She left the warning unfinished. Her death would be on Jack's head but not on his conscience. He wouldn't waste time regretting the removal of one more lowlife from New Orleans' streets. He wouldn't mourn her passing, wouldn't be driven by grief or guilt to seek vengeance on her killers. His only regret would likely be that it hadn't happened sooner, before he'd even met her.

Obviously relieved, he swung his feet to the ground, then stood up. "We'll start tomorrow. I'll pick you up at noon. Be prepared to dazzle the gullible Mrs. MacDougal."

Evie heard his footsteps move away, heard the creak of the iron gate set in the brick wall behind her, but she sat motionless, staring at nothing. Abruptly, a chill swept over her, making her shiver and leaving a fresh wave of pain in its wake. Jack's desire to bring William MacDougal to justice had become an obsession. He would make sure no one would die, he'd said, but it was a promise without substance, and they both knew it. He hadn't been able to stop Celeste Dardanelle's death. He hadn't been able to keep the accountant safe, and he wouldn't be able to keep *her* safe. But he was determined to use her anyway. To risk her life. To damn near guarantee her death.

Now she knew just how much he hated her.

It was shortly after twelve when Jack walked into Evie's shop the next day with a bag in hand. The waiting room was empty except for her cousin, and the door to the back room was closed. He wondered if they closed for lunch around twelve or if this was just a slow time in the scam business.

Anna Maria gave him a look of pure derision, then stabbed the air in his direction with the pointed end of her metal nail file. "What do you want?"

He stopped a few feet inside the door. "Is Evie ready?"

"For what?"

"We had an appointment for noon."

She looked pointedly at the clock. "You're late."

"Yeah. So is she ready?"

"She's with a client. You'll have to wait." Her gaze narrowed. "And this time you can't barge in. The door is locked."

He glanced around the room—small, plain, with walls painted pale yellow. Ten folding chairs with padded seats and backs were lined along two walls, and inexpensive shelves filled the remaining space. He moved close enough to read the titles on the bookshelves and scowled. "I thought she didn't play around with voodoo."

"She doesn't. But some of her clients are believers. Others

are merely curious." Anna Maria's voice cooled. "I consider myself a little of both."

"So you believe in curses."

"How could I not believe? You're here, aren't you?"

He picked up one title, thumbed through it, then returned it to the shelf. "So why don't you put a curse on me to make me go away?"

"I know a few conjures," she said airily. "But your kind of trouble requires the services of a serious practitioner of the dark arts. I don't dabble in that which I haven't mastered."

Suddenly edgy, he glanced at the clock again. "How long till this client is done?"

Anna Maria responded in what was surely her show voice. "When the spirits have communicated through the great Evangelina all messages that must be delivered to the believers."

"How convenient that the spirits only communicate while the clock is ticking. Doesn't the great psychic unknown ever offer anything for free?"

"Here's a little free advice." Rising from her desk, she approached him with the same kind of fluid, comfortable-with-her-body ease that characterized Evie's movements. "A man should believe in something—his fellow human beings. His family. His friends. The woman he claims to love." She seemed to take great satisfaction in his involuntary reaction to the last. "What do you believe in, Murphy?"

"I believe in me."

She smiled cynically. "Then you're a fool."

Before she could say anything else, the door to the reading room opened, and a woman came out. She was wide-eyed, shaken and pale. She looked as if she'd gotten her money's worth and then some. Evie must put on a hell of a show. Looking neither left nor right, the woman left the shop. While Jack watched her go, Anna Maria slipped through the open door, then closed and locked it behind her.

He listened through the door, but heard nothing. Either the

two women were whispering, or the damn room was sound-proofed. After an exasperating moment, he banged on the door with his fist. "Come on, Evie. Let's get going."

The door silently swung inward, and Anna Maria, still playing her role, invited him in. "Evangelina will see you now," she said, her voice equal parts theatrics and mockery. As he walked into the room, she brushed past on her way out and closed the door once more behind her.

Jack set the bag he carried on the table and began unpacking it. Evie, looking like some kind of damned gypsy queen on her throne, watched with little interest. "Your last client didn't look too happy," he remarked as he straightened a tangle of wires. "Did the great Evangelina fail her?"

"To the contrary." Her voice was cool, low in pitch but unmistakably female. It slid across a man's senses, seeped into his soul, crawled into the shadows of his mind. It made him trust, made him want, made him believe in lies, betrayed him even as it seduced him. It was a tool of her trade, as much as the room, the clothes, the crystal ball. "Evangelina fails no one."

He motioned for her to stand up and tried not to watch as she rose with a lazy, sensual grace that held him mesmerized. "You failed me," he disagreed.

"How could I? You never believed in me, never trusted me. Your failings are your own, Jack. You can't blame them on me." After a moment, she gestured. "What is that?"

"Wire. Mike. Transmitter."

"You expect me to wear those?"

"You expect me—or the courts—to take your word for what's said today?"

He didn't require an answer. He got one anyway, hushed and the faintest bit weary. "No. I don't." Then, in that cool voice again, "Do you want to go into the house?"

He'd thought about that—the bright interior of the house, compared to the gloomy, unwelcoming confines of this room.

The house, where he could see everything, versus this room, where he couldn't see too much. Under ideal circumstances, he wouldn't be doing this at all. Some female cop would be in charge of getting her wired for sound, and all he would have to do was make sure the equipment worked.

But there was nothing ideal about these circumstances. He couldn't ask any of his female associates to help out, because then he would have to explain how he'd gotten the equipment without authorization, why he was sending in an informant on a case from which he was temporarily removed and why he was working at all when he was on vacation under threat of losing his job.

"This is fine. Pull your shirt up."

She held his gaze for one long, still moment, then looked away and slowly pulled the shirt from the waistband of her skirt, lifting it high enough to expose her midriff, stopping just short of exposing her breasts. His hands were clammy and none too steady as he moved closer, too close, and pushed the fabric even higher. It was soft, silky, the color dark—maybe crimson. Blood red.

He tore off a length of tape, positioned the microphone between her breasts and secured it. He'd never known her to wear a bra, though if she'd had any idea that he'd planned to do this, he'd bet she would've started. So much for her powers.

After guiding the wire to her waist, he tucked it underneath the elastic band of her skirt, then moved behind her to fix the transmitter in the small of her back. Her skin was soft there— soft everywhere—and for one crazy moment as he worked, he fought the urge to step closer, to slide his arms around her, to stroke her breasts, across her belly and between her thighs. She would be hot in an instant, would sizzle and steam. She would open to him, would take him, claim him.

And how would he pay this time? What part of him would she destroy?

It took more strength than he knew he possessed to step back, to wait for her to pull her shirt back into place and turn. It was unlikely that the thin wire running between her breasts would ever be noticed. His concern was the transmitter. As small and flat as it was, it was still a protrusion where her body had none. "Do you have a wide belt? Something soft? Fabric?"

Without a word, she left the room. After a moment's deep breathing, he followed in time to see her disappear up the stairs. By the time he reached her room, she was coming out of the closet, a belt in hand. It was everything he'd asked for—wide, soft, fabric. It was long enough to circle her waist twice and still dangle its beaded fringe to her knees.

She stood in front of the cheval mirror, wrapping the belt with deliberately slow motions, tying it in a neat knot, adjusting the fringe where it fell against her khaki skirt. "How is that?" she asked, keeping her back to him for inspection.

He checked the placement of the transmitter, now thoroughly concealed. "Fine." With his voice hoarse and thick, he sounded anything but.

"Where are you going to be while I'm with Mrs. Mac-Dougal?"

"Nearby."

"Near enough to be of any use if something goes wrong?"

He didn't answer. He would be on the street, on the wrong side of the fence and the armed guards. If anything went wrong while she was inside, he would be about as much help as Anna Maria downstairs. If anything went wrong, she was on her own and she would have no one to blame but herself. She was the one who had sold out to MacDougal in the first place, the one who had gotten his best chance at closing this case killed. If something happened to her now, it would be her own fault.

At least, that was what he told himself. He hadn't yet learned how to dissociate himself from the guilt when someone who trusted him suffered for it. Sonny didn't feel guilty for Celeste's death. Neither did any of the other detectives working the case with them. They'd all been sorry and angry and more determined than ever that MacDougal would pay, but none of them had blamed themselves. Only Jack.

Though he said nothing, Evie understood his message. The evidence was in the taut set of her jaw, in the dark eyes that met his in the mirror. She was afraid, and he had no assurances to offer her.

Turning away from the mirror, she went to look out one of the French doors. "What exactly am I supposed to do today?"

He remained across the room from her. "When you get to the MacDougal estate, tell the guard at the gate that you're there to see Mrs. MacDougal. Tell him that Romanov sent you. That should be enough to get you inside. Then you have to convince her that you're the best candidate for Romanov's job." His voice turned cynical. "It shouldn't be too hard. You pull the same con downstairs every day." Hell, she had even pulled it on him. She'd made him think that he was the luckiest man alive.

She'd been no gift, though, but rather a curse from which he still wasn't free.

"Once you're in there," he went on, "do whatever it is you do. Play your games. Sucker your con. Pull out all your bells and whistles."

Evie continued to stare out. "This may not work, you know. Choosing an advisor is a very personal thing. You've got to have some sort of connection, some sort of bond, or it won't work."

"You fake it all the time. Fake it with her."

"I don't—" Abruptly she broke off and closed her mouth tightly. Surely she hadn't meant to deny his remark. As if any rational person would believe that she *connected* with all those gullible fools who frequented her shop. He found it difficult to believe that she'd ever connected with anyone, except dead presidents of the folding green paper variety.

Her arms folded over her chest, she finally faced him again. "Once I've established contact with her, I can leave?"

He nodded.

"Then let's get it over with."

They left her house via a side door and a short flight of steps that ended at the driveway. He opened the iron gates while she started her car. After closing them behind her, he went to his own car, parked out front.

He stayed a few car lengths behind her until they were within a mile of MacDougal's neighborhood. Then he slowed, letting her pull ahead and out of sight.

Though still in the city limits, the area had the look and feel of country living. The houses were few, and much of the land surrounding them remained in its natural state. To ensure that his house remained surrounded, MacDougal had bought the acreage on either side, more than doubling the buffer between him and his neighbors. Jack wondered how long those acres would keep their trees and undergrowth if MacDougal knew they provided cover to the cops who were trying to bring him to justice.

As MacDougal's iron fence came into sight, Jack slowed and turned off the road. The track he followed was used on occasion by the utility companies and consisted of nothing more than two trails of beaten-down weeds. It ran only a few hundred feet into the trees, but there was adequate cover. He could see the entrance to the house and the front gate, along with a portion of the patio where Irina spent much of her time.

He shut off the engine, settled comfortably and switched on the receiver in the passenger seat. Through the fence and trees, he watched Evie's car as the brake lights flashed, then the turn signal. She came to a stop in MacDougal's driveway, and the guard approached.

"Can I help you?"

"Hi. I'm here to see Irina MacDougal."

There was no hint in her voice of the fear she'd shown earlier in her voice. He wondered which was real—the fear or the absence of it. Had she put on an act for his benefit back at the house, or was she putting on one now for the benefit of the security guard?

He didn't know.

"Do you have an appointment with Mrs. MacDougal?" the guard asked as Jack focused his binoculars on them.

"No, but I'm sure she'll want to see me. Just tell her that Evangelina is here."

"Evangelina who?"

"That's all. Just Evangelina." She smiled, confident that the power of her name would open wide the gate and sweep her inside. Judging from the appreciative look the guard wore, another smile like that—warm, womanly, sensual—might get her everything. The man stumbled over his words and his feet as he returned to the guard shack and picked up the telephone.

Only a moment later, the elaborate arched gate began its slow inward swing, and the guard returned to the car. "Mrs. MacDougal is waiting for you, ma'am. Just follow the drive."

Evie smiled again, offered thanks in a tone that suggested the man had actually done something and drove through the gate. The guard watched her go. So did Jack.

As she parked in front of the house, the door was flung open, and Irina MacDougal herself came to meet her. The younger woman was smiling, her face flushed, and she greeted Evie by grasping both of her hands in her own.

Jack smiled as he listened to Irina's softly accented words of introduction. This would be easier than he'd thought. Irina had herself a new psychic advisor, Evie had a con who could afford her scams, and Jack had a new chance at stopping MacDougal. This time he would succeed.

Or die trying.

Chapter 3

The smells of the bayou were strong in Evie's nostrils. She could hear the soft lap of water against the banks, could feel the cooling shade of close-grown trees, could see the marshy ground, the lazy insects and wild undergrowth. The image was strong enough to overwhelm, strong enough to make her forget for a moment that she was standing under the blazing afternoon sun in the middle of a parking court miles from the nearest bayou.

Fighting the panic building inside her, she freed her hands from Irina's as quickly, as politely, as possible and folded them tightly together behind her. Every protective instinct she had was screaming that this was a bad idea, to run, run for her life, but she couldn't. She was locked inside the tall iron fence, effectively trapped, and even if she could escape, Jack would force her to come back. The best she could do right now was follow his instructions and hope—pray—that she got out of here without going into hysterics.

Irina was a true believer, Jack had said, and Evie knew that for a fact now, could feel it in the tingling in her fingertips, in the sickness deep inside. She hated true believers, *hated* them and their effect on her.

She hated this place, too. It was the most beautiful house she had ever seen—Mediterranean in style, massive in size, with no expense spared in either the building or the grounds— but its aura was dark. Bad things happened here. Bad people lived here. She had enough psychic disturbances in her life. She didn't need any, couldn't deal with any, of the sort she was likely to find here.

In an effort to regain control, she forced her attention narrowly onto Irina MacDougal. The photograph in Jack's file didn't do her justice. She was so much more beautiful, so much more dazzling and sensual. Even in her exuberance, she was the most graceful and delicate creature Evie had ever seen. She made Evie feel huge, though she was only an inch or two taller, made her feel clumsy, though she hadn't yet stumbled.

She felt as if she were in the presence of someone deserving of awe.

Irina treated her much the same way. "I've heard so much about you," she said softly, shyly. "Since coming to New Orleans, I've wanted to meet with you, but Alexei wouldn't have approved."

Romanov wouldn't have known, unless Irina had chosen to tell him. Of course, convincing his clients that he knew all and saw all was part of his game—probably the better part.

"But he's gone now," Irina continued as she led the way to the house. "His own advisor told him that it was time to move on, that his talents were needed elsewhere."

Evie wondered how Jack liked being referred to as spiritual advisor to a spiritual fraud. No doubt he was quite proud of what he'd accomplished in getting rid of Romanov. When all was said and done, how proud would he be of what he was doing to her? Whatever the outcome—whether she survived this physically or emotionally, whether she lived or died—she didn't think he would care.

A waiting servant opened the glass doors as they approached. Evie hesitated on the first step and again on the second. The house's cold, dark nature chased away the heat of the day and raised goose bumps on her arms. How could Irina live in this place and not feel its danger? How could she be unaffected by its aura?

Perhaps she simply wasn't attuned to it. There were as many variations on psychic ability as there were people on earth, as many facets to the simple act of believing as stars in the galaxies. Perhaps Irina's sensitivities were directed elsewhere or her spirit was strong enough to pay no heed to auras.

With a deep breath, Evie forced herself to take the first step inside. Before she came here again, she would visit her friend Martine, whose specialty was fetishes, amulets and charms. Though Evie had never been convinced of their power in the past, she needed it now. She had suddenly developed a well of faith directly proportional to her well of fear.

"We'll go outside. Bessie, bring us drinks, please," Irina said. She led, and Evie followed, dimly aware of tile floors, large rooms, exquisite furnishings and art. As soon as they stepped through a glass door onto a flagstone terrace, she blew out her breath, then filled her lungs with fresh, clean air. Immediately the chill began to disappear. So did the sense of menace.

"I hope you don't mind the heat. I'm used to it myself, and frankly…" Irina leaned forward as if offering a confidence. "I like it much better out here. The house is so…" She finished with a shrug.

"I don't mind at all," Evie said hastily. "This is lovely." And it was. The terrace extended the length of the house at various levels. This one, the highest, held tables shaded from the sun by oversize umbrellas. The next surrounded and bridged a huge pool, landscaped with waterfalls, boulders and lush plantings, and the lowest level held more tables.

"Shall we sit by the pool?"

Evie thought of the microphone and the waterfalls, gave an apologetic shake of her head and gestured to the nearest table. "Can we sit here?"

Once they were settled and Bessie had served fresh lemonade, Irina hesitantly spoke. "Can I ask you a question?"

Evie nodded.

"Why are you here?"

"I heard about Alexei leaving town."

"And you thought I might need a new advisor."

Evie studied her before giving the best answer she could. "I thought you might need a friend. It hasn't been easy— coming here—has it?"

Irina shrugged, a languorous, fluid movement that set her long curls asway before settling again. "I didn't have any family in St. Thomas. What was there to hold me?"

"It was your home, the place that helped make you who and what you are today. It's a part of you." The way New Orleans was a part of *her*. A few times she'd thought about leaving, about making a new start in a new place and becoming a new person—not Evangelina the psychic, the reader, the freak, but Evie the secretary, the schoolteacher, the shop clerk. After all, what was there to hold her in the city? Not family. Certainly not a man. Jack would throw a party to rival Mardi Gras if she left town.

But she stayed. She always would. Whatever she was, she would be in New Orleans. It was, she sometimes thought, the better part of her.

"No matter where I go, it will always be a part of me. I will always be who and what I am." Irina smiled, a breathtaking gesture, and returned to her original topic. "Your business is good. You don't need mine."

"You're right. I don't."

"Please don't misunderstand me. I'm honored you're here. But I'm also curious."

"Aren't we all?" If people ever lost the burning desire to know the future or the past, Evie would be out of business so fast that her head would spin. "I came because I was compelled."

"By whom?"

Knowing the truth wouldn't go over well—*by a cop who wants to see your husband in prison or dead*—Evie offered her own shrug. Shifting in her chair, she indicated the house. "This is a beautiful place."

"Yes, it is."

"But it's also a very dark place. There's a bleakness here, a negative energy."

Once more, Irina leaned toward her. "You feel it, too?" At Evie's nod, she sank back with a sigh. "My husband tells me it's my overactive imagination. He says houses are inanimate piles of concrete and wood that have no heart, no soul and no energy, negative or otherwise. I've done cleansing ceremonies, but they help only a bit. What do you suggest?"

"I'll talk to my friend. She'll have some advice."

With a satisfied nod, Irina clasped her hands. Her fingers were long and delicate, the nails unpolished and neatly rounded. Her wrists were delicate, too, and encircled with bracelets, the left with silver and gold chains braided together, the right with a broad, flat gold mesh. That was the only jewelry she wore—no earrings, no necklaces and, interestingly, no wedding ring.

She studied Evie with dark eyes that saw more than they should, then made a request with the faintest of smiles. "Tell me something about myself."

Evie opted for the obvious as a start. "You're a beautiful woman."

"I am." There was no vanity in her response, but merely

an acknowledgment of fact. She had been beautiful all her life, had been told so most of it.

"You were very close to your mother."

"Most girls are."

Evie's smile was just as faint. She hadn't been close to Antoinette since the day twenty-nine years ago when the doctor had delivered her from her mother's body.

"Tell me something specific to me. Something no one else should know."

Thinking back to their meeting by the car, to the contact that had lasted too long, to the connection they'd made, Evie chose one of the secrets she'd glimpsed. "You don't love your husband. He's too old, too American, too different from the man you'd imagined spending your life with. But you're grateful to him, and you know the ways to disguise gratitude as love."

Surprise flickered across Irina's face, then disappeared. If Evie hadn't been watching for it, she would have missed it.

"You might not have had family in St. Thomas," Evie continued, "but there was someone special—a man by the name of…" The name gave her a moment's trouble. It was there—exotic, lovely, not uncommon in this city's history—but she couldn't quite grasp it. The only name in her mind—good, solid, American Steven—didn't fit the—

"Etienne," Irina supplied. "That was his given name. For the American tourists, he called himself Steve."

"He was important to you."

The pensive look she wore in Jack's photograph settled over her features. "He was. Even after he left me."

Though she concentrated, Evie couldn't divine any further information about Etienne. Had he left as in packing up and moving away, or had his leaving been the more permanent loss of death? She wasn't sure, but she thought it mattered. She could find out her own way, through a thorough psychic probe, or she could ask Jack to use his connections.

She opted for Jack.

With a sudden outrush of breath, she stood up and, once again, clasped her hands. "I have to get back to my shop, so I won't keep you any longer, Mrs. MacDougal."

Irina stood, too. "I'll walk you to your car. We can go this way and avoid the house."

As they descended the steps to the lawn, something on the far side of the fence caught Evie's attention—not an object, not movement, but a presence, a force as powerful as any she'd ever known, so familiar that she would know it in her sleep. So that was Jack's hiding place—those tall sugar pines, those bushes grown wild. Locked outside the fence and too far away to come running if she needed him.

But Jack didn't give a damn if she needed him. He didn't give a damn about anything except revenge. He sure as hell didn't give a damn about *her*.

"Are you all right?"

Irina's soft, solicitous voice broke into her bleak thoughts and sent a tiny shiver down her spine. Forcing Jack out of her mind, Evie smiled cheerily. "I'm fine. Why do you ask?"

"For a moment you looked…" She seemed to try several words in her mind before settling on one. "Disturbed."

"No, I'm fine. Really." Stopping beside the car, she pulled her keys from the small purse she wore bandolier-style before facing her hostess again. "Thank you for your time, Mrs. MacDougal."

"Will you come again?"

"That's up to you."

Irina smiled another of those million-watt, make-you-feel-honored smiles. "Then you will return. Tomorrow? For lunch? Twelve o'clock?"

"I'll be here."

Irina clapped her hands with delight, an action that should have seemed silly and juvenile but instead was simply charming. "Thank you so much. I'll look forward to it."

She certainly wouldn't, Evie thought as she climbed into the car and drove away. She would be happy if she never set foot in this part of town again, would be ecstatic if she never set foot on this property again. If only she could find some way to get Jack off her back...

She could try appealing to his innate decency, but that wouldn't work. He believed in a system of reciprocal behavior. If people treated him right, then they were treated well in return. If someone betrayed him, he made them pay. He was looking to make her pay dearly.

She could go ahead with a complaint against him, but, as he'd pointed out, that would take time that she and her bank balance couldn't afford. Besides, she knew him too well to believe that a court order would stop him from going after what he wanted.

She could try to convince him of her innocence in Celeste Dardanelle's death. But how? What evidence there was weighed in against her. All she had on her side was her love for Jack at that time and her own innate decency, neither of which he believed in.

As far as she could tell, that left her with two options—she could walk away from her house, her business and New Orleans, or she could continue to cooperate with him. Much as she hated it, it was an easy choice.

She would stay, would help him, and then, if she survived, he would be out of her life forever.

Even so, she would never forget how she had loved him, would never forget how he hated her. She would never be free of the pain or the sorrow.

She would never be free of *him.*

Jack was more than halfway back to the Quarter when he recognized Evie's car parked at the far edge of a convenience store lot. He hit the brakes, earning an obscene gesture from the woman behind him, and swung in, parking the Mustang beside her.

She was sitting behind the wheel, her head bowed, her face hidden by her hair. He circled both cars, reached through the open window to unlock the door and climbed into the passenger seat. "Why did you stop here?"

She took a couple of deep breaths before raising her head. Her face was flushed and damp with sweat, but she didn't look hot. In fact, if he touched her, he knew he would find her skin chilled. If he pried her fingers from the steering wheel, they would tremble.

"What's wrong?" He wasn't worried, not about her. Evie was like a damned cat, always landing on her feet. The things she did made other people suffer, not her. But his case—yeah, he was concerned about that. If she screwed this up, he would have to find some other angle. With one informant dead and another missing, it would be hard to go that route again, and bringing in another psychic after two had bowed out would surely make MacDougal suspicious, if not Irina.

She breathed again, heavy, loud. "Nothing's wrong."

"Then why did you stop here?"

Finally she looked at him. Her eyes seemed a shade darker than usual, a shade wearier and about fifty shades less open. He half wished for the days when he could read her so easily, but the other half of him was glad they were gone. He didn't want that kind of insight into a woman who could do the things Evie had done.

"I needed gas," she said flatly.

He glanced at the dash, where the fuel gauge indicated a tank three-quarters full. "The pumps are back there. You can probably get all of three dollars' worth in the tank."

She looked away again and made a good show of ignoring him.

No one could have said something to upset her without him hearing it. Until the moment she'd driven out the gate, he'd been listening, and after that, she'd been alone in a moving car with no means of communication.

Had some part of the conversation with Irina upset her? What hadn't been meaningless chitchat had been worse-than-meaningless mumbo jumbo. He'd listened to it all, watching them like a spectator at a tennis match, swinging the binoculars back and forth from one beautiful woman to the other.

And they *were* beautiful. Each of Jack's partners harbored his own fantasies about Irina, and he had lived his fantasies with Evie. The two of them, sitting across the table from each other, had been enough to make a nonreligious man fall down on his knees and thank God for creating such sights.

Evie alone had been enough to bring *him* to his knees more than a time or two. The last time he hadn't been sure he could get back up. Between the grief, the guilt and the betrayal, he hadn't been sure he *wanted* to get back up.

And here he was back again.

"I need to get the equipment," he said, wiping sweat from his forehead that seemed excessive for the afternoon temperatures.

"Take it now."

"Not here." He climbed out, closed the door and bent to see her through the window. "I'll meet you at the house. We'll talk there."

She gave him a long, hostile look, then backed out, narrowly missing his feet on the way. For a moment, as he'd watched Irina do, he stood where he was and watched her, then he gave the convenience store a longing look. If he had any sense, he'd go inside and buy every cold beer in the place. Then, instead of going to Evie's place, he could head home, stopping at every liquor store on the way—and he knew them all—and, at home, he could drink himself senseless. He could forget William MacDougal. Harold Greenley. Celeste Dardanelle. He could forget Evie—loving her, wanting her, losing her, hating her. He could forget all the ways she'd betrayed him, all the lies she'd told him, all the sorrow she'd caused him.

But there wasn't enough booze in the world to make him forget Evie. He had tried before, and damn near killed himself in the process.

Giving the beer display inside one last look, Jack got in his car and left.

Fifteen minutes later he parked one street over from Evie's shop. In spite of the heat, there was a fair number of tourists outside. He joined a crowd wearing matching ball caps and strolled down the street, around the corner and down the next block. When they went straight, he turned onto Evie's block and studied each person on the sidewalks, each storefront and every window. He checked the cars for any that he might have reason to know, then ducked around the corner again and went back the way he'd come.

This time he approached her place through the alley. The word was a generous description for what was really just a narrow space that ran the width of the block, separating the buildings fronting one side street from the buildings fronting the next street over. He let himself into her courtyard through the iron gate and climbed the side steps to the gallery.

She had left the door unlocked behind her. He secured it, then went looking for her. He found her in the kitchen with a tall glass making good progress on a bottle of Scotch.

He watched her drain the glass and fill it halfway from the bottle. The smell made his mouth water and his stomach heave. "Better take it easy on that stuff."

Her eyes narrowed as she focused on him. "Strange advice from a man who drinks like a fish."

"Drank," he corrected. "Not anymore."

If he were foolish enough to expect sympathy or concern from her, he would have been disappointed as hell. "What happened? You try to drink yourself into Celeste Dardanelle's grave and couldn't do it?"

The muscles in his neck tightened with anger that she could speak so easily and so callously about Celeste's death. "Actually, I would have preferred *your* grave—after putting you in it, of course."

"But you couldn't do that, either, could you?"

"I could have." He moved closer, pulled her shirt up and yanked the microphone free. She didn't even wince when the tape took skin with it. She turned around, and he yanked the transmitter loose, too, then leaned close to her ear and murmured, "But you weren't worth it, Evie. You weren't even worth killing."

He was halfway to the side door when she spoke. "I had nothing to do with that woman's death." Her voice was thick with tears and quavered with gut-deep sincerity.

He stood motionless a moment, then tucked the equipment under his arm, turned and clapped. "Very good. If I didn't know you for the liar you are, I might have actually believed you." As tears filled her eyes and her shoulders crumpled, he steeled his voice. "I'll be here at eleven tomorrow. Be ready."

He walked out the door, through the gate and to his car. Once in it, he made turns as necessary, not having any clue where he was going until he recognized the stone gates that led into the small country cemetery.

Celeste's grave was in the back row, next to her father's. The marker was cheap, with no lovely sentiments inscribed thereon—just her name, the date of birth and the date of her death. Weeds grew high around the base of the above-ground tomb, and there were no flowers, no sign that anyone had visited in the last twelve months. Her mother hadn't given a damn about her when she was alive. There was no reason to think she cared now.

He closed his eyes and tried to rub away the grit that made them ache. Unfortunately, with his eyes closed, it was too easy to see images—Celeste, young, excited, full of dreams. Lifeless and battered, her body showing the effects of twelve hours in the warm waters of Lake Pontchartrain. And Evie, in tears, immeasurably sad and defeated.

He had nothing to feel guilty for where Evie was concerned. He had looked at the evidence, had shown her the facts and given her every chance, had *begged* her, damn it, to prove them wrong, but she couldn't do it.

He hadn't wanted to believe that she was guilty. When Sonny came to him with the first evidence against her, Jack had accused him of fabricating it because he'd always thought Evie was bad news. He had been convinced that she would never hurt anyone, had sworn that she wasn't that kind of person, had known that she wouldn't betray him because she loved him.

But the evidence kept mounting, and she had offered nothing in her defense. *Nothing,* except to say, "I didn't do it." The bank lied. The phone company lied. Everyone lied except her.

And finally he'd had no choice but to believe that no one had lied.

Except her.

It had damn near killed him.

Feeling unbearably weary, he sank down in the grass and leaned against the sun-warmed brick. In the early months after Celeste's death, he'd come out here often, usually bringing a bottle, and he'd talked aloud to the woman who had trusted him, who had been eager to help him, who had died because of him. Sometimes he'd thought he was going crazy with the heartache and the guilt. Other times he'd known that he would never go crazy, because that would be too easy, and for John Dylan Murphy, life was never easy.

He didn't have a bottle this afternoon, and he had nothing to say to Celeste, and so he simply sat there. Sat there with the sun filtering through the branches of a giant live oak. Sat there and watched the Spanish moss sway to a breeze that he couldn't feel. Sat there and felt Evie's chill, heard again her anguish, saw her tears. She was so damned good. Another man would have been suckered in, the way she'd suckered him time and again in the past.

But never again. He would use her, as coldly and unforgivably as she'd used him a year ago. Then, if they both survived, he would cut her out of his life.

And if they didn't both survive? What if she died because he'd forced her back into this mess? How would he deal with the responsibility of one more death on his conscience?

He wouldn't. Because if they killed Evie, they would have to kill him, too.

It was that simple.

He remained where he was for a half hour, an hour, another hour more, before pulling himself to his feet. He was thirty-four years old and felt every day of it and then some. It was the case, he knew. When it was over, once he'd found justice, the darkness would go away. The obsession, the guilt and sorrow would all be gone, and he would once again find some sort of normalcy in his life. He would become human again.

If anything normal and human survived inside him.

He walked the few yards to his car, then drove slowly through the cemetery and back onto the highway. Back in the city, he bypassed his own neighborhood and drove into the Quarter, maneuvering through crowded streets. He pulled to the curb a few yards back from Evie's shop, his foot on the brake, and looked.

He'd thought she might have closed up for the day, but the door was propped open, and he could see a number of people inside. So much for her anguish and tears and gut-deep sincerity. She hadn't been so torn up that she couldn't go back to fleecing the tourists at twenty bucks a pop. Whatever had upset her hadn't been enough to distract her from her games and scams.

Gunning the engine, he peeled away from the curb with a squeal of tires. This time he went home, went to bed, but he didn't sleep. Sleep brought nightmares from which he couldn't escape. He simply lay on his back, staring wide-eyed at the ceiling.

And he waited.

Before the shop opened Friday morning, Evie went out for breakfast, then stopped at the small shop owned by her friend Martine. The majority of the merchandise in the shop was tourist-oriented—postcards, pralines, T-shirts and posters. Louis Armstrong CDs filled one shelf, while the Neville Brothers and Beausoleil filled another. Mardi Gras posters from years past shared wall space with ceramic and feather masks, and strings of purple, gold and green beads hung everywhere.

The interesting stuff, though, Martine's real stock in trade, was in the back room. There were oils and candles, powders, potions and lotions, along with small red cloth bags waiting to be filled with power and luck.

The room was dimly lit, its temperature increased by the candles burning on every counter, and it smelled of incense, smoke and wax. It was a room that tourists walked into and looked around wide-eyed before quickly walking out again. Occasionally they bought some item for a novelty—a voodoo doll, a love potion, a dressing or anointing oil for luck or quick money or protection from the law. Primarily, though, it was only Martine's regular customers who selected their purchases here, just as it was only Evie's regulars who got the full benefit of her psychic curse.

Martine stood behind one counter. With her black hair pulled into a ponytail and wearing shorts and a Big Easy T-shirt, she looked like a teenager, though she was several years older than Evie. She glanced up to greet her customer, then grinned when she saw it was Evie. "Ah, Madame Evangelina. You honor my humble establishment with your presence," she said, bowing low as she spoke.

"You sound like an extra in a B movie."

"The same B movie whose wardrobe department provided your clothes, I'd bet. How's tricks, Gypsy?"

"The usual."

"Interested in some good fortune oil to dress a black devil candle?"

"And what would I do with a black devil candle?"

"Burn it to drive your enemy away." The mischief left Martine's expression. "I hear he's back."

Evie's nerves tightened. "News travels quickly."

"Anna Maria stopped by yesterday. She's worried about you."

"She worries about everyone. It's her hobby."

"She saw what he did to you last time. So did I."

Evie tried to pull off a casual shrug, but it was a failure. "Don't worry. I know better than to trust him this time. I'll be fine. Listen, I'm here on behalf of a client."

"Like that's a surprise. You wouldn't even burn the white candles I gave you a year ago."

"I did burn them. Last spring when the big storm knocked out the power for the night. And I felt very peaceful, too." She grinned as Martine rolled her eyes. "Back to my client... She needs something for her house."

"To protect it?"

"To cleanse it."

Martine began rummaging behind the counter. "Considering that you don't have much faith in my conjures and charms, I'm honored that you thought to come to me."

Evie ignored the mockery in her friend's voice. "I've been to her house. It's...evil."

Martine stopped to look at her. "Evil?"

Feeling a sudden chill, Evie rubbed her bare arms as she nodded.

"You're not particularly sensitive to those things. It must have a hell of an aura."

"It does."

"Is it an old place or new?"

"Relatively new."

"So it's not haunted—though, of course, the ground where it's built could be."

"It's not haunted. It's…contaminated." Hearing the strangeness of her answer, she shrugged awkwardly. "My client's husband…"

Martine simply nodded and continued selecting items. While she waited, Evie picked up a glass jar filled with gray-green powder, shook it, then returned it to the counter. Next to it was a painted tin, so old that most of the lettering was worn off, and candles of every color imaginable, some plain, some with designs in contrasting wax. She picked up a pure white one, similar to the ones Martine had given her last year, then a green one.

"Dress the green candle with money-drawing oil, then burn it to improve your finances," Martine said without glancing her way. "Burn the white one to St. Peter in the morning, then scrub your shop from front to back with water containing parsley and thyme. When you finish, burn green incense—" she gave a wave toward the opposite corner "—at the back of the shop and you'll have more business than you can deal with."

"You really believe that?" Evie asked skeptically, and her friend's only response was another wave toward the corner, where a cone of green incense smoldered. "So how's business?"

Finally Martine looked at her and grinned. "Up fifteen percent over the same period last year." Finished at her worktable, she gathered an armful of items and brought them to the counter. "Here you go. Tell your client to sprinkle this powder at the exterior corners and in the interior corners of the house and to burn this drive-away-evil incense, along with these candles. Also, she should carry this in her pocket at all times."

That explained the tin, the incense, the candles and one small red flannel bag. "What's the rest of this?" Evie asked.

Martine picked up the second flannel bag. "This is for you. For luck and protection."

"What's in it?"

"Do you really want to know?" she asked with a grin, then told her. "Dragon's blood, incense, steel dust, powdered sugar and a little High John the Conqueror root. Keep it in your pocket. And wear this." She leaned across and slipped a silver chain over Evie's head. From its middle, held in place by a knot in the chain, dangled an old dime, minted the year Evie was born. "Washing your face with rose water increases the efficacy of the charm. And scrubbing your front steps with red brick dust will help bring luck and ward off evil—though, since *he's* back, we may be a little late for that. But not for this—I hope. Sprinkle a little salt over your mattress before you make the bed to keep evil from finding you there."

"Or give me a bad's night sleep."

"I know you're a skeptic, but humor me." Martine came around the counter and slipped the flannel bag into Evie's skirt pocket. "If this doesn't help your client, she may need to have someone come in to cleanse the place—though it sounds as if her first, best defense would be getting rid of her husband."

Evie should be so lucky. If William MacDougal were no longer in Irina's life, then Jack would get out of *her* life. "How much I do owe you?"

At the cash register in the front room, Martine rang up only Irina's things. When Evie protested, she merely shrugged. "We'll consider it a professional trade. I'll come over sometime, and you can tell me why I keep having dreams about my ex."

"It's a deal," Evie murmured on her way out, though she already understood Martine's hang-up with her ex-husband. Their breakup, like Evie's breakup with Jack, had come abruptly, unexpectedly and had been completely unwanted on her part. Martine's ex was even more of a skeptic than Jack and, being a politician to boot, more aware of her unsuitability for him. Jack had known a French Quarter psychic wasn't the ideal lover for him, but at least her record had been clean. People could frown on their involvement, could suspect that she was a fraud and a con artist, but they couldn't prove anything, and without proof, they couldn't make him quit seeing her.

Unfortunately, the voters didn't need proof, and neither did the ruthless men running Jake Lassiter's campaign. They'd believed it was easier to get a divorced man elected to office than a man married to a flake and a fraud like Martine, and they'd convinced him to divorce her. Evie thought he was a self-centered bastard and Martine was well rid of him, and Martine returned the favor by thinking the same of Jack.

But Martine had loved Jake and Evie had loved Jack, and losing them had broken both their hearts.

This time Jack wasn't interested in her heart. This time she was only risking her life.

When Evie arrived at the shop, Anna Maria was already there. She unlocked the door for Evie, then secured it again behind her. "Where have you—" She looked at the plain brown bag and the silver chain around Evie's neck. "Oh, you went by Martine's. Good. The dime should really be worn around your waist, but close to your heart... Yeah, that's good. You look better already."

Evie smiled faintly. She'd been in pretty sorry shape yesterday after Jack left. She'd put away the Scotch, because she knew it wouldn't help, and instead had curled up in the darkest corner of her bedroom until the pain and panic eased to a bearable level.

Finally Anna Maria had tracked her down, coaxed her downstairs, fed her lunch and talked her into the reading room. It was always easier in the reading room with clients, because in there she was no longer broken-hearted Evie. She left herself at the door and put on the other persona, the powerful, mysterious, all-knowing Evangelina. It was an act, perfected over nearly thirty years of being different, of feeling unloved, and, more often than not, it helped keep her under control.

"I'm fine. Jack is coming over at eleven. I'll be gone until probably about one."

Anna Maria scowled. "I don't suppose he's paying for your time."

"I don't want his money. I just want him out of my life."

"Do you? Really?"

"Really." Evie glanced past her to the sidewalk outside, where a group of elderly women were gathered, reading the price list posted on the plate glass. "Let's open a little early. Just give me five minutes to get ready."

She stowed the bag with her purse, then got the usual overload of jewelry from upstairs before settling in the reading room. Only a moment after she signaled that she was ready, Anna Maria showed the first of five customers in.

They were friends, all from Scottsdale, Arizona, free from the demands of their husbands and families for a girls-only vacation in New Orleans, and their readings were easy. Evie played her role for all she was worth, slipping a few truths into each reading, using information gathered from the ones before to surprise the ones after, adding enough generic assurances to round out the time. It was an easy way to pass the morning.

Until the last one.

The instant the white-haired woman sat down across from her, Evie felt the room shift. The other women had come in on a lark, to do something wild and daring that they would never dream of back home in Scottsdale, Arizona, where they were sensible wives. But this one, this Mrs. Woodlawn, was a believer with a capital *B*.

Evie did her best not to connect with true believers, tried to keep everything on the most superficial of levels, but once it happened, she couldn't back off. She could tell this woman things that would dazzle her, things that would frighten her. She could tell her damn near anything she wanted to know about her life, past, present or future.

Anna Maria referred to that kind of response in less-than-technical terms as getting zapped, as appropriate a description as any. Too often the exchange of psychic energy was too powerful for Evie to bear. She learned things she didn't want to know, was more drained than she could afford to be.

This morning, before facing Jack, she couldn't afford to be drained at all.

"Shall we get started?" she asked, her voice husky and noticeably devoid of enthusiasm.

"Yes, of course. Would you like to take my hand or have some article of mine?"

Evie remembered the instant Irina MacDougal had taken her hands—the visions, the sounds, the sensations—and revulsion curled through her. Keeping her expression serene and cool, she waved one hand languidly. "That's not necessary, Mrs. Woodlawn."

She focused on the woman, with her white hair, cotton dress and straw hat. On her left hand, resting on the table top, she wore a wedding band. On her lapel, she wore a grandmother's pin with five bejeweled boy/girl figures.

"You and the other ladies have been friends a long time. They've helped you through many rough times...like now."

The woman bobbed her head.

"You're concerned about your daughter."

Another eager and totally unnecessary nod.

"She's having problems in her marriage. She and her husband have separated and are considering a divorce. He thinks he's outgrown her while she's stayed home with the children. He regrets all the things he might have done if he hadn't been tied down with a family. She feels cheated and unappreciated, and she fears he's having an affair with someone more attractive, more exciting, than an overweight housewife.''

Mrs. Woodlawn was staring at her, shock and discomfort, just a little, in her eyes. "How do you know all that?" she whispered.

Evie's smile was thin and false. "I know many things, Mrs. Woodlawn. For example, I know your son-in-law isn't having an affair, and he and your daughter aren't going to divorce. Your daughter will have a chance to return to school, to be something besides a wife and a mother, and your son-in-law will come to appreciate everything she's done for him in the last seventeen years. They'll be fine, and your grandchildren will be fine."

The old lady sat motionless, her gaze locked on Evie's face. After a time, she nodded, and the worry was gone. "I believe you. But how do you know?"

Evie shrugged. "I know." Damned if she wanted to, but she did. "Our time is up, Mrs. Woodlawn. Enjoy the rest of your stay in our fair city." When she stood, she slid her hands into the deep pockets of her skirt so the old lady wouldn't be tempted to offer her own hand. When she was halfway to the door, Evie spoke again. "That's a lovely hat, but be careful around the carriages. Some of the mules are quite fond of straw flowers."

"Thank you, Evangelina. Thank you so much."

For a long moment after the door closed, Evie remained where she was, her right hand clenching the flannel bag in her pocket. It was for luck and protection, Martine had said. She suddenly felt a desperate need for both.

With no other customers waiting in the outer room, Evie slipped behind the velvet drapes and through the door into the house proper. She needed a jolt of sunshine and a blast of the Quarter's muggy summer heat, needed to clear away the darkness where she spent her days and to reacquaint herself with life, bustling and intense and unconcerned with her. To that end she walked out the front door and onto the small stoop.

Tourists clogged the sidewalks in spite of the mid-nineties temperature and the low-nineties humidity. To her right the clip-clop of hooves on pavement signaled the approach of a mule-drawn carriage. Ten feet to her left the front door of her shop was propped open, but drawing no takers.

The carriage drew nearer, and the driver called her name and waved. As the wagon wheeled past, he changed his usual spiel to insist that no visit to N'awlins was complete without a visit to Evangelina, the best psychic in the world. For the free publicity, she owed him cookies for Rickey, his mule, the next time she saw him.

She was turning to go inside when a scream down the street stayed her. The carriage had reached the corner, but instead of turning as he'd obediently done a thousand times in the past, Rickey had veered to the sidewalk, where a group of elderly women waited to cross the street. The scream had come from Mrs. Woodlawn, who alternated between looking back at Evie and watching with chagrin as Rickey chomped down on her straw-flower hat.

Feeling immeasurably better, Evie started to return to the house. She stopped short when she saw Jack lounging in the open doorway. Curling her fingers around the charm again, she scowled at him. "Where did you come from?"

"I let myself in the back way."

"Let yourself—" She broke off when he held up his keys. At some point in their relationship, they'd traded keys, though she had been to his apartment only once. For all practical purposes, he'd moved in with her here and used his place primarily for storing his belongings. When their affair had ended, it ended so quickly that she'd had no chance to give his key back or to get her own back. His she had thrown someplace. A drawer? The trash?

She held out her hand, and after a moment, he removed the key and dropped it in her palm.

"What makes you think I don't have a copy?"

"What makes you think I won't change the locks?" She passed him, careful not to touch, and went inside. After retrieving his bag from the hall table, he followed her into the dining room, where he laid out his equipment.

He had to come close, unbearably close, to rig the microphone and transmitter. As his fingertips brushed her breast, she fixed her gaze on the wall and concentrated on not breathing, not responding, not moving so much as a millimeter. When finally he moved around behind her, she let her eyes close, let a tiny whisper of relief shiver through her.

"Isn't this normally done by female officers?" she asked, glad to hear that her voice had substance and a sarcastic edge.

"Normally."

"Then why isn't there one here?"

"Because there's not a woman on this case. Which of my partners would you rather have instead of me? Haskins? Gomez? How about Sonny Roberts?"

She cringed at the last name. Sonny had disliked her presence in Jack's life from the beginning. He had counseled Jack against getting involved with her, had refused to socialize with her. He had been, she was convinced, the driving force in the case Jack had made against her.

"I see you remember Sonny." He smoothed a wide strip of tape across the transmitter and the small of her back, then asked, "Does it bother you that it's me doing it?"

"Of course not."

"Not at all?" He leaned closer, and she felt his heat on her back, her shoulders. His breath brushed across her neck as his fingers combed her hair from her ear. "Not even a little bit?" he whispered. "It doesn't make you remember all the wicked things we used to do, all the hours we spent naked and hot and sweaty, all the times I made you explode?"

She tried to control her body's responses, but they were too immediate, too strong. A shudder rippled through her, goose bumps popped up from her ear down her arm, and, before she could stop herself, she leaned back against him, pressed herself against him.

He stepped away, cold and hateful and mocking. "You're so easy, Evie."

She wanted to curse, throw things, stamp her feet, slap him. She settled for a smile that matched his mockery. "So were you, Jack. You gave me everything I wanted, and I didn't even have to ask." Except forever. She'd wanted forever with him, but he'd denied her that.

His humor disappeared, and his features settled into a mask so forbidding that it chilled her blood. The intensity of his hostility was breathtaking. Once he had loved her with that level of intensity. Now he hated her. She could never let herself forget that.

Jack Murphy hated her.

And he just might get her killed.

Chapter 4

Jack slumped down in the Mustang's driver's seat, his head tilted back, the necessities of surveillance scattered around him. The receiver and tape recorder filled the passenger seat. Trash from his lunch—a deli sandwich wrapper and a soda can—was on the floorboard. His sunglasses were on the dash, next to his binoculars, and his gun rested, grips up, between his legs.

It was a hellishly hot and humid afternoon. His damp clothes stuck to the seat when he moved. His head was starting to ache. He needed to get out and stretch his legs, but he couldn't afford the risk.

And he couldn't forget those few brief moments back in Evie's dining room.

Lucky for him that she had leaned only her shoulders against him, that she hadn't taken a couple of steps back to bring her entire body into contact with his. He never would have been able to hide his response, never could have kept her from discovering that touching her—not sexually, but sim-

ply in the performance of his job—aroused him as quickly, as
fully, as if it *were* purely sexual.

On the one hand, he should be grateful for the incident. It'd
been a hell of a long time since he'd had the slightest sexual
urge. He'd blamed the grief, the guilt, the sedatives, the booze,
the long hours. He'd blamed his obsession with punishing
MacDougal, with finding justice for Celeste. Mostly he'd
blamed Evie, and he'd wondered if he would ever want sex
again.

On the other hand, he was disgusted because the only
woman he'd shown the least interest in was the one woman
he could never let himself have.

He didn't have much experience with wanting something
he couldn't have, which was surprising, considering he'd
grown up in a house where struggling to make ends meet was
a way of life, and he'd put himself in the same situation by
becoming a cop. Fourteen years in the department, and his pay
was low enough that if he ever figured it on an hourly basis,
he'd probably just shoot himself and be done with it.

But however little he earned, it was enough. He'd never had
many expenses beyond rent, utilities, food, car insurance. He
had no hobbies, didn't care to travel, had no desire for a newer
car or a nicer apartment. He had no responsibilities—no ex-
wives or children to support, no family who would take his
money if he offered it. All he had was work—the beginning
and end of his life.

A year ago he'd wanted more. He'd wanted to give up his
apartment and complete his move into Evie's house. He'd
wanted to try his hand at marriage, to see if he was better at
it than his parents were, to find out what kind of father he
would make. He'd wanted the American dream.

And instead he'd gotten a nightmare.

He didn't believe in dreams anymore. He knew he wasn't
cut out for marriage, and he didn't want some poor kid punished by having him for a father. He wanted only what he'd

always had, what had always been enough. Work. Being a cop. Nothing more, nothing less.

Two hundred yards away a servant was clearing away the dishes from lunch, refilling glasses with some sort of tropical drink, adjusting the umbrella to keep the two women in the shade. All through the meal they'd made small talk—admiring each other's jewelry, comparing off-the-wall shops that sold unusual and one-of-a-kind outfits, discussing ideal places to spend New Orleans' long, hot summers.

Now, as Jack trained his binoculars on her, Irina MacDougal stretched, a slow, lazy, indolent move. When she settled back into the chair again, she gave Evie a smile. "I hope you don't mind, but I made a few inquiries about you."

Jack's stomach muscles clenched. Evie, magnified by the thick lenses, didn't react at all other than to smile. "I don't mind at all. What did you find?"

"A puzzle. Some say you're the best, a seer of incomparable talent, a genuine clairvoyant in a city full of fakes."

"And what do the others say?"

"They say you're fun and games, smoke and mirrors, a fake of the first degree. My housekeeper says you're a fraud. She says her sister went to see you and you played charlatan's games."

Though he listened to Irina's softly accented words, he kept the binoculars focused on Evie, studying her face as she shrugged gracefully. "I have no control over what others think or say. In the end, the only opinion that matters is yours. What do *you* think? Am I legitimate? Or am I a fraud?"

Irina's response was slow in coming, as if she were seeking the answer even as she spoke. "Your clothes, your jewelry, your props at the shop are all a bad American movie version of a psychic. You con people. You play games and tricks. But I believe *you're* the biggest trick of all—a genuine psychic masquerading as a fraud masquerading as a genuine psychic."

The answer should have pleased Evie. It didn't. She covered

well, though, with another shrug and smile. What was it about the answer that displeased her? The fact that she had successfully suckered Irina into believing her scam? A twinge of conscience from the woman who had helped bring about Celeste Dardanelle's death?

Hard to believe, but easier than accepting the other possibility: that Evie disliked Irina's answer because it was right. Because she had real, honest-to-God psychic powers but preferred being thought of as just another con artist in the Quarter. *Much* harder to believe.

"And what do you think about that?"

Irina's voice was as warm and fluid as Evie's was stiff. "I knew a person or two in the islands who did the same thing—humored the tourists who were so eager to part with their money and saved the genuine talent for those who truly sought advice and not a few minutes' entertainment. Frankly, it increases my respect for you. It proves you take your gifts seriously and treat them accordingly. You don't prostitute your psychic talent, merely your acting talent."

Jack watched Evie nod slowly, regally, then lowered the binoculars and simply listened for a time.

"It isn't easy being psychic, is it?" Irina asked sympathetically.

"Given a choice, I'd rather be so shortsighted that I couldn't see beyond the tip of my nose."

"What about the people in your life? Are they supportive?"

"My father's not interested. My mother thinks I'm cursed. She's afraid of what I might unleash on her, and so she keeps her distance."

Jack scowled. Was she trying to gain Irina's sympathy with made-up stories? She'd told him about her parents, and she'd never mentioned curses or fears. And what was the point? Irina was already clearly on her side. She should stop the other woman's questions and start asking questions of her own, start gathering the information he needed to close this case once and for all.

"And the men in your life?"

Evie laughed. "What men?"

"Surely there's been someone."

"Not for a long time. Not anyone who ever bothered to learn anything about me."

"I didn't learn anything about you because you lied to me," he muttered derisively. She'd scammed him just like she'd scammed everyone else, just like she was scamming Irina.

And he wasn't learning anything today, either. After a few minutes more, Evie said she had to go, and, as she stood up from the table, they made arrangements to meet the next morning. He focused the binoculars once more, just in time to see Irina offer her hand. When Evie hesitated, Irina picked up her hand, clasped it in both of hers.

Though she continued to smile, Evie paled, looked dazed, frantic. She took a step back, then another and another, until Irina had no choice but to let her go. The instant the contact was broken, relief, faint but recognizable, washed over Evie, and the wattage on her smile went up about a hundred percent.

Interesting.

Jack laid the binoculars on the back floorboard, switched off the receiver and tape recorder and put on his sunglasses. After returning the pistol to his holster, he started the engine and, as soon Evie cleared the MacDougals' gate, he pulled onto the street. After a mile or so, he swung around a corner, cut through a parking lot, then came out a half-dozen cars behind her.

She didn't go straight home, but stopped at the farmer's market. Always suspicious, he stopped some distance away and switched the receiver back on to listen to the sounds of vendors and tourists as she bought bags of fresh produce. They'd shopped here often in their months together. Sometimes a vegetarian, she'd wanted the freshest food available, and he'd been more than willing to accommodate her.

In every damn way.

Coming back out of the open-air market, she paused on the curb and looked straight at him. He'd watched her park, go inside, make her selections, without ever glancing in his direction. How had she spotted him?

It was the first question he asked her when they were once again inside her house. He was in the dining room, resting his hands on the counter that separated them. She was in the kitchen, putting away the fruits and vegetables she'd purchased. "Maybe your surveillance skills have gotten a little rusty."

"Not likely." He might not be good at anything else in his life, but he was damn good at being a cop and all it entailed.

"Then how do I know that when you're watching the MacDougal house, you park in that wooded lot to the east? Where a stand of sugar pines and a clump of overgrown shrubbery provides cover?"

"You saw me pull out of there today."

"I knew yesterday."

He muttered one obscene word that precisely summed up his opinion of that.

Her sarcastic smile was cloaked with sweetness as fake as her powers. "Thank you, Jack, for that refined and oh, so succinct response. You can go now."

"How did you know?"

For a moment she looked as if she intended to walk away. Then she sighed. "I *felt* it. At Irina's yesterday and at the market today, I felt you there."

She expected him to make some sneering comment—he could see her waiting for it—but there were some things a person couldn't argue with. From the moment he'd first laid eyes on her, he'd experienced some sort of extraordinary awareness where she was concerned. He had literally felt her presence whenever she was near. Even in sleep, he'd known when she was beside him and when she'd left him.

But he hadn't known that she was lying to him, using him, betraying him. He'd never had a clue.

Was that possible? Was she that good? Was he that dense?

She must be, and he must be, because the only other option was that she hadn't lied to him, hadn't betrayed him. No matter how desperately he wanted—*had* wanted—to believe that, the evidence was against her.

"So she's coming to the shop tomorrow," he said in a stiff change-of-subject. "You should have insisted on going to her house. You're not going to find out anything about Mac-Dougal here."

Expecting an attack on her earlier response, she needed a moment to regroup, to give him an answer he'd already heard from Irina herself. "She wants to see the freak in her natural environment. She wants the full effect of the bad American movie psychic."

He ignored the freak comment and the uncomfortable twinge it triggered in his gut. "You played her well today."

The look she gave him was weary, somehow disillusioned. "Is it all games to you, Jack? Do you think everyone's playing games and scams and cons with everyone else?"

"I don't know about everyone else. I know *you*. I know what you did to me."

"And what did I do to you? I loved you. I trusted you. I believed in you, and you—"

He circled the bar and advanced on her, forcing her away from the counter, never slowing until her back was against the wall and he was looming over her. "You screwed me, literally and figuratively. You took the information I told you in confidence, you sold it to William MacDougal, and you got an innocent woman killed. Love had nothing to do with it, except your love of money."

Though she'd backed away, she didn't cringe, didn't tear

up or tremble. She simply looked unbearably forlorn. "So those are my sins," she whispered. "What about yours? You helped get that innocent woman killed. You helped put that accountant's life in danger. You betrayed me, and now you're risking my life. You're willing to sacrifice me to bring down MacDougal. How will you sleep, Jack, knowing that you've caused another woman's death? How will you live?"

He didn't mean to pull away. He simply couldn't help himself. Regardless of his feelings for Evie, he didn't want her death on his conscience. Celeste's death had almost killed him. He couldn't live through it again.

But he also couldn't give up his obsessive need for justice.

And he couldn't find justice without risking Evie's death.

He withdrew to the hallway, then fixed his gaze on the wall beside her. "I need the equipment."

Peripherally he saw the blur of movement as she removed her belt, pulled up her shirt, pulled off the tape, the microphone and the transmitter. She laid them on the counter halfway between them, then returned to the wall as if she needed its support. He picked up the equipment and headed for the side door. He had almost escaped when she spoke.

"Did you ever consider the possibility that I might be innocent?"

He stopped only inches from the door but didn't turn. "I considered it every time they showed me new evidence pointing to you. I considered it long past the time a reasonable man would have given in and accepted the facts." Slowly he turned so she could experience the full exposure of his anger where she stood. "I considered it until I had no other choice in the world but to believe the proof that left no doubt how damnably and unforgivably guilty you were."

She drew in on herself, suddenly appearing smaller, frailer, less substantial. "Then why are you trusting me now?"

"I'm not trusting you. I'm using you. And if you die—" He forced a casual shrug, though there was nothing casual about the lie he was about to tell, about the emotions that were destroying him inside. "As long as you help me get Mac-Dougal first... I'll get over it."

At six-thirty, Evie closed and locked the door behind Anna Maria, left one dim light burning in the front room, then went into her house. She locked the dead bolt on the reading room door before making her way upstairs.

It had been a long, exhausting week, and she wanted nothing more than to shower, curl up in bed and vegetate with only the television for company. But in the last year, Friday night had become girls' night. In an hour or so, Anna Maria and Martine would be knocking at the door, full of plans and ready to unwind. It was a routine they'd started soon after Jack had walked out of Evie's life, one that had helped save her. It was one she needed now that he was back.

She showered, pulled her hair back in a braid and dressed for comfort in shorts and a cotton top. They might stay home, order in dinner and watch rented movies on the VCR, or they might go clubbing in the Quarter. Sometimes they dressed to the nines for dinner in a fancy restaurant. Once they'd stocked up on snacks and canned sodas, loaded into her car and driven the night away, heading east into Mississippi and Alabama before finally returning. For a time, she hadn't wanted to come back but had wished she could drive forever.

There would be no long drives tonight, or this time she really might not come back.

As she reached the bottom step with sandals in hand, the doorbell rang. Anna Maria and Martine were standing on the stoop, arm in arm, ready to celebrate the end of the week. "Get your shoes on, Gypsy, and grab your bag," Martine said in greeting. "We've got places to go and people to see."

"What places? What people?" Evie leaned against the wall to tug on her shoes, then slung her palm-sized purse over her head and one shoulder.

"Any place that looks good," Anna Maria replied.

"And any people who look bad," added Martine.

Evie joined them on the stoop, locked the door, then followed them down the steps to the sidewalk. It was a hot July night, barely seven-thirty, and already the streets were crowded. She didn't like crowds—it was too easy to get jostled, too easy to get zapped—but they were a part of life in the Quarter, one that she minimized tonight by taking a position between her two friends.

Their first stop was a crowded café for a dinner of sandwiches and sodas. When they were back on the street, Martine asked, "Blues, jazz, booze?"

Evie declined to vote. She didn't enjoy it so much when they hit the clubs. Anna Maria and Martine usually abandoned her for some guy, and she spent the evening alone, listening to great music and wondering if she would ever be interested in men again. Usually they returned to accompany her home, but on occasion she'd been left to take a cab alone.

On a hot night like tonight, she would prefer to sit on a bench in front of St. Louis Cathedral and watch the tourists for the next few hours. Or on a bench overlooking the Mississippi watching the river traffic. Or stretched out on a chaise longue in her courtyard watching the sky...

Except that the last person to stretch out on that chaise longue had been Jack, who might have left some lingering essence to haunt her.

Not that she needed anything but her own memories to be haunted.

"Martine to Evie," her friend called in a low voice. "Come on. We're going to hear some blues." Careful not to touch anything but clothing, she hooked her finger through Evie's belt loop and gave her a tug to catch up with Anna Maria.

Evie loved the blues—too often she lived them—but for the past year she'd avoided the clubs where the music could be heard. After all, that was where she'd met Jack, who also loved the blues. Normally her friends respected that. Tonight she respected their choice.

The club they chose was new to her. She followed them inside, claimed a seat between them at the bar and ordered a beer. The air was warm and smoky, the music hot and mournful. Most of the tables were occupied by tourists out for an evening of music, beer and fun.

She felt as if she'd forgotten how to have fun.

Within ten minutes Anna Maria had gone off to the table of a young man who looked as if he were on summer break from high school. Her cousin always did attract the younger men, and Martine always drew the attention of the older men, and Evie got the guys who couldn't possibly interest her.

Of course, for a year now, *no* man had interested her.

"You keep looking like that, you're going to scare your prospective suitors away."

She swiveled sideways on the stool to face Martine. "I'm not interested in prospective suitors. Most of these guys are from out of town. They'll be gone in a couple of days, and you'll never see them again."

"That's the best kind of man to get involved with—one who's not around long enough to break your heart."

"If he's not going to be around long enough to break your heart, then why bother getting involved at all?"

Martine gave her a chiding look. "Sex, Evie. Haven't you ever used a man for nothing but sex?"

"No."

"Why am I not surprised?"

Evie finished her beer and ordered another. "I have two requirements for a sexual partner—I can't get zapped when I touch him, and I have to care about him."

"Funny. I have two requirements, too. He can't remind me of my ex, and I don't even have to know his name." Martine slid off the stool and picked up her drink. "And if you'll excuse me, I think I've found a good candidate right over there.''

Smiling faintly, Evie watched her cross the room, slide into the empty seat at a back table and introduce herself to the man there. Within minutes they looked as if they'd known each other all their lives.

That kind of instantaneous connection had been present the night she'd met Jack. At the time, she'd thought it was something really unique—destiny, fate, meant to be. Now she knew that men and women made that connection all the time. The only problem was that she'd been foolish enough to get emotionally involved, while most people felt only a physical link. She'd gotten her heart broken, while most people got nothing more than a good night's sex.

"Hey, darlin'."

Reluctantly Evie shifted her attention from Martine to the man who'd claimed her stool. He was too much for her tastes—too handsome, too happy, too drunk. She didn't respond to his greeting but looked away and silently wished him away.

"With your friends otherwise occupied, you look a little lonely here all by yourself."

"I like being alone."

"Sure, you do, darlin'. That's 'cause you haven't met me. I'm Grant."

"And I'm not interested."

He feigned an injured look. "Ow, darlin', that was cold. I bet if I touched you, I'd get frostbite. But that's okay, 'cause I got exactly what you need to thaw out. Why don't we have another drink, then go someplace quiet? Bartender, a beer for me and another for the lady."

He laid his hand on her shoulder, and Evie's senses went on full overload. Images bombarded her, nothing significant, nothing interesting, but overwhelming all the same. "Don't touch me!" she hissed as she jerked away, stumbling to her feet, heading for the door. He called after her, and from the back of the room, Martine called her name, but she ignored them both, intent only on escape. She was almost there, almost free, when abruptly she stopped.

Jack was standing inside the door, his expression absolutely impassive, his hazel eyes blank. She knew he'd seen the incident at the bar, knew he'd witnessed her panicked escape. After a long moment, he looked past her and she knew Grant had stopped a few yards back, knew he brushed her off with an impatient gesture, muttering, "Hey, forget it. She's not worth the trouble." She knew, too, when he'd left her comfort zone, when he'd turned his attention elsewhere.

"Are you all right?" Martine hovered beside her, emanating concern as thick and cloaking as the smoke. After a quick scrutiny of Evie, she shifted her suddenly scornful gaze to Jack. "What is *he* doing here?"

Still feeling shaky, Evie ignored the second question. "I'm fine."

Her gaze came back, along with the worry. "Are you sure? Just let me tell Bill that we're going, then I'll walk you home, okay?"

Evie stopped her without touching her. "It's okay. Stay here. I'm perfectly capable of getting home by myself."

"But that guy—"

"Won't bother her." Jack's words were as hard and cold as he'd become. They made her feel queasy inside.

"You don't need to bother her, either," Martine said hotly. "You should stay hell and gone away from her. She doesn't have to put up with this crap—"

"Martine." Summoning her courage, Evie took her friend's hand. The action startled her into silence. "Go back to Bill and don't worry about me. I'm going home. I'll be fine."

"Gypsy—"

"Please. Go on. Have fun. I'll see you later." With a smile, Evie released her, walked past Jack and out of the club. With her hands shoved into her pockets, her right fingers curled around the charm, she started toward the corner. She was half-way there when she felt Jack approaching. He caught up with her, stopped at the red light beside her.

"Your house is the other way."

She didn't look at him but merely clutched the charm tighter. "Are you following me now? Making sure I'm not meeting with MacDougal to sell you out again?"

Jack felt a flush of guilt because she was partially right. He had followed her tonight, though not intentionally. He'd just left his car on his way to check in with one of his regular informants when that awareness they'd talked about earlier had warned him that she was nearby. A quick sweep of the street, and he'd seen her and her friend Martine, had noticed Anna Maria some yards away. He hadn't meant to follow them. In fact, he'd stood beside the car and watched until they'd gone inside the bar. He had finally moved away with every intention of locating his informant.

Two minutes later he'd found himself standing just outside the door, watching her with Slick. Up to old habits. She'd found *him* in a similar club only a few blocks away.

But she'd taken him home. All she'd wanted from Slick was to get away. It was surely a sign of weakness that he found some satisfaction in that.

The light changed and tourists swarmed past, but Evie didn't move. "Why were you there?"

He shrugged. "I was watching."

"What did you expect to see?"

"You." It was too simple an answer, so he untruthfully added to it. "With a man."

Her laugh was shaky. "Glad I didn't disappoint you—for once." She spun around and headed back the way they'd come, but he didn't let her go alone.

He waited until they were crossing St. Ann to speak again. "What's this thing you have against being touched?"

"I don't have a problem with being touched."

He caught her wrist and pulled her to a stop on the curb. She gave him a disdainful look as she lifted her hand and his. "See? You're touching me. No problem."

"Oh, yeah? Then why are your muscles so tense? Why is your pulse racing?"

Holding his gaze, she consciously relaxed her muscles, slowed her heart rate. Then she smiled coolly. "Better?" Still very calm, unnaturally so, she freed her hand. "I don't need an escort home."

"I don't have any other plans."

"Then why don't you go back to the club? I'm sure you can find someone there who *wants* to spend time with you."

"I don't pick up women in bars. I got burned the last time." When she started walking again, so did he, instinctively matching his stride to hers. "Is that what you do for fun? Pick up men in bars?"

"You know, my conning Irina for you doesn't give you the right to snoop into the rest of my life."

"I'm not snooping. I'm making sure you get home safely."

She gave him a sharp look, but didn't reply. In fact, she remained stiffly silent the rest of the way to her house. She was unlocking the door when he broke the quiet.

"I saw the way you reacted when Irina took your hand today, and you practically fell over your own feet to get away when that guy touched you. Why?"

For a long moment, she stood motionless. Then, with a sigh, she pulled her key from the lock and swung the door open. She went inside, leaving the door open in silent invitation. By the time he closed it behind him, she was already in the kitchen. As he came down the hall, she turned in front of him with two cold sodas and went out the French doors to the courtyard.

They were settled in chairs, their sodas half gone, before she spoke again. "Do you remember the night we met?"

He resisted the urge to laugh derisively. "Which part? The dance? The drinks? The sex?"

She stared into the distance, showing no reaction to his sarcasm. "Before all that. When you first approached me."

He remembered. He'd gone to the club strictly for the music, with no intention of meeting anyone. He'd nursed a beer through the first set and the band was halfway through the second when he'd seen her, sitting by herself, lost in the music, oblivious to the looks every man in the place was giving her.

Looks were all she was getting. No one spoke to her, asked her to dance, tried for more. Except him. He'd sat down at her table, and she gave him a faint smile. He introduced himself, and she offered her first name only.

"I told you my name. You gave me yours."

"And we shook hands."

He'd thought it a little odd at the time. He couldn't remember any other time that he'd shaken hands in a pick-up situation, but she'd insisted on it, and he... Hell, he'd been eager for an excuse to touch her—any excuse.

"That's the last part of this answer that you'll accept without ridicule," she warned. She glanced at him as if to make certain he understood, then gazed away again. "Sometimes— too often—when I make physical contact with people, I get...flashes. Feelings. Visions. Usually, it's nothing important. Always it's more than I want to know. So, for my own peace of mind, I try to avoid contact as much as possible."

As answers went, he'd heard worse—and better. He sat still for a long time, considering it.

He was a skeptic. Always had been. He knew little about paranormal phenomena and believed even less. He'd dealt with Evie's claims of being psychic during their three months by not dealing with it. They'd kept their jobs totally separate from their life together—at least, hers was separate. He'd talked cop business, and she'd listened, but he'd never asked a single question about the psychic business. He hadn't wanted to know, hadn't wanted to even acknowledge what she did for a living.

Truth was, he'd been uncomfortable with it. Being in love with Evie DesJardien was fine, normal, understandable. Being in love with Evangelina, great psychic and fraud extraordinaire, had been... Hell, it'd been embarrassing.

So was it possible that touching someone could cause the kind of response she'd described? He didn't have a clue. How could he, when he didn't believe?

But *she* believed. Wasn't that what counted?

And she *did* believe. She'd done everything possible to avoid contact with Irina this afternoon, and she'd panicked over a simple touch like Slick's hand on her shoulder. And there was more. When he'd first seen the three women tonight, Martine had walked back to pull Evie along with them, but she hadn't taken her hand or arm. She'd pulled her by her clothes. And after the incident with Slick, Martine had almost touched her but hadn't. When Evie had taken her hand, it'd been enough to surprise the woman into silence.

So she believed. But was it *real?*

Seeing no answers and knowing no way to find them, he changed the subject. "Who was your friend?"

"He wasn't my—"

"I meant the woman. Martine."

"Oh. Martine Broussard." She slid lower in the chair, propped her feet on the edge of the fountain and stared up at the dark sky. "Yes, she's single, but I have to warn you—she's into auras, charms, amulets, rituals."

"She's not my type."

"She's beautiful, intelligent and has a healthy regard for sex. She's *every* man's type."

"Not mine," he repeated.

Another silence settled. He finished his soda, set the can on the grass, then folded his hands over his stomach. The high walls blocked much of the noise from the street, but there were occasional shouts, the sweet sounds of distant music, the clop of a carriage passing by. It was a hot, still night, the air muggy, the faint smell of rain mingling with the heavy fragrance of confederate jasmine blooming nearby.

All in all, it was a good night to be in New Orleans.

A good night to be in a private courtyard with a beautiful woman.

Even if that woman was Evie.

"What is your type?"

Her voice was soft, pure Louisiana, perfectly suited to a hot summer night. He listened to it in his head until it faded, then answered. "I have no type."

"I assume that means you've become so obsessed with your case that you don't have time for unimportant little things like regular meals, sleep and sex."

It was a good comment to ignore. He couldn't say why he didn't. "I owe her…justice. She was trying to do the right thing, and they killed her for it. She was only twenty-five years old, and she deserved better. She deserved to live." Feeling her gaze on him, he looked up and saw that she was watching him with a million or more emotions on her face and not a single one that he wanted to identify.

He stared at her a moment longer, then pushed to his feet. "I've got to go."

She continued to watch as he walked into the shadows of the live oak, as he let himself out the gate into the alley. He closed the gate and headed toward the noisy, busy street and told himself that she hadn't spoken as he walked away, that the whispered words had been a product of his guilt and his imagination. But he could still hear them, as clearly, as damning, as if they'd gone straight from her mind to his.

I deserve better, too.

He could reassure her that she wasn't going to die, that she would come out of this intact, but it was a promise he couldn't keep. He knew it, and so did she.

Or he could do the smart thing and let her go. God help him, he didn't want to find himself a few weeks or months from now, saying, ''She was only twenty-nine years old, and she deserved to live.'' He didn't want to bear the enormous responsibility of her death.

Or he could take the easy way out, the coward's way, and tell himself that she hadn't said anything at all. It had simply been the stirring of the wind in the trees. The delicate splash of water in the fountain. The rustle of the night through the flowers.

Not a whispered plea. Not words shrouded with fear as dark as the night, as oppressive as the heat. Not an entreaty that would haunt him as long as he lived.

Just the wind. The water. The night.

Chapter 5

Evie awakened Saturday to a gray morning and the sound of rain. Leaving the warm comfort of her bed, she slipped through the French doors onto the balcony, ignored the fact that the rain was blowing underneath the eaves and leaned against the railing. The air was unusually cool for July, the rain unusually refreshing. It dotted the tank top and thin cotton shorts she slept in, turning the soft gray a dozen shades deeper. It misted over her face and seeped into her hair until she was wet from the top of her head all the way to her toes.

It was a lovely way to start the morning, so lovely and peaceful that she wasn't even particularly surprised to see Jack in the courtyard, leaning against the live oak's trunk, looking up at her. He wore a navy blue slicker to protect his gun from the damp, but the hood hung down his back, leaving his hair to darken in the rain.

She wondered how long he'd been there. A few minutes, a few hours, all night? With Jack there was no telling.

She wondered why he'd felt compelled to wait there. Again,

there was no way of knowing. She wouldn't be surprised if he didn't know himself. He was a complicated man.

She just wished he would go complicate someone else's life and leave her be. He'd promised to do just that if she helped make his case against MacDougal. If she survived MacDougal. And if she didn't survive...

Her smile was thin. Some believed that death was the ultimate peace. She would be free of these damn powers, free of her family, of all life's disappointments and hurts, free of Jack. She would be—for once, forever—at peace.

Turning away, she returned to her bedroom, to the bathroom. She pulled her hair back in a ponytail, dressed in her fortune-teller's clothes, added all the layers of jewelry. Downstairs in the kitchen, she started a pot of coffee, transferred a loaf of raisin-studded cinnamon bread from the pantry to the oven, then finally crossed the room and unlocked the French door. She didn't open it, didn't offer any invitation at all, but immediately returned to the kitchen.

A minute passed. Two. Three. She was taking her morning vitamins with bottled water when at last the door swung open and Jack came in. He hung the slicker on the outside knob, left his soaked running shoes and socks on the throw rug just inside, and came to the counter, sliding onto the barstool there, drying his face and hair with the dish towel she set there.

She leaned against the counter and watched the oven timer count down on the bread. "You know, those jackets have hoods for a reason."

"They obscure your hearing."

And he couldn't stand to have any of his senses obscured. Except his common sense, at least when it came to *her*. "How long has it been raining?"

"It started about midnight."

And how long had he been out in it? she wanted to ask. How long had he stood in her courtyard watching the balcony outside her bedroom? "Any flooding?"

"A little."

She had waded through calf-deep water in the streets before, had watched manhole covers dance inches above the streets from the force of the water rushing through the underground drainage canals. It slowed the tourists some, but it didn't stop them completely. Nothing could stop them completely, a fact for which she was most grateful.

The timer beeped three times, and she removed the bread from the oven, spread it with a powdered sugar glaze, then tore off chunks for each of two plates. She'd put one in front of Jack and was turning away to get the coffee when he caught just her fingertips.

"Why doesn't it happen when I touch you?" He asked it with a fierce scowl, directed at himself, she suspected, because he was curious enough to ask. "Why don't you get flashes or feelings or visions from me?"

Oh, she did. Hot flashes, erotic feelings, visions of the two of them, wicked in bed. She had from the very beginning, straight up through the very end. Hell, even past the end. Every time he touched her, no matter how innocently, she *felt*.

But that was her secret. Besides, that wasn't what he wanted to know. He was asking—actually wanting to know—about the psychic stuff. This was a day she'd thought she would never see.

"I don't know," she said, pretending a calmness she was far from feeling. "My own personal theory is that there's got to be some level of openness for it to happen. You're the most cynical, distrusting person I know. You don't believe in anything you can't see with your own eyes, touch with your own hands. Your world operates according to the rules—your rules, but rules all the same. You're not open to anything other-worldly, to anything requiring faith."

While he considered that, she poured two cups of coffee and added scant sugar and a few drops of milk to hers, using a more liberal hand with his. After everything that happened, she still remembered how he liked his coffee. That he would pick the raisins out of the bread. That, unshaven, he looked dangerous and dissolute. That he liked sex fine in the morning but wanted it most at night, when he'd finished a long day's work and needed to feel human again.

She knew so many things about him, and he knew practically nothing about her. If he could believe her guilty of the crimes he'd already damned her for, he couldn't have known her at all.

But how could he not believe she was guilty? There had been real, physical evidence against her—phone calls made from her house, money deposited into her bank account, the fact that he had confided in her and no one else information that had gotten Celeste Dardanelle killed. The evidence had been in black and white, hard, cold proof—the only thing in the world Jack Murphy could believe in. The one thing in the world he couldn't *not* believe in.

And all she'd had to offer were pathetic denials—denials that the phone records and bank records and Jack's own words disputed. She'd had no proof, nothing but weak pleadings for trust and faith, tearful declarations of love, frantic insistences that she would never hurt him or anyone else. Was it any wonder that he'd chosen tangible evidence over claims that had to be taken on faith?

"So was that the attraction?"

Jarred from her thoughts, she finished her bread, rinsed her fingers, then leaned against the counter once more with her coffee. "What attraction?"

"Mine. To you. Because there weren't any flashes?"

It was such a ludicrous suggestion that she wanted to laugh—or cry. She did neither. "It *is* rather difficult to have sex with someone whose life has invaded your brain," she acknowledged. "But, no, that wasn't part of it. It was…" She shrugged. *"You."* The feeling of completion she'd felt that night, as if she'd found what she'd been missing and was finally whole. The immediate kinship. The certainty that he was the man she'd been looking for, the one she needed, the one she would need forever.

He stared at her for a long moment, his face utterly empty of emotion. When he looked away, she felt actual physical relief, as if a great weight had been lifted.

Before she could think of anything else to say, the door down the hall opened and Anna Maria's voice, bright and energetic and indicating a satisfying night, filtered through the air. "Good morning, Evie. Isn't it a gorgeous day? Well, of course, you have to look the past the rain, but trust me, it *is* gorgeous. Oh, you wonderful person, you read my mind. I really need some of your hot cinnamon-raisin bread this morning and a cup—" She passed the kitchen, turned the corner at the end of the hall and instantly became still.

Evie knew exactly what she was seeing—Jack, all comfortable on the stool, finished with breakfast, his jaw unshaven, his hair uncombed, his feet bare. She also knew exactly what Anna Maria was imagining. Her cheeks grew hot as she took refuge in fixing a plate and coffee for her cousin.

Anna Maria didn't take a seat on the remaining barstool but stood with one arm resting on the counter. "Well…isn't this cozy?" she asked in a voice that indicated it was anything but.

"Not as cozy as you and that boy were last night," Jack drawled. "Did you check his ID to make sure he was of legal age before you took him home?"

"As a matter of fact, I did. I always do, and throw back the ones too young to keep," Anna Maria replied sweetly. "I don't have to ask if Evie was of sound mind when she brought you home, do I? Obviously, she wasn't."

"She didn't bring me here. I found the way on my own."

Anna Maria joined Evie in the kitchen to get sugar for her coffee. While stirring it, she directed her conversation to Evie as if Jack weren't there. "Listen, honey, I've never tried to tell you how to run your life, but *this*… You're too smart for this. God knows, you've got enough problems without inviting the king of all problems into your life again. He's bad luck and bad news, Evie. He's dangerous, and you don't need that, girl.''

Feeling awkward, embarrassed and damn near feverish, Evie tried to occupy herself with rinsing dishes. "He'll be gone soon enough."

"Oh, I don't doubt that. He hasn't had a single long-term relationship in his entire adult life. It's the damage he'll do before he leaves that worries me."

"Then you don't need to worry. This is strictly business."

"Though if we wanted to make it personal, it wouldn't be any of *your* business," Jack added helpfully, earning him a scowl from both women.

It was past time to take control, Evie decided. She dried her hands, then planted them on her hips. "Though it's nobody's business but my own, he didn't spend the night here, Anna Maria. He's here because I have an appointment this morning with the woman who's connected to his investigation. When she's gone, he'll be gone, too. And when this case is finished, he'll be gone permanently. You have nothing to worry about, no reason to play mother hen—at least, not with me. Now do me a favor, would you? Finish your breakfast, then call Martine and make sure she's all right. I'm going to get the reading room ready. My client will be here at nine. When we're finished, I'll see her out the front door to avoid anyone who might be waiting in the shop. Okay?"

After Anna Maria's reluctant nod, Evie left the kitchen and headed down the hall. She switched on the reading room lights, too dim to make much difference, lit a cone of incense on the library table shoved against the back wall and aligned the two chairs across from each other. That was about the extent of "getting ready"—that, putting out the incense before the fragrance overpowered the small room and, for this one appointment, getting wired for sound. Also just for this one appointment, she lit the white candles in each of the room's four corners. White was for peace, according to Martine, and she could use all of it she could get.

When the velvet drape over the door moved, she glanced that way. For once she couldn't be sure that the knotted muscles and taut nerves meant it was Jack. This morning she was just as reluctant to share Anna Maria's company as his.

She was sitting in her thronelike chair when he stepped into the room. He walked around the perimeter of the room, from candlelight to lamplight to shadow. The furniture—two tables against the walls, the center table and two chairs—was all too large for such a small room, too elaborately carved, too dark. The Persian rug in a dark crimson and navy pattern stretched from one black wall to another to another, and dustcatcher drapes in crimson velvet covered the fourth wall end to end.

Jack sat down opposite her. "This is a hell of a place to spend your days."

"I'm not sure it's any darker than the world where you spend your days."

"Maybe not." He touched the crystal ball, but didn't pick it up. "Your cousin's right about one thing. The long-term relationships. I never managed to keep one going past six months."

She knew that. She had thought she would be the exception to the rule, until the night he'd stormed in, so distraught and enraged that he'd barely been able to speak. Before the night was over, she had known she would be an exception, all right. She would be the first of his lovers that he'd hauled off to jail in handcuffs.

"Me, either," she admitted. "I always wanted…" More. Before meeting Jack, she thought she'd set her standards too high. After meeting him, she'd thought perhaps they were too low. After all, when the first and foremost requirement for a relationship—trust—was missing, there was a problem.

Though she didn't finish her sentence, he agreed with a nod

and a grim, "Yeah." *I always wanted...* Then, with a surge of energy, he got to his feet, retrieved the gym bag from inside the door and laid out his equipment on the table.

Everything was taped in place and her shirt tucked back into her skirt when Anna Maria came in from the house. Wearing a scowl, she ignored Jack and said, "Martine's fine. Bill's gone, the shop is open, and she also thinks having *him* here is an extraordinarily bad idea."

"Thank you, dear," Evie responded a second before Anna Maria slammed the waiting room door behind her. She doused the incense, pulled the fringed scarf from the library table, draped it around her waist and knotted it over one hip. The exotic pattern woven in dark threads complemented her navy skirt and burgundy top and hopefully would camouflage the transmitter.

Jack walked in a slow circle around her, then, surprising her, reached up to pull the band from her hair. It fell to her shoulders, thick and damp, and he nodded once, murmuring, "Gypsy."

Martine had called her by the nickname since they'd first met, but it sounded so different coming from him. So much huskier. More intimate. Sensuous. Shivering, she took a step back, sought the safety of distance even though she knew in her heart that all the distance in the world couldn't protect her. "Irina should be here soon. Where are you going to be?"

"In the kitchen or dining room."

"Make sure she doesn't see you when she leaves."

He nodded again, then took his bag and left. The instant the door closed behind him, Evie gave a great sigh of relief. It came too soon, though, for almost immediately the other door opened a few inches and Anna Maria slipped inside.

"There's a beautiful woman out there who arrived in a Mercedes driven by a gorilla in a suit. She says she's your nine o'clock appointment, but she wouldn't give a name. All she'd say was that you're expecting her," she said in a whisper.

"Who is she? And why do I keep thinking the gorilla has a gun under that jacket?"

"Trust me, you don't want to know. Send her in and send him away."

Only a moment after Anna Maria left, Irina appeared. She closed the door behind her, gave the room a long look, then directed a brilliant smile at Evie. "I can see why the tourists love you—and why some believers think you're a fraud. This is perfect. You even have a crystal ball."

"Actually, I think it's meant to be a paperweight. It's a gift from a client with a sense of humor. Sit down, please."

"Is this where you meet with your regular clients?"

"No. Usually we go in the house or sit in the courtyard. But you wanted the full effect." She waited until Irina was settled to ask, "Have you used the items I brought you for the house?"

"Yes. I think it may have helped. You'll have to see for yourself Monday. Lunch? Noon?"

"That sounds fine. Shall we get started?"

"Please."

Evie drew a deep, calming breath and consciously narrowed her focus onto the other woman. Even as she concentrated she became aware of the change in the air—the sudden closeness, the heaviness, the darkness. "You're worried about your husband. His business... Business is good, but there are problems. Always problems."

For an instant, she froze, distracted as images hovered at the edge of her awareness—the soft, mesmerizing sound of water, the heat of a sultry day, the smells of rich earth, lush growth, decay. But the very distraction that caused her to notice the images also drove them further away until they were nothing, until she couldn't swear they'd ever existed.

"My husband is in the gambling business," Irina offered.

"Gambling... Yes, the *Scotsman's Queen*. It's a lucrative business, more so for him than for others."

"He's a very talented businessman. He devotes himself to his job. His hours are long, but business is good."

"You spend all those long hours alone. But you don't mind. His absence is a fair trade for his success."

Irina looked embarrassed, but only slightly. "That makes me sound rather mercenary."

Evie shook her head. "You grew up with little in St. Thomas. You never knew your father, and your mother died when you were barely more than a child. You learned the hard way that a life with money is better than a life without."

"It's as easy to fall in love with a rich man as a poor man," Irina said with a delicate shrug.

"But you don't love William MacDougal. He frightens you." All too aware of Jack in the house listening, Evie deliberately shifted the conversation in the direction he wanted to go. "There was another young woman, before you met him, who was killed. According to rumor, your husband was somehow involved in her death, and you think it might be true."

"No. I don't believe..." The denial trailed off, as if she couldn't bring herself to complete the lie.

"You suspect that some of his business activities are less than legal. You worry about the people he's involved with. You blame that—blame him—for the negative energy that surrounds the house."

Irina leaned forward, an anxious look on her face. "Can you tell me? *Is* he involved in something illegal?"

"I can only tell you what you think, what you already know. I've—" Evie caught a quick breath "—I've never met your husband. I can't read him secondhand."

"But if you did meet him? Then could you tell?"

"I don't know. I can't read everyone. You know that."

"But if you met him... You could try."

Feeling sick deep inside, Evie nodded. "I could try."

"I'll ask him to join us for lunch Monday." Irina sat back

again, satisfied that the issue was resolved for now, and asked conversationally, "What do you see in my immediate future?"

Each deep breath Evie took filled her lungs with the sweet heavy scent of the incense, with panic, with dismay. She wanted to call the session to a halt, wanted to run from the room into the courtyard and stand in the rain until she was calm again, until she could breathe again. But she couldn't run, and so she used every trick in Evangelina's book to regain control. She was almost there, almost settled into the unflappable Evangelina persona when Irina touched her hand and, in a rush of panic, the answer to the woman's question became crystal clear.

Death. She saw death.

But whose future was she looking into?

Irina's?

Or her own?

Jack lay on the sofa, a pillow under his head, and listened to the conversation taking place down the hall. Irina's voice was soft, gently accented, pleasing to the ears. Evie's was also soft, also accented and pleasing to the body. Many were the times she'd seduced him with nothing more than her voice—no touches, no sensual moves. Just her sweet, sultry, Southern-womanly voice.

It was just another trick of her trade, he reminded himself even as his body started to react. It was a prop, like the crystal ball, the candles, the clothes. She sounded calm, serene, supremely assured, and it made people want to believe her—to believe in her.

And knowing that believing in her was the biggest mistake he'd ever made did nothing to protect him from the power of that voice.

"I have an image," she was saying. "Just an impression really, of water. Does that have any particular significance for you?"

Irina answered in all seriousness. "Before coming to the United States, I lived all my life on an island. Now I live in a state that's largely covered by water, and I have a pool and waterfalls in my own backyard. I don't have any special connection to it, though. I've never had any bad experiences, never suffered any frights, never known anyone who drowned."

"Can you swim?"

"Oh, yes. I learned as a small child. I'm quite a strong swimmer."

There was a rustle of clothing as the sensitive mike picked up Evie's shrug. "As I said, it's simply an impression. It may not have anything to do with you. It could be nothing or, for all I know, it could be significant to one of my other clients or even to me and I just haven't realized it yet."

"Can *you* swim?" Irina asked.

"No." Jack heard the faint smile in Evie's voice, saw it in his mind, felt it in his body. "I've never been in water deeper than my bathtub."

"You should learn. It's one of those basic skills that everyone should know. You never know when it'll come in handy." There was a scraping sound as Irina scooted her chair back. "I see our time is up. I'll speak to my husband about lunch Monday. If he agrees, you'll tell me whatever you learn?"

"Are you sure you want to know whatever I learn?"

Irina's answer came slowly, quietly. "Yes." But she didn't sound convinced. Right now all she had was suspicions that her husband wasn't quite what he seemed. What would she do when Evie confirmed them? Leave him? Try to reform him? Learn to live with him?

Maybe help them stop him?

The door from the reading room into the hallway opened and he no longer needed the receiver to hear their conversation. Quietly he shut it off. Then, for safety, though he knew they couldn't see him, he threw the afghan from the back of the sofa over the equipment.

"I could send my driver to pick you up Monday," Irina was saying as Evie closed the door.

"No, thank you. I prefer to come on my own."

Irina murmured acceptance of the refusal, then gave a soft sigh. "After the darkness in there, all the light here is a relief. This is a lovely house. Oh, and you have a courtyard with a fountain. May I take a closer look?"

Jack rolled to his side, burrowing his face between the pillow and the back cushions. For good measure, he bent one arm up over his head, then lay utterly still.

"No, I'd prefer—" Two sets of footsteps on the wood floor came to a stop at the same time Evie's protest abruptly ended. There was a moment of silence, then Irina's whisper.

"I didn't know you had company. I won't disturb him." Then, with humor, "And you said there was no man in your life."

The footsteps went back the way they had come, and the whispers continued. A moment later he heard the front door close, then Evie returned alone. He rolled over, then sat up as she dropped into the chair nearest the sofa.

"I'm having lunch with William MacDougal Monday."

"I heard."

"What can I expect?"

Jack shrugged. "You tell me."

"How should I know? I've never met the man. I know very little about him."

"Then who did you deal with?"

There was nothing serene about her now as a muscle clenched in her jaw and her voice grew cold. "I dealt with *you*—a mistake for which I'm still being punished."

"Who were the phone calls to? Who agreed to the payoff? Who made the deposit into your account?"

She clamped her jaw shut, curled her fingers into fists and stared away.

He knew he should let the subject drop, but there was one more question he had to ask, one answer he needed to know. "What did you do with the money?"

After a deep, fortifying breath, she looked directly at him. "I gave it to her family."

"Her family," he repeated blankly. "Celeste's family? Why?"

"Because they lost their daughter. At the very least, they could use it to pay for her burial. *I* sure as hell didn't want it. It wasn't mine. I'd done nothing to earn it."

His smile was thin and unamused. "You want to know about her family? Her father died when she was a kid. The wife of the man her mother was sleeping with came looking for her with a gun and her father got in the way. Her mother is an alcoholic and drug addict who never gave a damn about any of her kids. She taught them to beg and steal for her and gave them a stepfather whose idea of discipline involved a wide leather belt and a lot of pain. He raped Celeste when she was twelve and continued to use her on a regular basis until she ran away at the age of sixteen. At the time she died, she hadn't had any contact with her family for nine years. They didn't care when she was alive, they didn't care that she was dead, and they for damn sure didn't pay a penny toward her burial."

He knew that for a fact, because he'd paid the funeral expenses himself. Besides some anonymous priest, he'd been the only mourner at her graveside. Disgusted, he shook his head. "And you gave them the money that paid for her death."

Her shoulders rounded and a look of defeat crept across her face, making him feel like a bastard. However belated it was, she'd tried to make some atonement for the tragedy she'd caused. It hadn't been necessary to point out that she'd atoned for nothing. The important thing was that she hadn't kept the money. She hadn't profited from Celeste's death.

Or was it?

"Why didn't you keep it? You were greedy enough to sell us out. You killed her. You damn near killed me. And then you gave the money away. You did it all for nothing. *Why?*"

Looking fragile and weary, she slid to the edge of the cushion, then stood up, removed the wire and walked away. At the hallway, though, she looked back and twisted his words. "You're right, Jack. Everything I did was for nothing. Absolutely nothing."

A moment later the reading room door closed behind her. Even from this distance he could hear the lock click.

Did you ever consider the possibility that I might be innocent? she had asked yesterday afternoon. He had believed in her innocence in the beginning, but the evidence had kept piling up until he'd had no choice but to accept the truth, no matter how he hated it.

But what if she *was* innocent? What if her claims, weak as they were, were true? What if someone else had betrayed Celeste to MacDougal, had made those phone calls and deposited that money? What if he'd put her through all this hell and she really, truly was innocent?

Then God forgive him.

But the chances for her innocence were somewhere between zero and none. The cold, hard fact was she had betrayed him. Of course she continued to lie about it. Added to the other evidence, an admission of guilt would be enough to bring a charge of murder against her. And giving away the money was the logical thing to do—the innocent-victim-wanting-nothing-to-do-with-blood-money thing to do. Nothing more.

Picking up the bag he'd left under the coffee table, he packed up his equipment, zipped it shut, then sat back. He was exhausted—physically, mentally, spiritually. The last year had been the worst of his sorry life, and it wasn't going to get better until MacDougal had paid for Celeste's death. *Then* he would be able to put to rest the nightmares that haunted him. *Then* he would find some peace.

Then he would get over Evie.

And what would that leave him? He had nothing but a burning desire for revenge and an obsessive need for justice. When his revenge had been satisfied and justice meted out, he would have nothing at all. No reason to live. No woman to love. No hope for the future.

He knew he should leave—should pick up the bag, put on his wet shoes and his damp slicker and let himself out the back and into the alley. He should go home, get some rest, but his apartment wasn't the most restful place these days. The photographs of MacDougal taunted him. The snapshot of Celeste haunted him. And Evie… Evie made him bleed, way deep down inside where nothing could staunch it, where nothing could help him.

He sank lower on the sofa, put his head back, closed his eyes. No sounds filtered from the shop at the front or the buildings next door. There was only the low rumble of the air conditioner and the relentless pounding of the rain. The gray skies made it a good day for staying put—just until the rain let up. Just long enough to gather the strength to make it home.

Just for a little while…

"Listen to this. 'To keep an unwanted visitor from returning, sprinkle salt in his trail as he leaves, then sweep it out the door after him. As you sweep, call his name and implore him to never return.'" Anna Maria looked up from the book she'd taken from the shelf to pass the slow afternoon. "I've got a saltshaker in my bottom desk drawer, and there's a broom in the utility closet."

Evie smiled faintly. "If you're referring to Jack—"

"Who else?"

"—you would probably have better luck throwing the salt

in his eyes and then, while he's disabled, beating him senseless with the broom."

"Treating you the way he has proves that he's already taken leave of his senses," Anna Maria said with a scowl. "Besides, he'd just slap the handcuffs on and drag me off to jai—" Abruptly she caught her breath. "I'm sorry. I didn't mean—"

Evie brushed away the apology. Once she'd given Anna Maria and Martine all the shameful details of that night, by tacit agreement, they'd never discussed it again. It had been the most terrifying, humiliating, heartbreaking experience of her life. She'd seen the man she loved become a stranger who despised her. His own personal code wouldn't allow him to physically crush her and so he'd done it emotionally. His hatred had been palpable, his words cruel, and they'd devastated her.

"He put me in jail," she said, pretending an ease with the idea that she would never feel. "He's a cop. That's what he does."

"He's supposed to put *guilty* people in jail!"

"People make mistakes."

"And sometimes they don't learn from them," Anna Maria pointed out quietly. "Sometimes they repeat them."

"Sometimes they don't have any option." Evie stared out the plate glass window. It was late in the afternoon, she'd had only six customers, and though the rain had slowed to little more than light showers, it showed no signs of stopping. It was a day made for curling up with a book and pretending to read while gazing out the window and dreaming.

Thanks to Jack, she'd run out of good dreams over a year ago. He'd left her only the nightmares, the sorrows, the might-have-beens.

She gave a deep sigh that reverberated all the way down to her toes. "Why don't you go on home while the streets are still passable?"

"And leave you alone with any customers who happen along?" Anna Maria shook her head. "I'll stay until closing."

"Then I'll close early. I'm not much in the mood for telling fortunes anyway."

"You mean it?"

"We haven't had a customer in three hours. We're not likely to get anyone this late." She slid her feet to the floor, then stood and stretched. "Don't bother with the sweeping or the bank deposit. We can do it tomorrow."

Anna Maria tidied her desk, stashed the hundred and twenty bucks they'd taken in a hidden cubbyhole there, then took her raincoat from the closet. "Want to get an early dinner?"

"No, thanks."

"Catch a movie? Listen to some music? I promise I won't abandon you for the first handsome young man who catches my eye."

Evie grinned. "You mean you'd wait for the second or third? No, thanks. I wouldn't be very good company tonight."

"Are you sure? I can pick up a pizza and bring some videos over—"

"Go, Mama Anna." She held open the door. "I'm going to lock myself in and be blue. I'll see you in the morning."

As soon as she closed the door behind Anna Maria, Evie locked it, waved, then flipped the Closed sign over.

She wasn't more than five feet into the house when she realized that she wasn't alone. Everything was untouched and normal in the kitchen and the dining room, but the living room... Her unwelcome guest was there, stretched out on the sofa, sleeping as soundly as he'd pretended to this morning when Irina barged in.

And you said there was no man in your life, Irina had teased. *He* was the reason. He was the only man she'd ever wanted, the one man she couldn't have. He was the most stubborn, most skeptical, most so-damn-sure-of-himself man she'd ever known. He would require proof of her innocence from

God Himself, and even that wouldn't make things right between them. If he ever came to accept that he had falsely accused her, had wrongly damned her, his guilt would keep him away as surely as his hatred had.

Either way, she was alone. She was afraid sometimes that she would always be alone.

She didn't go closer, didn't watch him sleep. She'd indulged in that pastime often enough in the past while she spun dreams of their future. Instead, she crossed the room silently and let herself onto the gallery. She pulled a wicker chair from its protected corner close to the railing, curled up in it and stared across the courtyard as the rain misted over her.

She couldn't remember the last time the scene had matched her mood so precisely, she thought. Then, with a melancholy sigh, she corrected herself. It had been a sunny April morning—one of those rare mornings so perfect that she'd wanted to somehow capture it and keep it with her forever. The day had been warm, the light so clear and sharp. Everything had looked, tasted, smelled, felt absolutely perfect.

All because the night before she'd met Jack.

The fear of getting zapped had kept her from developing the careless, casual attitude toward sex that her friends embraced—that, and the fact that she thought the most intimate act two people could share should be shared with someone you cared about, someone whose story you knew, whose future was interwoven with your own. She had never even imagined getting intimate with a stranger.

But by the end of the first dance, Jack had no longer been a stranger. She'd known little about him beyond his name, but she'd instinctively known the important things—that she wanted him. That they belonged together. That they were good and right.

So much for instincts.

The hell of it was, if she could go back in time, she wouldn't do it any differently. She would still go to that club, still dance with him, still bring him home and fall in love with him.

Well, she would change one thing—when he tried to tell her about his case against William MacDougal. She would change the subject, distract him, stick her fingers in her ears and sing loudly to drown out his words. But all that would accomplish was delaying the inevitable. If it hadn't been MacDougal and Celeste Dardanelle, eventually it would have been something else, because the simple truth was Jack hadn't trusted her.

That knowledge still had the power to break her heart.

The French door opened with a creak, then closed. She didn't look over her shoulder, didn't want to see him standing there silhouetted against the glass. His bare feet made little sound as he pulled another wicker chair from the corner, positioned it a few feet from her, then sat down. She turned her head a fraction of an inch, cutting him out of her peripheral vision.

"I didn't mean to fall asleep here."

She knew that. Asleep he was vulnerable, and he would never willingly make himself vulnerable to her again.

"Has it rained all day?"

"Yes."

"Was it a slow day?"

"Yes."

"Maybe tomorrow will make up for it."

"It's supposed to rain then, too."

He fell silent for a time, then so easily tossed out another of his unbearably tough questions. "Do you have any regrets?"

Finally she looked at him. "What do you want me to say? That I regret telling MacDougal about Celeste? I can't regret that, because I never did it. That I regret how it ended between you and me? I wasn't responsible for that, either. It was all your doing. That I'm sorry I ever knew you?" The words caught on the heavy air and hung there before slowly fading away. When she spoke again, her voice was softer, less vehement, but no less certain. "I'm not."

For three months, she had been happy and in love and couldn't have felt more normal. Three months out of twenty-nine years. It wasn't much, but it was all she had, and she could never regret it.

She wiped a splash of rain from her face. He was silent, waiting for her to turn the question back on him, to ask about his regrets. She wasn't going to. She couldn't give him the chance to name her among them. She wasn't strong enough to bear the hurt tonight.

After he'd had his fill of silence, he leaned forward as if to get up. The wicker creaked under his weight. "Want to get something to eat?"

Her look was sharp and quick. "Do you think you can share a meal with me without choking on it?"

He ignored her sarcasm and simply waited. She should say no. The last thing she needed was more of his company. But the very last thing she needed was to be alone on a night like this. When she was feeling so hopelessly blue, anyone's company—even Jack's—was better than her own.

She stood up, scooted the chair back against the wall and walked to the French door before looking back at him. "All right. Let's have dinner."

Chapter 6

It took a little effort Monday morning, but finally Jack tracked down Sonny Roberts, sitting down to a late breakfast at one of the many restaurants that served cops for free. The waiter brought him a cup of coffee as he slid into the seat opposite his partner and offered a menu. Jack waved it away.

"J.D."

Everyone in the family had called Jack by his initials when he was a kid. That was why he allowed it from no one now—except his partner. "Sonny."

"How's vacation?"

"I've had better times."

"And worse. You know, if you'd find yourself a woman and settle down, you might come to appreciate time off."

"You're not settled with one woman," Jack pointed out.

"The ladies love me too much. I couldn't bear to break their hearts by choosing only one." Sonny stabbed the air with his fork. "Why don't you make this a real vacation—go somewhere and relax? Jamaica, Hawaii, the Bahamas?"

"On what the city pays? Yeah, right."

"You just don't get it, do you, Murphy? What the city pays is just a starting point. You're supposed to supplement it with details and friendly contributions. It's a time-honored tradition—the New Orleans way."

Jack knew his partner was kidding. Since making detective, neither of them ever had time for details—off-duty jobs such as providing security or protection—and, even before making detective, neither had ever been interested in friendly contributions. Time-honored or not, payoffs were illegal and immoral, and the one cop less likely to take one than Jack was Sonny. That was one reason—one of many—they were able to work so well together. They were able to trust each other in ways they couldn't trust their fellow officers. It was hard to turn your back on someone with a gun when you didn't know exactly whose payroll—besides the city's—he was on. But, with Sonny, Jack always knew.

"What's up at work?" Jack asked.

"Nothing much. Everyone's keeping a low profile lately. Maybe they've heard that you're out of commission for a while, and they're waiting for you to come back." Sonny sprinkled pepper sauce liberally over his eggs, then pointed the fork once more at Jack. "You look like hell, J.D. Getting any sleep?"

"Some." Over seven hours straight on Evie's couch Saturday—the best rest he'd had since the last night he'd spent in her bed. Maybe he could extend their deal to gain rights to her couch for the duration of his investigation.

Yeah, and the next thing he knew, he'd be wanting to extend it even further—up the stairs and right into her bedroom. Right into her bed.

His head knew better than to want sex with her—knew all the reasons he could never want her. And his body knew all the reasons he did want her—all the teasing. All the torment. All the pleasure.

Sonny waved a butter knife a few inches in front of Jack's face. "You're falling asleep with your eyes open," he muttered as he spread butter and jelly on a piece of toast. "Did you come by here for a reason, or did you just get lonely for the sight of my handsome face?"

"Yeah, right. I just thought I'd touch base—see what's going on. What's on the schedule for today?"

"Court. At eleven. The Rossiter case. Me and Haskins and Gomez all got subpoenaed."

Jack had been so buried in the MacDougal case that he hadn't also caught the Rossiter case—a favor for which he was most grateful. If everyone else was going to court, then they couldn't be watching MacDougal at lunch. They wouldn't find out—yet—that Evie had wormed her way back into MacDougal's life or that she'd done so at Jack's request.

Of course, one of these days they *would* find out. They were too good not to. Jack had to have something to offer when they did, or they'd shut him down.

"How's the case look?" he asked.

"Good. All my cases are good." Coming from anyone else, it would sound boastful. Coming from Sonny, it was fact. He did good work. "Why don't you come by O'Hara's tonight and help us celebrate?"

O'Hara's was a good Irish bar popular with good Irish cops and others. Jack had been a regular there for years—though not when doing his serious drinking. Then—out of guilt, out of shame—he'd gone to forgettable dives across the city. He'd needed places where no one knew him or his problems, where no one sympathized or worried or tried to make things better. Since then, he hadn't spent much time at O'Hara's. He wasn't sure he could resist the temptation.

That uncertainty didn't keep him away from Evie, though, did it?

"You don't have to drink, J.D. I'll stay sober with you. Hell, it'll keep me clearheaded for work tomorrow."

"I—I don't know. I'll see." Jack finished his coffee, then slid his chair back. "I think I'm going to head home and to bed. I could use another few hours' sleep."

"Another twenty or thirty hours," Sonny muttered. "I'm tellin' you, man, you need to find a woman. A pretty little thing that'll raise your blood pressure and lower your resistance and make you forget all about things like work and bad guys and winning and losing. You remember those times, J.D., when you used to be able to lose yourself with a woman?"

"Yeah," he said stiffly. "I remember them."

"Hell, I don't mean with—" Breaking off, Sonny grimaced. No one ever said Evie's name to him. Once they'd accepted that they couldn't make a case against her, it was as if she'd never existed. "I don't mean the serious stuff. I'm talking about the good times—the love-'em-and-leave-'em times. Somebody who can make you forget for a day or two or three, and then *you* forget *her*." Suddenly he grinned. "I've got some names and numbers."

"Keep them for yourself. I'll see you later." Dropping a dollar bill on the table to cover the coffee, he headed for the door.

"Don't go around the bend, J.D.," Sonny called after him. "We need you back on the job."

And what had made his partner think that he was about to go around the bend? Jack wondered as he left the restaurant and crossed the street to his car. His obsession with Mac-Dougal? His unhappiness with the enforced vacation? His inability to put the case aside for a while? Or—most likely— his lack of interest in easy sex with forgettable partners?

If Sonny knew where Jack was headed right now, he wouldn't think his sanity was on the line. He'd *know* it.

Fifteen minutes later, Jack pulled into a parking space around the corner from Evie's and entered through the shop door. Anna Maria, seated at her desk with a magazine, gave him a dark look, then pointedly ignored him. The lone customer watched him as he prowled the small space. Finally the woman, old enough to be his mother, gave him a calming smile. "Nervous?"

He frowned at her. "No."

"It's all right to be nervous, especially if it's your first time. Evangelina will calm you down. You'll find the most incredible peace with her."

He wanted to sneer, to make some blunt comment about the kind of peace he had, thanks to Evie. He wanted to tell the woman in excruciating detail just what kind of peace Celeste had found, just how deceitful and cold and greedy her precious Evangelina really was. Only one thing stopped him—he knew exactly the peace the woman was talking about. He'd felt it the first time he'd held Evie in his arms, the first night and every night he'd slept at her side. He'd felt it when he was with her, and it had stayed with him when they were apart.

Peace.

Now he hadn't felt it since.

Shoving his hands into his hip pockets, he stopped in front of the bookcase and skimmed the titles. Crystals, auras, chakras, amulets, spells and potions. He didn't believe in any of it and would have guessed that Evie didn't either.

It wouldn't have been the first time he was wrong about her.

The overwhelmingly sweet scent of incense moved him past the second set of shelves and brought him uncomfortably close to Anna Maria's desk. She looked up from her magazine, her malevolent gaze making contact somewhere around his knees and moving slowly up. By the time it reached his face, he was receiving the full effect of her animosity.

"Evangelina's not expecting you until eleven." Each word was separate, distinct, icy. "We would both be more comfortable if you came back then."

"I'm comfortable, Anna Maria," he lied. "If you're not, perhaps you should go someplace until then."

''Perhaps you should go to he—'' With a glance at the customer, she bit off the words and substituted a cold, ugly smile.

In spite of the smile, she was pretty. He'd never really noticed that before. Of course, after one dance with Evie, he'd never noticed other women at all. There was no physical resemblance between the two. Evie was gypsy dark, Anna Maria blond with blue eyes. Evie was exotic, Anna Maria girl-next-door. Evie was slender, with small breasts and a narrow waist. Anna Maria was about twenty pounds over what society dictated as her ideal weight, but just about perfect for men who liked lush curves. Anna Maria loved to party, and Evie loved…

There was a time when she'd claimed to love *him*. He wondered if she ever had and thought—wanted to think—that the answer was yes. He wanted to believe that some part of their relationship was real. He wanted to believe that her betrayal had come only at the end, not that it'd been in her plans from the beginning.

What did she love now? Scamming people like the old woman across the room? Taking money from well-heeled tourists and from locals who needed it to live? Preying on people's beliefs, on their weaknesses?

''Who is this woman?''

Blinking, he focused on Anna Maria. ''What woman?''

''The one who was here Saturday.'' She glanced at the customer to make sure she wasn't eavesdropping, then lowered her voice for good measure. ''The one Evie's going to see today. The one you're manipulating for the sake of your investigation.''

''Doesn't she confide in you?''

''Of course she does. *I've* never betrayed her.''

Jack opened his mouth to make his own denial, then closed it again. If Evie was innocent, what he'd done to her went far beyond betrayal. It was unforgivable, and it would leave him beyond redemption.

He returned to the subject of Irina. "Then I guess telling you who she was just slipped Evie's mind. Or—here's a possibility—maybe she doesn't want you to know."

"I know everything about her, Murphy—unlike you. You lived with her for three months and learned nothing more than her sexual preferences."

"Yeah, *me*. She always preferred me—in her bed, in her life—over everyone else. Including you." He expected her to argue. He was disappointed.

"She did," Anna Maria agreed. "She loved you. She would have happily spent the rest of her life loving you. And you destroyed her. You screwed up. You couldn't keep your mouth shut, and it caused that woman's death. You had to put the blame somewhere because you weren't man enough to accept it yourself, and so you dumped it on Evie, whose only crime was loving you."

He ignored the guilt that pricked at him—*Did you ever consider...that I might be innocent?*—and focused on Anna Maria's argument. "'That woman' has a name—Celeste. Celeste Dardanelle. You think I caused her death because I couldn't keep my mouth shut?"

"It seems a strong possibility."

"Better rethink that," he warned. "Because I told only one person in the world about Celeste. If that's what got her killed, then Evie was behind it."

Bright spots of color appeared high on Anna Maria's cheeks. "That's a lie."

"Then prove it."

"I can't. But neither can you."

She had a point. Once he'd accepted Evie's guilt, he'd busted his butt to gather enough evidence to take to the D.A. He hadn't found it. "I don't have to prove it. I *know*."

"You *think*. And that's enough for you? That justifies putting her life in danger?"

The level of his guilt increased a notch or two and turned his voice defensive. "What makes you think her life is in danger?"

"I saw the goon who brought that woman here. Normal people don't have guys like him on the payroll."

"Normal people don't have frauds like Evie on their payroll, either."

Before she could make a retort, the door behind him opened and a middle-aged woman came through. Looking shaken, she reached out to the old woman, who took her hand, patted her arm and ushered her outside into the sun.

When he started toward the door, Anna Maria jumped to her feet. "Wait— She needs a minute— You can't—"

As he closed the door, he heard her last, vicious words. "Damn you, Murphy."

"Too late." The soft response came from Evie, seated at the table and looking for all the world like a queen. "You've been damned a long time, haven't you?"

"A long time," he agreed. He walked around the table, taking in her clothing, then sat down across from her. "Dressed up for MacDougal?"

She shrugged. "It's not often someone like me gets invited to lunch with one of the most powerful—"

"And most corrupt."

"—businessmen in the city."

"Trying to impress him?" he asked stiffly.

"Maybe I'm trying to impress you."

Oh, he was impressed. The outfit was as theatrical as any he'd ever seen—a white blouse that hugged her shoulders, with full sleeves that puffed out before catching in a ruffle at her elbow; a matching skirt with yards of fabric embroidered white on white; three scarves—teal, green, purple—woven through the links of a metal belt; and leather sandals. With her hair down and her usual jewelry, the image she projected was somehow both innocent and purely sexual.

Heat burned through him—lust, desire, hunger. He clenched his hands to stop from reaching for her, clenched his jaw to keep from ordering her upstairs to change into a different outfit. She would want a reason, and he could give only one— he didn't want MacDougal to see her like this.

He didn't want to watch from a distance and know that the bastard was seeing the same things he was—the sexuality made infinitely more potent by the innocence. He didn't want to know that the murdering son of a bitch was looking at her in her white dress and thinking about taking it off her, about stripping down and taking her hard and fast, about claiming her, filling her, possessing her. He didn't want to think about doing those things himself.

He opened his mouth and forced words—hoarse, thick— into the superheated air. "Why would you want to impress me?"

"Because you're my only chance at coming out of this alive. It would be so easy for someone else to die. You've already lost two informants. No one would blink twice if the third one died, too."

He answered with more confidence than he felt. "MacDougal isn't going to kill you."

"MacDougal isn't the only one I have to worry about, is he?"

For a moment, Jack was too stunned by what she was suggesting to do more than stare. Then he scowled. "You think *I* might kill you?"

"Or let someone else do it." She shrugged. "My death would suit your sense of justice."

He stared narrowly at her, then abruptly leaned back. "You don't believe that."

Time slowed as she returned his look, then slowly, regally shook her head. "No, I don't believe it."

Before he could feel much more than a hint of relief, though, she added more.

"But I also don't believe you would grieve too much if someone else took care of me for you."

"I don't want you dead."

"Since when?"

He wanted to say that he'd never wanted to see her dead, but it wouldn't be entirely true. The night Sonny had presented him with the final damning piece of evidence against her, he'd wished for it then. The brutally hot, humid summer day when he'd stood alone beside Celeste's casket and listened to prayers from a priest who'd never known her, he'd made the wish then, too. And all those nights when he'd tried to sleep but couldn't, when he'd tried to drink himself into oblivion, when he'd been convinced that the hurt, the anger and the loss were destroying him one agonizing day at a time…hell, yes, those nights he'd wished her dead.

A few of those times, he might even actually have meant it.

"No one's going to die."

"Someone is." She said it flatly, as if she had no doubt.

"What? You see it in a vision?"

"Yes."

She spoke so quietly, with such certainty, that the mockery he'd displayed drained away. If she were anyone else, any other subject in any other investigation, he would trust his instincts that said she was speaking the gospel truth. But she wasn't someone else. She was Evie, who lied as easily as she breathed, who'd made a fool of him time and again, who was so immersed in her scams and tricks that she wouldn't know the gospel truth if it bit her.

But, even knowing that, his instincts still said she was being truthful.

Before he came up with a response, there was a knock at

the door, then Anna Maria stuck her head in. "Evie, do you have a few minutes for Vernell?"

"Sure. We'll go out in the courtyard."

As Evie stood up, Anna Maria pushed the door open farther and an elderly man came into the room. When he saw Jack, he gave him a narrowed, disapproving look but didn't slow his steps.

Anna Maria returned to the front. Evie and Vernell went out back. After a moment of drumming his fingers on the black cloth that covered the table, Jack headed toward the back, too, stopping in the kitchen for a soda, standing at the sink, watching them through the French doors.

They sat side by side on an iron bench while they talked. Evie, who too often these days gave the impression of fragility, looked absolutely strong compared to the old man. His ebony skin gleamed in the sun, and he required both belt and suspenders to hold up his neatly pressed black trousers. He was thin, insubstantial, as if in his long life he'd seen far more than his share of sorrows.

They talked ten minutes, maybe a little more, then looked as one toward the house. Even though he knew they couldn't see him, he felt uncomfortably as if he'd been caught spying and turned away.

A moment later, Evie returned to the house alone, sliding onto one of the stools at the counter. Wordlessly he offered her a soda and a beer. She took the soda and he returned the beer to the refrigerator—though not without a moment's craving.

"What was that?" he asked dryly. "A psychic emergency?"

"You might say that."

"Unfriendly old guy."

"He wasn't happy to see you here."

"Why? I don't even know him. What does he know about me?"

"He knows you're a cop. He knows you're trouble." She drew her fingertip down the side of the can, collecting moisture, then looked at him. "You weren't the only one whose friends found it necessary to warn you away from our relationship. They told you I was bad for your career. They told me you were bad for my business and bad for my life."

She knew from personal experience what his partners had thought about her, Jack remembered. One night they'd run into Sonny, Haskins and Gomez in a bar and joined them for a drink. Their hostility toward Evie had been so intense that Jack had taken her away before they'd finished even one beer.

But somehow, he thought with a cynical smile, it had never occurred—

"It never occurred to you that my friends disapproved of you, did it?"

His smile slipped. The similar choice of words was coincidence. Nothing more.

Sliding to her feet, she began unfastening the belt around her waist. "We'd better get going. We don't want to keep the MacDougals waiting."

He quickly secured the mike and transmitter, trying not to touch her any more than necessary—trying not to breathe, to think, to want. Once she was ready, she told Anna Maria they were leaving, then they went their separate ways.

He was parked in his usual spot near the big house, binoculars trained on her car, when she turned off the street. The guard waved her through, then secured the gate behind her, leaving her locked inside. With William MacDougal.

For the sake of the case, he hoped nothing went wrong. *Only* for the sake of the case.

Right.

As she approached the house, she spoke softly, barely moving her lips. "Why only five thousand dollars, Jack? Look at this place. If he was buying information that would save him from ruin, don't you think he'd be willing to pay more than five thousand dollars? Don't you think I'd be smart enough to ask for more?''

Slowly he swung the binoculars to the house. He knew how much MacDougal had paid for the land and how much more to build the house. He knew the value of the antiques that furnished it, knew how much income the man had claimed to Uncle Sam since coming to New Orleans and had a ballpark figure on the millions he hadn't claimed.

She was right. Five thousand bucks was pocket change to a man like MacDougal. He spent far more than that on household staff every month, dropped five times that on a single race at the tracks. Information on a traitor in his ranks should have been worth at least fifty thousand, maybe two or three times more. Why had she asked for such a paltry sum?

One answer was so obvious that it came immediately to mind. He didn't want to consider it, wanted to focus instead on more convoluted theories, but he was too good a cop to overlook the obvious. No matter how the possibility disturbed him, he had to face it.

Maybe she hadn't asked for such a paltry amount.

Maybe she hadn't asked for any money at all.

Maybe she was innocent.

And if that was the case, the betrayal—the guilt and the unforgivable blame—was his. All his. And he was unredeemably damned.

A servant escorted Evie through the house and onto the patio, where a table was set underneath a giant umbrella on the upper level. She laced her fingers tightly together, drew a couple of deep breaths, then put on her best-customer smile as she approached.

"Evangelina. Darling, she's here." Irina came to meet her, catching her hand. Evie felt a rush of sensation that faded the instant the contact was broken, when Irina traded her hand for her husband's arm. "Evangelina, this is my husband, William

MacDougal. Darling, this is Evangelina… I'm sorry. I don't know your last name.''

"I don't use one. Mr. MacDougal, I'm pleased to meet you.''

He sized her up in one look and deemed her harmless. She wished she could say the same about him.

He offered his hand, and she stared at it. It was soft, unmarked by calluses—the hand of a man who never did his own dirty work. If he was guilty of even half the deeds Jack believed, the simple act of shaking his hand could send her into nightmares she didn't need. But in twenty-nine years, she hadn't yet learned an easy, gracious, non-suspicion-provoking way to avoid a handshake—and the *last* thing she wanted to provoke in this man was suspicion—and so she slowly reached out.

His palm was warm, dry, his grip firm. Those were her only impressions. *Thank God.*

Irina called to the servant to serve their meal, then they seated themselves around the table.

"Evangelina.'' The syllables dropped off MacDougal's tongue, each distinct. "Is that what people call you?''

"It's my name.''

"Was your mother a fan of Longfellow's *Evangeline?*''

"It's a family name. Tell me, Mr. MacDougal…'' She paused briefly, giving him an opportunity to say, Oh, call me William.

He didn't.

"Are you skeptical of all psychic gifts or just mine?''

His smile was smooth and easy and turned an average face into a handsome one. "Did Irina tell you that I'm a nonbeliever or did you divine it?''

"A person doesn't need psychic powers to notice the obvious. Have you ever had a reading?''

"No, I never have. You want to try to convert me?''

Smugness prevented his expression from coming off as the

friendliness he pretended. The look alone tempted her to give him the benefit of her best performance. She fooled tourists with cold readings all the time, and this wouldn't even be completely cold. Thanks to Jack, she knew a lot about MacDougal that your garden variety psychic shouldn't know—things she would bet Irina didn't know.

But convincing William MacDougal—criminal, murderer, dangerous man—that she could uncover his secrets didn't seem the best way to stay healthy, and she wanted very much to stay healthy.

He was waiting for her answer. She gave it with a smile. "I never read skeptics when they know they're being read. They're too tempted to play games."

"Wonderful policy. Of course, it allows you to insist that you *could* do it, if only you were willing to try."

"Of course," she agreed.

He laughed. "I like this one, Irina. She's much more interesting than that Romanov character. What do you think of him, Evangelina?"

"I make it a policy to neither criticize nor compliment the competition. Being in business yourself, I'm sure you understand."

"I criticize the competition all the time. The best gambling in New Orleans—anywhere in the South—is on the *Scotsman's Queen*. Why don't you come over some evening? I'll give you a personal tour."

For one moment there was something more than congeniality in his expression—some subtle suggestion of intimacy, of possibilities. The idea made the muscles in her stomach tighten, but through sheer will she kept the revulsion from her expression. "I appreciate the invitation, but I'm not a gambler, Mr. MacDougal, and I prefer to keep solid ground under my feet."

He continued to dominate the conversation throughout the

meal. Once the dessert dishes had been removed, though, he immediately stood. "I must return to my office. Evangelina."

She accepted his handshake and silently congratulated herself for not pulling back when he held her hand seconds longer than necessary.

"It's been a pleasure. If you change your mind about that tour…"

"I'll let you know." *When hell freezes over.*

He bent over Irina, touching her long wild hair, brushing a kiss to her cheek. For such simple touches, it was an intimate farewell. It made Evie wonder—since she already knew how Irina felt about him—how *he* felt about Irina. A week ago she'd scoffed at the idea of William MacDougal in love. Right this minute it didn't sound so ridiculous.

So why the predatory-male look he'd given *her?*

"Dinner at eight," he murmured as he straightened.

"I'll be here." Irina watched until he was inside, then eagerly leaned toward Evie. "Well? Did you learn anything?"

Evie delayed her answer by reaching for her tea. Though they'd known this question was coming, she and Jack hadn't discussed her answer. Did he want her to tell the truth—that she knew nothing more about William MacDougal now than she had an hour ago, except that he was smug, charming and somewhat interested in a little extramarital entertainment? Or would Jack prefer that she pass off information learned from him as her own psychic discoveries?

She didn't have a clue, and looking in the direction where he waited and listened didn't provide one.

Returning the glass to the table, she wiped her fingers on the napkin, then folded her hands in her lap. "Skeptics are difficult to read, as you can imagine, especially when they're on guard. However… I don't believe he's exactly what he seems. He has secrets, and they're dangerous."

"What kind of secrets?"

She smiled gently. "If I knew that, they wouldn't be secrets

anymore, would they?'' Then she shrugged. ''I don't know.
Something to do with his business—perhaps with the woman
who was killed. What do you know about her?''

Irina gazed off into the distance. ''Very little, actually. She
worked for him at the *Scotsman's Queen,* and she was murdered. It happened about a year ago. Don't you remember, or
are there so many murders in New Orleans that you lost
track?''

''I had problems of my own a year ago. I had no time to
follow someone else's.''

Irina's sigh was delicate and made her shiver. ''People made
a point of repeating the rumors to me when I first came here—
my hairstylist, my masseuse, my maid. They all told different
stories—that the woman was blackmailing him with evidence
of his illegal doings, that she was working for the police, that
she was having an affair with him—all with the same ending.
That he killed her.''

''And what did William say?''

''That he didn't know her. He said she worked in the casino.
One night she disappeared, and the next morning her body
was found in the lake. He said he didn't even know which of
the dozens of young women who worked for him she was.''

''But you're not convinced.''

Looking faintly embarrassed, Irina shrugged. ''As you said,
my husband keeps dangerous secrets. He didn't like being
questioned. And this house…''

She gestured and Evie turned to look. The house was a
reflection of the man who lived there, and part of what it
reflected was evil.

Wishing for the full effect of the midday sun, she looked
back at Irina. ''Are you sure you want to know his secrets?''

Instead of answering, the woman picked up her drink and
gestured toward a nearby table sans umbrella. ''Do you
mind?''

Evie took her own drink and moved to another chair. Its

cushions were sun-warmed and went a long way toward easing the chill inside her. Once they were settled, she prodded her client for an answer. "Irina? Are you sure?"

"I need to know."

"And what will you do with the information?"

For a moment Irina's expression was pure anguish. Because her fairy-tale marriage was more likely a nightmare come to life with a husband who was certainly no prince? Or because she might have to give up all this luxury and return to the island where she'd grown up, poor and alone, with little to show for her marriage but disillusionment?

"I don't know," she said at last. "I just don't know."

And Evie believed her.

When she was finally able to take her leave, she started around the house to her car. She was halfway there when Irina caught up with her.

"I forgot to give you this." She held out a check folded in half. "We never discussed your fees, but I think this should be sufficient. It's what I paid Alexei."

Evie took the check and hid her tiny shudder of revulsion. Once again William MacDougal's tainted money would be residing in her bank account, and once again she was fairly sure she couldn't keep it. His cash could buy nothing she wanted in her house or in her life.

Without looking at the amount, she folded the check in half once again, then closed her fingers around it. "I'm sure it's more than enough."

"Can I see you again on Wednesday?"

Evie nodded and set a time, then climbed into her car and, with a wave, drove away. The young guard at the end of the drive opened the gate and gave her a shy smile as she drove through. He looked so young, innocent and smitten. She wondered if he had a clue that he worked for a murderer.

She made it home without so much as a glimpse of Jack. Maybe he had other business to take care of. Maybe he would trust her to remove his equipment and put it someplace safe until they needed it again. Maybe she wouldn't have to face him again until Wednesday.

Cutting through the house to the shop, she found Anna Maria reading a magazine over the remains of a chef's salad. "What's so interesting?" she asked as she filched a strip of turkey slathered with blue cheese dressing.

"'Fifteen Christmas wreaths to make with items found around any household.' And 'Lose ten pounds in fifteen days.' Not off *these* hips. Or how about 'How to ask your boss for a raise'?" Anna Maria subjected her to a long, judging look. "How'd it go?"

"Okay."

Whatever she saw must have convinced her, because she nodded in agreement. "Are you ready to work?"

"Actually, I thought I might close up for the rest of the day."

"So you can spend it with *him?*"

"So I can spend it alone. I want to laze around and do nothing. It's called a day off, Anna Maria, remember? We used to take one every week." She summoned a smile. "Surely there's something you'd rather be doing than sitting here and sweltering."

"Sure, but I don't think Tom Cruise is in town." But she closed her magazine and began clearing her desk. "If he comes over here, don't answer the door."

Evie laughed. "Honey, if Tom Cruise rings my bell, you can be darn sure I'm going to answer."

"I mean Murphy. If he shows up—and, like bad luck, he keeps coming back—pretend you're not here."

"Yes, ma'am." It sounded like a plan she could live with.

They closed up quickly, then, alone in the house, Evie went upstairs. After changing into shorts and a T-shirt, she settled on the chaise longue in the courtyard, crosslegged, spine straight, eyes closed. She'd been meditating longer than she'd known the name for it. It calmed her, balanced her, helped her find some measure of peace and control. She wasn't fanatical about it—didn't have a set time and place—but rather used it as necessary to make it through the day.

Today it was *very* necessary.

She was drowsy, her breathing slow and measured, her body heavy and drained, when abruptly she realized that she was no longer alone. Her guest made no sound. He wore no fragrance that she could smell and didn't stand where he shaded her from the sun, but she knew he was there as surely as if he'd done all those things. Worse, she knew who he was without looking—knew it from the loathing that crept along her skin and seeped underneath.

Drawing one last breath, she opened her eyes. Her gaze went directly to William MacDougal, seated on the bench where Vernell had sat a few hours earlier. In his elegant summer suit, he looked at home in the courtyard. She was the one who felt out of place.

"Invite yourself in," she said coolly. "Make yourself comfortable."

"I knocked. When you didn't answer, I came back here."

"Generally when a person doesn't answer the door, it's because she doesn't want to be disturbed."

"Or perhaps she's out back and didn't hear." He nodded toward the iron gate. "If you really don't want to be disturbed, you should put a lock on that gate and use it."

"What do you want, Mr. MacDougal?"

"This is more like it," he said with a gesture indicating her clothes. "The other outfit was a bit dramatic, don't you think?"

"My clients expect a certain image. You should understand. Your clients also have expectations."

"That they do—though they have little to do with me and everything to do with the games and the *Queen*."

"The product you're selling is gambling. The product I'm

selling is myself.'' She regretted the words the instant they left her mouth, regretted the way they made his gaze narrow and focus more intensely on her.

"And you don't sell yourself cheap, do you?'' he asked softly.

"I don't sell myself at all in the way you're thinking.''

"And how do you know—'' He smirked. "Oh, yes. You have psychic powers.''

"What do you want?''

A layer of friendliness slipped away, revealing a tougher surface underneath. "My wife is a trusting soul—gullible, you might even say. An unscrupulous person might try to take advantage of her.''

"Lucky for us, I'm not unscrupulous.''

"Aren't you?'' A perplexed look came over his face. "As I recall, a young woman who worked for me was murdered last year. The authorities were convinced that a psychic down here in the Quarter was involved—a woman by the name of Evie DesJardien. That's *you,* isn't it?''

She felt a chill in spite of the heat. "I was never charged with anything.''

"For lack of evidence, not because they believed in your innocence.''

"If you recall, the same authorities were convinced that I was working with *you.* They were wrong.''

"Wrong about any connection to me,'' he pointed out, and she wished fervently that she was still wired and Jack's tape recorder was taking down every word. "But wrong about the first part? I have no way of knowing.''

"So you've come here to warn me away from Irina.'' Good. Then Jack would leave her alone—and MacDougal, too—and life could return to normal.

"Not exactly. Just to warn you in general. Don't hurt my wife. Don't disappoint her. Don't scam her anymore than you already have. And, most importantly…'' He left the bench and came to stand very near her chair, forcing her to tilt her head back to see him. "Don't try to come between us. I won't allow that to happen. Do you understand?"

She nodded.

He smiled pleasantly. "Don't bother getting up. I'll let myself out."

Chapter 7

Why only five thousand dollars?

The question had been in the back of Jack's mind ever since Evie had asked it. Maybe the five thousand had been only a portion of the payoff, with the rest hidden in accounts that they hadn't been able to find. Maybe she simply hadn't known better, hadn't dreamed big enough. Maybe the five grand had merely been a down payment, then, with suspicion cast her way, MacDougal had known that paying more would bring them both down. Maybe they'd come up with some sort of deferred payment plan from the beginning.

Or maybe she hadn't asked for any money at all, which meant the money had been planted by the real killer. Maybe five thousand was all he—or they—could afford to lose. And if that was the case, Jack was even guiltier than he already felt, because he could think of only one reason anyone would frame Evie for Celeste's murder, only one connection that tied the two women together: him. She could have been set up—their relationship destroyed, her honor and honesty called into question, her life disrupted—for no reason beyond the fact that she'd been a part of *his* life.

Lacking the strength to deal with such possibilities right then, he pushed the questions back where they belonged as he turned the corner onto Evie's block. He'd parked in a public lot on Toulouse and walked the rest of the way. Just in case anyone was curious, he hadn't wanted his Mustang anywhere around her house.

But William MacDougal didn't share his reluctance.

Jack stepped into a recessed doorway and stared at the car illegally parked in front of Evie's shop. MacDougal's wasn't the only chauffeured gray Mercedes in the city, but it was the one Jack was most familiar with. He'd spent so many hours tailing it that he knew it, and its driver, in his sleep. This was one place he'd never imagined finding it.

As he watched, MacDougal came out of the alley and climbed into the backseat. The instant the door closed, the driver pulled away from the curb. Jack turned his back as the car drove past, then watched through the plate glass until it turned the corner and disappeared. Muttering curses, he headed for Evie's, covering the few hundred feet in record time, shoving the gate open with enough force to make it swing shut again behind him.

Just inside he came to an abrupt stop. Evie was lying on her stomach on the chaise longue, hair falling to hide her face, utterly motionless. His heart stopped, then resumed beating at double time, and his lungs felt as if they would burst. Pure panic washed over him, then receded when he saw the slow, deep movement of a breath. He started toward her, his movements jerky, his hands unsteady. "Evie?"

For a moment she didn't move, then a great sigh shuddered through her and she raised her head. "It's impossible to meditate out here anymore."

"No one meditates lying facedown."

"Meditation is extremely personal. You do it however suits

you.'' Slowly, she sat up and moved into a more traditional pose—cross-legged, spine straight, palm to palm. If he didn't know her so well, he would think she was as calm as she looked, but he noticed the tightness of her jaw, the white spots in her fingernails where her fingers pressed together, the unnatural stiffness in the way she held herself.

He pulled a chair closer. "What the hell was he doing here?"

With great control, she restrained a shiver. "Proving my claim of innocence. He knew that I was a suspect in Celeste's death. He acknowledged that the police were wrong about my working for him. Unfortunately, I'd already removed your wire and you weren't here to record it even if I hadn't. Where were you?"

He was half embarrassed to answer. "I stopped to get some lunch." He'd thought it would be best, after lusting after her from a distance for more than an hour, to give himself a break before facing her up close again. He'd eaten a fast-food burger and fries and distracted himself with questions about the money, until he couldn't delay any longer.

Until he hadn't *wanted* to delay any longer.

"Great. My alleged accomplice unequivocally states that I wasn't working for him, and you're having a burger at the time." Her gaze narrowed on his face. "But it doesn't matter. You wouldn't have believed him even if you'd heard him, would you?"

Not answering seemed his best choice. Truth was, he didn't know what he would have believed. Even compulsive liars told the truth sometimes. Part of his job was figuring out which times were which. Maybe he could have guessed with MacDougal. With Evie, he'd lost all perspective—and there were five thousand and one reasons why.

Five thousand dollars…and one hell of a long time without her.

She settled back in the chaise, stretching her legs out

straight. The clothes she'd changed into—denim shorts, a faded Mardi Gras T-shirt—didn't belong in the same closet with the white dress they'd replaced. They were loose, faded, not the least bit flattering—and they didn't do a damn thing to cool the heat curling through him. The idea of removing these clothes was just as appealing as removing the white dress, because the end result would be the same—Evie, naked.

Wiping the sweat from his face, he wished for a cold shower and a colder drink. He wished for some magic potion that would leave him immune to her, for some amulet that would keep her at a distance. Failing that, he wished for one that would absolve him of responsibility for bringing her closer.

But there was no shower cold enough, no magic or amulet strong enough. There was nothing that would grant him absolution. *Nothing.*

But punishing MacDougal was a start.

With his reasons for being here—MacDougal, Celeste, justice, revenge—clearly centered in his mind, he asked, "What did he want?"

She repeated the conversation, from her sarcastic greeting to MacDougal's cool goodbye. Jack's instincts said her story was complete. She hadn't left anything out.

For a time they sat in silence. A horn sounded on the street. Voices passed by on the sidewalk. Cooking smells drifted from an open window next door. Outside these walls life went on as normal. Inside, thanks to him, it didn't.

"Was he threatening me?" Evie's voice was small, disguised as calm but just the slightest bit unsteady.

"MacDougal's not that subtle. Having his goons grab you off the street, take you someplace blindfolded and shove a gun in your mouth while telling you what he wants—that's more his style."

She didn't look as if she found any comfort in his response—and she was right not to. Goons with guns were MacDougal's style for people who double-crossed him, who stole from him or threatened him. But such a warning to a woman as fragile as Evie appeared, a woman no more dangerous than she appeared, would be overkill.

"Do you feel threatened?" he asked.

Her smile was as phony as the crystal ball inside, and it faded before it fully formed. "Yes," she admitted. "I do."

"Okay. Then let's put new locks on this place, including on this gate and the one across the driveway. The ones you have are so flimsy that anyone with a few minutes on his hands can pick them."

Her gaze turned speculative, and he knew beyond a doubt that she was remembering part of the evidence against her—the phone calls to MacDougal's office from her house. Someone else must have made them, she'd insisted, because *she* hadn't. Who else? he'd asked. She'd claimed that the house was empty, and no one had keys—at that time, at least—but her and him. How could someone else have gotten inside?

Maybe, she had replied stiffly, they had picked the lock.

He had examined all the exterior doors for telltale scratches, gouges or signs of jimmying. He'd found nothing and had dismissed her explanation. He had dismissed all her explanations.

"Do you think new locks will keep out MacDougal's people if they want to come in?"

"No. But it might slow them down."

"I can't afford—" Breaking off, she reached into her pocket, withdrew a small rectangle of paper and offered it to him. "Do something with that."

He unfolded the paper. It was a check made out in Irina's hand for an amount that made him blink. He stared at it a moment, feeling a surge of hatred for the woman's husband. Killing Celeste had been so damn unnecessary. All she'd been trying to do was make a new life for herself, one where she got to choose who she had sex with, where no one could use her as a punching bag, where she didn't have to live in fear that people she was supposed to be able to trust would hurt her. MacDougal could have offered her money—less than the amount of this check would have been sufficient—and she would have disappeared from his life. She would have apologized to Jack and taken off to a place better than this one, and he would have understood. He would have let her go and found some other way to nail the bastard.

Resisting the urge to tear the check to pieces, he returned it to Evie. "Sign it and put it in the bank."

Revulsion edged into her expression. "I don't want his money."

"If Irina were a regular client, you'd be taking her money."

"Not this much."

"You didn't ask for that much. She offered. Romanov had no problem accepting it."

"Of course he had no problem. He's only in it for the money."

"And why are you in it?"

A startled silence settled between them. She was surprised that he'd asked the question at all, Jack guessed, instead of assuming that she was in it for the money, too. He was surprised that he'd asked in all seriousness, with none of his usual skepticism or mockery.

After a time, she shrugged. "I can't stop being psychic, no matter how much I would like to. It influences everything— how people feel about me, what I can do, who I can get close to. It's made me a freak. Since it's cost me so much over the years, I thought it only fair that it give something back. So I set up shop, started calling myself by my first name and for the first time in my life began using the abilities instead of trying to hide them."

"You can't get rid of them, so you may as well profit from them." When she nodded, he leaned forward, put the check in her hand and folded her fingers over it. "There's this week's profit."

"I don't want his money!"

"So give it away. Just give some of it to a locksmith to beef up the security on this place." He suspected even as she returned the check to her pocket that she would give it all away and pay the expenses out of her own pocket. Personally, he would find a certain satisfaction in using the bastard's own money to protect herself from him. But Evie had to do what she could live with.

For a long time, he'd thought she was perfectly capable of living with blood on her hands.

Right this moment he wasn't so sure.

Because that was a line of thought he didn't want to pursue, he deliberately changed the subject. "MacDougal offered you a private tour of the *Queen*. Why did you turn it down?" He'd sworn aloud when she refused. Getting close to MacDougal was her whole purpose for being there, and the bastard had just offered her the opportunity to spend an entire evening with him. How the hell could she turn that down?

On the other hand, some part of him had been glad that she'd refused, because he'd seen through the binoculars—

"Because I saw the way he was looking at me."

The muscles in his neck tightened as he pushed for confirmation that she'd seen the same thing he had. "And how was that?"

"As if..."

When she didn't finish, he did. "As if he was much more interested in the private part than the tour."

The look she gave him was apprehensive. "I'd hoped I had imagined that."

"Hell, how could any man look at you and not want you?"

Her answer came quietly. "You manage."

He laughed. It was unexpected, sounded rusty and foreign, but it was unquestionably a laugh. "You think so? If you believe that, then you're looking in the wrong direction." He stood up and headed for the gate. "I'll call a locksmith in the morning, and I'll see you Wednesday."

Before the shop opened Tuesday morning, Evie left the house on foot. It was a hot, humid morning, with clouds in the sky that offered the promise of relief. She wouldn't mind a gentle rain, but, please, no thunder, lightning or deluges. After a slow Saturday and most of Monday off, she could use a full day's business.

Then she thought of the check in her purse and snorted. It was enough to pay her bills for a month or two. She could even take a vacation—something she hadn't done since the day she'd decided to go into business ten years ago. But the only place she wanted to go was back—or ahead—in time. Back to when she and Jack were happy or ahead to when she might be over him. But time travel definitely exceeded her abilities and the abilities of everyone she knew.

She reached her destination—the bank—and deposited the check. It made her account look appealingly healthy. It would remain that way—oh, until noon. By then, she would have written a check to the locksmith who'd called to arrange an appointment and another to her favorite women's charity, and her balance would once more be dangerously close to insufficient, where it usually resided.

When she came out onto the sidewalk again, she stood for a moment and simply looked around. She had a strange feeling—the hairs on her neck standing on end, a quiveriness to her nerves—that someone was watching her, but not Jack. He generated a whole other set of strange feelings. MacDougal, perhaps, or some of his goons? Jack's partners who were working the case with him?

She looked down one side of the street, then up the other. There was no sign of Jack or the Mustang. No vaguely familiar faces. No one standing around trying to look inconspicuous. No one sitting in parked cars as if waiting for someone. It was a perfectly normal morning scene, undeserving of such paranoia.

But the feeling was hard to shake. It didn't completely go away until she was safely inside her house, with her inadequate locks secured behind her. Breathing a sigh of relief, she walked down the hall, only to come to a sudden stop in the kitchen doorway. She couldn't stop the startled gasp that escaped before it registered that the person sitting at the counter was her cousin. "You startled me," she said reprovingly.

"Sorry. I brought beignets from Café du Monde, croissants from La Madeleine and fruit from home."

Evie turned into the kitchen and picked up a slice of sweet cantaloupe. Her choice made her cousin frown and reach for a berry-filled croissant. "No wonder you're thin and I'm not. It's unnatural, I'm telling you, to prefer cantaloupe over this stuff."

"There's a lot about me that's unnatural. Just ask Antoinette. She'll tell you."

"Aunt Toinette is the unnatural one," Anna Maria said loyally. "She doesn't have a maternal bone in her body."

"She just wanted a different kind of daughter, that's all." Evie reached for a napkin to wipe the juice from her chin, then changed the subject from her mother. "I've got a locksmith coming by this morning."

"It's too late, honey. The danger has already walked right in and set himself down."

Evie smiled faintly. "Jack's not a problem."

"Everyone who knows him thinks Jack Murphy is a problem—from the criminals he arrests, the cops he works with, the lawyers he keeps in business to the family he has nothing to do with."

"How do you know about his family?"

Anna Maria switched to the voice normally reserved for tourists. "Mama Anna knows all, sees all, hears all." At Evie's wry look, she laughed. "Well, she hears all—at least, all you say to her. There was a time when Murphy was your one and only topic of conversation. I knew more about him than the men in my own life.''

"I must have been an incredible pain."

"You were in love." Anna Maria's voice softened. "You know, I kind of thought I was in love back then, too, but I wasn't. My heart didn't break anything like yours when it ended.''

Evie stared at her. "I never knew—''

"I never told you. You were wrapped up in Murphy, and I was wrapped up in—'' She swallowed, then said the name delicately, as if it might hurt "—James. It was a very private relationship. Truthfully, I don't think he approved of what we do here. He didn't think it would do his reputation much good to be connected in any way with the mysterious and slightly notorious Evangelina.''

"He was probably right. Being slightly notorious certainly hasn't done *my* reputation much good." Evie rinsed her fingers and dried them, then squeezed Anna Maria's hand. In the instant before she drew back, she felt a rush of emotion—love, hurt, disappointment, regret, anger. "I'm sorry. You should have quit your job. If you loved him…''

"I'm not sure I did. And why should I quit a job I like because some guy has problems with it?''

"What's to like? It pays a fraction what you're worth. The hours are long. It's disreputable.''

"I like dealing with tourists. I like working with you.'' Anna Maria grinned devilishly. "And where else can I get paid to give Jack Murphy a hard time every time he walks through the door? Speaking of the devil, is he going to show up today?''

"I don't think so.'' Not that she would mind if he did. His response to her comment that he managed to not want her— *If you believe that, then you're looking in the wrong direction*—had intrigued her. Of course, it was a long way from wanting to believing in, trusting, having. Jack could want until a weaker man would die from it, but it would only make him stronger and more determined than ever.

She became aware of Anna Maria's steady, all-knowing look a moment before the question came. It was asked in a soft, comforting, intimate-best-friends tone, but that made the answer no easier to consider. "Are you going to fall in love with him all over again?"

Evie shrugged uneasily. "I've never had much restraint where he's concerned."

"Oh, I don't know. I thought you showed admirable restraint in not bringing a thousand curses down on his head. Not waiting outside the station and running him down in the street showed considerable restraint. Not meeting him at the door with a shotgun loaded for bear shows tremendous restraint."

Evie couldn't even smile. "I don't want another broken heart. I'm still dealing with the last one."

"What are the chances of avoiding one this time?"

"Oh, I think it's pretty much guaranteed. He's going to use me to get what he wants, and then he's going to leave."

"Maybe not. Maybe he'll come to his senses. Maybe he'll see what everyone else who knows you has known all along— that you could never betray someone you love. That you could never hurt anyone."

Evie shrugged again. "If he ever comes to believe that, then it'll be himself that he can't forgive. Either way, I lose." And she'd lost so much—the future they'd intended to spend together, the family they'd planned to have, the happily-ever-after she'd looked for all her life.

Before Anna Maria could make more than a sympathetic murmur, the doorbell rang. "I'll get it," she announced, sliding off the stool.

Evie was content to let her go. She busied herself with setting a pan of water on the stove to boil, then counting out enough bags for a half gallon of tea. While she stared into the pan, she idly noted the voices in the front hall—the locksmith's low, definitely male, and Anna Maria, sounding her most charming Southern belle-ish.

So the locksmith was young and handsome, she thought with a faint smile, envying her cousin's easy manner with young, handsome men, wishing she shared it. If she did, if she'd known countless men before she'd met Jack and countless since, maybe she wouldn't have been—wouldn't still be— so susceptible to him. Maybe she wouldn't have fallen in love with him so quickly, and maybe losing him wouldn't have broken her heart so thoroughly.

"Don't you know a watched pot never boils?"

Speaking of the devil... She glanced over her shoulder. Jack was leaning in the doorway. "Where did you come from?"

Anna Maria answered before he could. "Jeez, you leave the door open for two minutes, and look what wanders in."

"I came in with Bobby." He nodded toward the locksmith, trailing behind Anna Maria. "He's my cousin."

Bobby—definitely young and handsome—gave her a nod as Anna Maria finished the introductions. "Bobby, this is Evie, your customer and *my* cousin, but she's busy, so we won't bother her. Come on outside and I'll show you those gates you were asking about."

Evie watched until the French door closed behind them, then glanced at Jack. "How old is he?"

"Old enough to take care of himself." He circled the counter, sat down on a stool and helped himself to one of the croissants.

"Old enough to take care of himself and old enough to deal with Anna Maria are two vastly different ages."

"He's twenty-six, twenty-eight, somewhere around there. Your water's boiling."

She dropped the tea bags in, then removed the pan from the burner. "I thought you weren't coming by until tomorrow."

"I changed my mind."

"Why aren't you working?"

He gave her a dry look. "Don't worry. The city's getting an honest day's work out of me."

"Which is more than they can say about a fair number of your fellow officers." She ignored his sharp look and went on. "But they always get their money's worth from you. You're dedicated to the job, you give a hundred and ten percent, you never take a payoff, never blow a case and never let a bad guy walk free."

"But I got an innocent woman killed."

She had started to wipe a counter that didn't need it, but his words stilled her. "No, you didn't," she quietly disagreed. "A number of people share the responsibility for Celeste Dardanelle's murder, but you're not one of them."

"I put her in that job. I convinced her that I could protect her. I promised her a new life." His voice grew tighter, colder. "All she got was a painful death."

"But it wasn't your fault. William MacDougal is to blame, and the people who actually killed her and the person who betrayed her, but not you." *And not me.* But she kept that plaintive little denial to herself. "You're a good cop, Jack."

He tried to lighten the moment with an uneasy smile and a not-quite-teasing warning. "Careful. You're starting to sound like you respect what I do."

Tearing her gaze from his, she resumed the unnecessary cleaning job. "I always respected you. If you'd respected me, things might have turned out differently."

"I did—"

"No, you didn't. You were embarrassed by Evangelina. You wanted to pretend that that part of me didn't exist. You never could quite trust me because you thought I was a fraud and a con artist, and that made it so much easier for you to believe the worst when Celeste died."

She expected an argument or denial, or some sneering comment about how the evidence proved her guilt. What she got, after a moment, was a weary agreement, one that seemed to surprise him as much as her. "You're right. I used to wish you were a waitress or a nurse or—hell, anything but a *psychic*." He said the word as if it were obscene, as if simply saying it might contaminate him. "You should have heard the jokes, the comments, the warnings. Everyone thought I was a fool for getting involved with you. When the evidence started coming in against you, it proved they were right. I *was* a fool."

Leaving the washcloth on the counter, Evie took a watering pitcher from under the sink and filled it. She needed to move, needed to find something to occupy her or she was going to sink to the floor, curl up in the corner and not come out for a long, long time.

What a wonderful way to start the day, she thought morosely as she carried the can to a large ivy in the living room— finding out that not only had she been responsible for ending Anna Maria's relationship with the unknown James, but, in a roundabout way, she'd been responsible for her own broken heart. Did Jack think she *wanted* to be this way? Didn't he realize that she would give anything to be normal, to wake up tomorrow and have nothing but the usual five senses? Didn't he understand how badly it hurt to know that he'd been ashamed of her, that he'd been unable to trust her solely because of something she had no control over?

He reached around her and tilted the spout of the can up, stopping the flow of water, even as, below, water trickled from the pot onto the tabletop. "It's not your fault. You never tried to hide what you were. I just couldn't accept it."

And he still couldn't accept it. Tears seeped into her eyes as she stared at the wall straight ahead. He still couldn't believe in her. He thought she spent eight hours a day in her shop, ripping off anyone foolish enough to walk through the door. He thought she played on people's beliefs and fears when they were at their most vulnerable. He thought she was worse than a thief, because she played mind games with her customers while relieving them of their cash.

He thought she was so many things except the one thing she'd always been: a woman who had loved him more dearly than life itself.

"So…" She was relieved that her voice sounded fairly normal. "If I'd been a waitress or a nurse, would you have trusted me? Would you have believed me when I said I didn't betray you?"

He backed away, making no sounds for her to hear, but she felt the distance grow between them. "I believed the evidence."

"Then that's the difference between you and me," she said with a calmness she didn't feel as she turned to face him. "All the evidence in the world never could have convinced me that you'd played a part in a woman's murder. Evidence can be manufactured. Innocent people can be framed. But I trusted you. I would have believed in you forever."

"You think I should have ignored the evidence because I loved you?"

"No. I think you should have looked past it to the truth." She started to walk away, but turned back to ask one more set of questions. "Tell me something, Jack. That love of yours—was that the best you're capable of? Or was it the best you thought someone like me deserved?"

He didn't answer. But it was just as well. She wasn't sure she could handle any answer he might give.

Jack was trying to ignore the discomfort in his gut and the ugly certainty that once again he'd let Evie down—and trying to convince himself that it didn't matter—when distraction came at the same time from both the front and the back of the house. The doorbell rang at the same moment Bobby and Anna Maria returned from outside.

After giving Evie a wary look and him a black one, Anna
Maria went to answer the door. She returned a moment later
with her arm around an older woman—elegant, lovely, with
familiar exotic eyes—whose mere presence was enough to in-
crease Evie's stress level a few notches.

So this was Antoinette DesJardien. Though he'd never met
either of Evie's parents, he would have recognized her from
the eyes alone—or from Evie's tension. She had even less
contact with her parents than he had with his own, and she'd
told him little about them. At the time he hadn't been particularly interested. All he'd wanted to know about was *her*. Not
her business, not her family, not her abilities. Just her.

A year ago that had seemed like enough. Today he knew it
wasn't.

"Your mother will be happy to hear that I've seen you,"
Antoinette was saying to Anna Maria. "She says it's been a
long time."

"Less than two weeks, Aunt Toinette. I was there on the
Fourth."

"And she's wrong, you know," her aunt continued, raising
one hand to brush Anna Maria's hair back. "I don't think
bleaching your hair makes you look cheap. You have the coloring to carry it off. And that style doesn't make you look
heavier at all."

Anna Maria rolled her eyes, which Evie took as her cue to
break in. "Mother." She approached the woman with open
arms, but Antoinette stepped back and to the side, gracelessly
avoiding the embrace by putting Anna Maria between them.

Evie gave him a look that she meant to be defiant. She
succeeded there, but along with the defiance—and unintended,
he was sure—was hurt of the ages-old, relentless, never-gets-
easier variety. My mother thinks I'm cursed, she had told Irina
at their second meeting. *She's afraid of what I might unleash
on her, and so she keeps her distance.* At the time he'd been

scornful, thinking it was an obvious ploy to gain Irina's sympathy. Apparently, he'd been wrong.

Sometimes he feared he'd been wrong about everything.

Evie stopped a half-dozen feet from Antoinette. "I wasn't expecting you."

The older woman looked at Bobby, then Jack, and dismissed them as unimportant, a part of her daughter's life she didn't want to know about. "I had an appointment in the area and thought I'd drop by and see if we could arrange an evening for dinner. Your father's birthday is coming up, you know."

"The twenty-eighth. I know. Same place, same time?"

Antoinette looked vaguely uncomfortable. "Actually, we're having dinner with friends on the twenty-eighth."

"Oh, and you want me to join you," Evie said, feigning surprise and increasing her mother's own stress level a few notches. "How nice. I've never met any of your friends. I bet they don't even know you have a daughter, do they? This will be the perfect occasion to make their acquaintance."

Antoinette had the decency to blush, and she had to clear her throat to speak. "Actually, we were hoping you would be free on the thirtieth. Same place, same time?"

Tell her no, Jack silently urged. But Evie's features settled into a resigned look. "Sure," she said flatly. "Of course."

With relief that her daughter wasn't going to be difficult, Antoinette smiled. "Well, I'd better be going or I'll be late for my appointment. Anna Maria, it was wonderful seeing you, dear. Call your mother. Better yet, go see her. Evie." Halfway across the room, she turned back. "I almost forgot... You know, Evie, you really should do something about those— those tourists lined up out front. They're drawing attention to the place."

"It's a business, Aunt Toinette," Anna Maria pointed out. "We *want* attention."

"Yes, of course, but…well, couldn't you be a little more discreet about it?"

"I'll take care of it, Mother," Evie said, her tone impatient, as if they'd had this conversation before. "I'll hustle them inside and fleece them of every spare dime in their pockets with my games and tricks."

Antoinette turned huffy. "Well, there's no call for insolence. I was merely making a comment, but obviously my input isn't wanted here. I'll see you on the thirtieth, if that's not asking too much of you." Looking affronted, she sailed out of the house, closing the door with a solid thunk behind her.

For a moment there was silence, then Anna Maria asked, "Why don't you tell her to go to hell?"

His thoughts exactly.

"Because she's my mother."

"You say that as if it matters," Jack said scornfully.

Evie glared at him. "Get out. Go away." Turning to Bobby, left wide-eyed by the exchange, she gestured toward the French door. "Get to work. See Anna Maria when you're finished. She'll write you a check. And you—" She pointed to her cousin. "Open up. There are people waiting to part with their money. Let's help them do it."

Bobby obediently went to work. So did Anna Maria. Jack followed Evie into the kitchen. "Who did you piss off to get both your mother and me on the same morning?"

She set the watering can in the sink hard enough to splash out water, then snatched up a towel. When she started to squeeze past him, he put out an arm to stop her. "Anna Maria's right, you know. You should tell her to go to hell. Me, too. Why don't you?"

"Because she's my mother," she said wearily. "And you don't listen."

"When was the last time she let you touch her?"

"The first time she realized I could see things through physical contact.'' Her smile was thin and strained and made him angry—with Evie for caring, with Antoinette for not caring. ''I was…I don't know. Nine. Maybe ten.''

''What about your father? Do you see things with him, too?''

''No. But then, he's not the touching sort.''

''I'm surprised you haven't found someone safe and held on tight.''

''I did. I tried. But it's hard to hold on when your hands are cuffed behind your back.''

Acting purely on impulse—because he knew better than to touch her—he laid his hand against her cheek. For a moment she closed her eyes and rested against his palm, breathing slowly, deeply. Then she pulled away. ''I have to get to work.'' She walked halfway down the hall, came back, dropped the towel in his hand, then disappeared into the reading room.

For a long time Jack stood where he was, feeling sick, angry, frustrated, regretful—and oddly hopeful. He wasn't even sure why.

Bobby walked past, giving him a curious look. A few minutes later, he came back, carrying a handful of dead bolt locks, and gave him another look.

Giving himself a mental shake, Jack went into the living room, drained the excess water from the ivy and dried the table, then turned to watch his cousin work.

''Interesting bunch,'' Bobby commented. ''What do you know about Anna Maria?''

''I know she'll eat you alive, son, and spit out the bones when she's finished.''

''Huh. Anna Maria's not the problem here. She's just looking for a good time. Good times are easy. The other one, though—'' He gave a low whistle as he tried the new lock in the old hole.

''What about her?'' Jack asked stiffly.

"Don't get defensive. It's just that she's the marriage-and-forever sort. You'd be a smart man to settle whatever's wrong between you, because, son, you're just delaying the inevitable."

Jack scowled at him. "What makes you think there's anything wrong between us? Hell, what makes you think there's anything at all?"

Bobby looked up from where he knelt on the floor. "How many times have you offered to give up a day off to help me with a job? And how much help have you given me on this job so far? How have you spent the time we've been here? And how many times last summer did I haul your ass home because you were too drunk to get there on your own? I heard enough about Evie to pick her out of a crowd blindfolded." He grinned. "I heard more than either of you would be comfortable with."

There were many nights in the months following Celeste's death that Jack didn't remember at all. He suspected he was better off not remembering most of them. No doubt he had made quite a fool of himself, mourning Celeste and hating Evie. Or was that mourning Evie, too?

"There's nothing to settle. She says she's innocent. I know she's guilty. End of discussion," he said with a grim finality that Bobby ignored.

"You know that, huh? How do you know?"

"The evidence—"

Bobby made an obscene sound. "How long you been a cop, Jack?"

"Twelve years."

"That long, and you still haven't learned that evidence can be made to prove pretty much whatever you want it to prove?"

Jack stared at the tiny pile of wood chips collecting on the floor as Bobby chiseled a deeper hole in the door frame for the bolt. He knew evidence could be manufactured and manipulated. Hell, he knew cops who'd done it. But that wasn't the case here. His partners were good cops. *He* was a good cop. All the evidence had said she was guilty.

And all his instincts had said she wasn't. Because he'd loved her, because he couldn't think straight about her, because his emotions were so deeply involved, he had trusted instead the hard, cold facts of the evidence.

And now he had to consider the possibility that he'd made a hard, cold mistake. One that couldn't be set right. One that he—and Evie—would have to live with for the rest of their lives.

Chapter 8

The smells of crab boil—a blend of spices tossed in boiling water for cooking shrimp, crawfish or crab—greeted Evie when she stepped into the hallway at the end of a long work-day. She'd kept busy all day, convincing herself that she wasn't hungry and taking customers straight through lunch. At the first whiff of the crab boil, though, her hunger made itself known with a loud growl.

She approached the kitchen warily, knowing what—who—she would find. When Bobby had appeared in the waiting room around eleven with a bill, she'd hoped Jack was leaving with him, if not already gone. She should have added the hope that he wouldn't come back, at least not until his job required it tomorrow.

No such luck.

She stopped in the doorway and drew a deep breath. A colander of crawfish sat in the sink. Ears of corn and boiled red potatoes slathered with butter and parsley shared a large serving platter, while shrimp cooked on the stove. Like hers,

Jack's culinary repertoire was limited, but this was one meal he did justice. It was the first—and also the last meal—he'd ever cooked for her.

He glanced at her but didn't speak. Instead, he drained the shrimp, dumped them in a waiting pan of ice water, then opened two sodas—the only difference. Before they'd always drunk beer with the meal.

And they'd always made love afterwards.

Of course, they'd always made love, period. Every chance they'd gotten.

With a sigh, she climbed onto a stool at the counter, peeled a crawfish and discarded the shell before eating the meat. "I suppose Cousin Bobby gave you a set of keys to my new locks."

"What's family for?"

Her family appeared to have many purposes. Helping her out, except with Anna Maria, didn't appear to be one of them.

"Would it do me any good to tell you to go to hell?" she asked wearily, referring to his comment this morning. *You should tell her to go to hell. Me, too.*

As he drained the shrimp once again, he gave the same response she'd offered then. "I don't listen. Where do you want to eat?"

There were several perfectly satisfactory choices—the counter, the dining table behind her. She chose the least ideal. "Outside."

She took the drinks and the vegetables. He carried the seafood, napkins and dishes, and they settled at a round wicker table next to the fountain. They ate in silence, at least until the edge was off their hunger, then Evie settled more comfortably in her chair, peeling shrimp and crawfish, piling them on the edge of her plate. "I assume there's a purpose behind this."

"We have to eat."

"Yes, but we haven't done it together, except for Saturday, in a long time."

He shrugged. "I felt like cooking."

"There must be plenty of other women you'd rather cook for."

"I haven't spoken to a woman not connected to this case in more than a year," he said with a hint of scorn.

She considered the implication of his statement. No dates. No social life. No sex. Not since her. Now *that* was a powerful thought.

After a moment's hesitation, he asked, "What about you?"

"I speak to women every day," she replied absently, lost in the fantasy of sex with Jack after he'd been celibate for a year. It would be incredible—not that she stood a chance in hell of being part of it.

"Have there been many men?" he asked impatiently.

She glanced at him. Dusk had settled, and the only lights on inside—in the kitchen and hallway—couldn't reach out here. She couldn't read anything in the impassivity of his expression. "What do you think, Jack?" she asked softly. "Though you insist on denying it, you *know* me. Maybe you don't trust me. Maybe you can't forgive me. But you *know* what kind of person I am. How many men do you think there have been?"

His answer came reluctantly, quietly, a bare whisper of sound in the night air. "None."

Though it wasn't necessary, she confirmed his answer with a nod as she drenched a crawfish tail in homemade cocktail sauce. He watched as she ate it, his gaze intense enough to feel in the dark. He wanted to say something—to ask something—but she made no effort to draw him out. She simply ate and waited and prepared herself.

But there was no way to prepare for the question he finally asked. "Where were you those days?"

Startled, she stared at him. She knew exactly which days

he was referring to—the two days those damning phone calls had been placed to William MacDougal from her house. A crawfish tail slipped from her fingers, landing with a soft splat of sauce on the tabletop. She left it, dried her fingers on her napkin and sat back in the chair. ''I told your partners that repeatedly.''

''Tell me.''

''All right.'' She swallowed, laced her fingers together. ''I don't know. There was nothing significant about the dates. All I can tell you is that I wasn't in the house. I normally worked during those times. If I wasn't in the shop, then I was out.''

''By 'nothing significant,' you mean you don't remember those specific days. So how do you know you weren't in the house?''

''Because I didn't make those calls to MacDougal and I don't know who did. That means I wasn't here when they were made.''

''It would have to have been someone who knew where you lived, who knew your schedule, who knew about your relationship with me,'' he said quietly, as if merely thinking out loud.

Evie stared at him. He was actually considering the possibility that she'd told the truth—actually looking for some other explanation. This was a day she'd thought would never come. Did it matter that it was a year late?

Or was it, for that reason, simply that much sweeter?

''I'm in the phone book,'' she hesitantly pointed out, ''along with my regular hours. And everyone we knew knew about us. We made no effort to hide our relationship.''

''It would appeal to MacDougal's warped sense of justice,'' he murmured grimly. ''Killing a traitor, then setting you up to take the fall. He'd have to know that it would damn near kill me…''

Evie sat, unwilling to move, speak or even breathe too loudly for fear that it would interfere with his speculation. One wrong question or too-eager comment, and he might revert to the black-and-white, right-or-wrong, evidence-is-everything cop he'd always been. He'd believed the worst of her for so long that these tiny seeds of doubt could be so easily destroyed in favor of the familiarity and comfort of the official theory that had found her guilty.

"But how could he have found out about Celeste? She was careful. She knew the risks. She never would have taken any chances. Someone must have told him." His gaze narrowed on her, and she knew the official theory was gaining strength with him. *She* had known about Celeste. The phone calls had come from *her* house. The money had been deposited into *her* account. She was looking guilty again.

"Were you and I the only two people in the world who knew about her?" she asked, hating the anxiety in her voice. A few more minutes of this, and she would be begging him to believe her, the way she had begged the night he'd arrested her. She had cried, pleaded, and he had simply stared at her so cold, so distant, so convinced of her guilt.

"Of course not. But you're the only one who shouldn't have known. Sonny, Haskins and Gomez knew. The lieutenant knew. But they knew all along, and nothing went wrong. Nothing went wrong until *you* found out. Until…" His voice turned darker, bleaker. "Until I told you."

"Somebody else must have known."

He shook his head.

"Someone *must* have, Jack, because I didn't tell anyone! I swear to you—" She broke off, and her shoulders sagged. Swearing meant nothing. He believed she was an accomplished liar, that she had no morals or decency, that she could bring about another person's death and not care. He wasn't swayed by vows or oaths.

"Maybe Sonny or Haskins or Gomez told MacDougal. Maybe the lieutenant did." She knew the suggestion offended him but went on. "Let's face it. Except for you, the New

Orleans PD doesn't have much of a reputation for abiding by the laws they've sworn to uphold.''

He shook his head. "We've got bad cops, but not *those* cops. I trust them."

"Lucky them," she said bitterly. "You slept with me. You said you loved me. You talked about marrying me. But you never trusted me." She stood up and started gathering dishes. He grabbed her hand.

"*Not these guys,* Evie. They're good cops. They want MacDougal as much as I do. They never would have done anything to jeopardize Celeste."

"But I would have." She wrenched free and grabbed an armload of dishes, but she didn't head for the house. Instead she faced him. "Why, Jack? *Why* would I have done it?"

"For the money," he answered lamely.

She snorted. "Five thousand dollars? You saw that check from Irina! I can make that much legitimately without even trying! Why would I risk losing you for five thousand lousy dollars?"

He opened his mouth, then closed it again.

"You don't have any other explanation, do you? You've never even considered it. Someone planted the evidence they wanted you to see, and you saw nothing else. You never wondered why. You never doubted their proof for an instant. You accepted it without question, without ever even acknowledging that there might be another explanation. You know what? You were right about one thing this morning. You *were* a fool. And I'm a hell of a lot better off without you!"

She stormed inside, kicked the door shut, dumped the dishes in the sink, then took the stairs two at a time to her bedroom. She kicked that door, too, so hard that it bounced open again. With the ball of her foot throbbing, she closed it quietly, then limped toward the dresser to remove her jewelry. She was only a foot away when the door opened and Jack stepped inside. Here in the light, she could see everything the night had hid-

den outside—the exhaustion. The confusion. The misery. Part
of her wanted to throw him out. Part of her wanted to wrap
her arms around him and help him find some peace.

She settled for a bitter request. "Please go away. Leave me
alone."

"I have questions."

Her gaze connected with his in the mirror. *You accepted it
without question...* But this time she couldn't find it within
herself to be hopeful. "I don't have any answers."

"So help me find them."

She removed her chains and rings, pulled the pins from her
hair and let it fall loose, untied the belt from around her waist,
then finally turned to face him. "You don't want to believe
that I'm innocent."

"Some part of me has always wanted to believe it." He
came a few steps closer. "That's what made it so hard. All
the evidence was against you. Everyone was telling me how
guilty you were. But part of me wanted to believe you, with
no evidence, no proof, nothing but your insistence that you
didn't do it. They told me my emotions were getting in the
way. They said you'd blinded me to the truth. They said I was
thinking with the wrong part of my body, that I was being a
lousy detective."

She didn't need to ask who *they* were. Sonny, Haskins and
Gomez. His partners who had hated his relationship with her
from the beginning. Who had made those jokes, comments
and warnings that increased his shame of her. Who had
jumped to a conclusion regarding the murder—exactly the
conclusion the killer wanted them to reach—and convinced
Jack to believe it.

"They said I didn't want to face the truth, because as long
as I could believe that you didn't betray Celeste, then I didn't
have to accept that her death was my fault."

"Bastards," she whispered. They knew him well—had
known exactly which buttons to push to sway him to their

side. And if it laid a load of guilt on him almost heavier than he could bear, well, that was acceptable as long as they got what they wanted. And they'd gotten it—an easy resolution to a murder case and her out of Jack's life.

"It's not their fault," he said, still speaking in that numb, emotionally and mentally exhausted voice. "I let them tell me what to believe, and I believed it. I didn't want to be responsible for Celeste dying. I didn't want to give up believing in the one constant in my life."

The facts. Everyone else might let him down, but the facts didn't. Truth was sometimes elusive and difficult to prove, but once proven, it remained proven. Phone records and bank records didn't lie.

But in this case they'd been manipulated, and the truth remained elusive. *She* was innocent, but somebody else wasn't. Somebody else had gotten away with murder.

She sat down in the wicker chair in the corner, rested her hands on the curved arms, took a few deep breaths to ease her tension. It didn't help. "Let me get this straight. You're not convinced that I'm innocent, but you're willing to at least consider it." At his nod, she bluntly asked, "Why?"

He flipped the switch that turned on the two fans overhead, then opened the French doors on his way across the room. It was a hot night, but the breeze helped. The filmy white curtains fluttering at the doors helped, and the fragrance of jasmine drifting in from the courtyard. They made the evening seem so normal.

Normal. In a life that was about as far from normal as it could get.

He pulled the footstool a few feet from the chair and sat down, his feet planted apart, his hands clasped loosely between his thighs. "We assumed you'd done it for the money—maybe because that was what MacDougal wanted us to believe. But you were right. Only a fool would sell such valuable information to such a rich man for so little. You could earn that kind of money and more without any of the risks. Hell, with people like Irina around, you could make a fortune, if you were interested in getting rich, which you aren't.''

She was surprised he understood that about her, when other basic truths had gone right over his head—like the fact that she wouldn't cause another person's death for all the money in the world, or that she would have died before betraying him in any way.

''You'd never met Celeste. Until I told you about her, you didn't know she existed, so it couldn't have been a personal vendetta. You'd never met MacDougal, either, so you couldn't have been trying to protect him. There was nothing wrong between you and me, so getting back at me is out as a motive. And then there's your mother.''

His last statement startled her. Antoinette was such a small part of her life—so small and so separate that, despite three months in a very intense relationship, Jack had never laid eyes on her until today. ''What does Antoinette have to do with this?''

''She treats you badly and you let her, because the fact that she's your mother means something to you. You feel a certain loyalty to her. It stands to reason that you would also extend that loyalty to—'' He swallowed hard and looked as if he wanted to use the most general terms possible, but couldn't. ''To me.''

''Yes,'' she whispered. ''It stands to reason.''

''You had no motive to hurt Celeste or to help MacDougal, and the evidence against you could have been...'' He hated to say it, hated to admit that the one constant in his life had, indeed, become inconstant. She understood how he felt, because one of only two constants in her own life had let her down a year ago, and it had almost destroyed her.

His knuckles whitened, and a tough, hard look came across his face. ''The evidence against you could have been manipulated,'' he said flatly. ''Someone could have set you up.''

Could have. It wasn't a one hundred percent vote of confidence, but it was more than she'd thought she would ever get from him. "So how do we prove it?"

He shrugged. "We bring down MacDougal and everyone who works for him. We make deals until we find out who told him about Celeste."

"And then, when you have more proof, you'll believe me."

He looked away guiltily and said nothing. She looked away, too, focusing her gaze on a small crack in the plaster wall. It was foolish to feel hurt. This wasn't a simple matter of trust. It was a question of murder. Of course he needed more than her word that she was innocent. She couldn't blame him for that.

But she did. For her, trust *was* a simple matter. It was part of loving. She gave it freely, and she couldn't take it back unless he proved he no longer deserved it. She hadn't given him such proof.

But for more than a year, he'd believed that she had.

"What if you never manage to bring down MacDougal? What if the people who work for him are more afraid of him than they are of prison?" She drew a steadying breath. "What if you never find irrefutable proof that I'm innocent?"

"He has to pay for what he's done. We'll nail him."

"But what if you don't?"

"That's not an option."

"Yes, it is. Some crooks are smart enough and careful enough to get away with murder. What if he's one? What if you never make a case against him?"

"I'll get him, Evie. I don't have a choice. It's either that…" He fixed his gaze on her, and an unholy light shone in his hazel eyes. "Or die trying."

Wednesday was a miserable day. The temperature edged over a hundred, the humidity wasn't far behind, and there wasn't a breeze anywhere in the city—for damn sure not in a stand of scrub brush just outside the MacDougal estate.

Jack leaned forward, peeling his soaked T-shirt from the Mustang's seat, then sank back. He'd been here more than an hour, had polished off two quart bottles of water, watched Evie and Irina looking as if the heat were no more than a minor nuisance and developed one hell of a headache. He wished he was home, in the quiet, cool dark of his bedroom, where he could die in peace from the throbbing in his temples.

He leaned his head back and closed his eyes. His stomach was queasy, his nerves taut. Even listening to the soft, soothing sounds of Evie's voice did nothing to ease the tension that gripped him. He'd awakened all wound up from a long night of bad dreams, and things had only gotten worse through the day. If he could sleep a few hours, he would feel ten times better…if the sleep were restful. Dreamless. Right this moment he didn't hold out much hope for finding such sleep.

Unless it was at Evie's.

With Evie.

He groaned aloud. That was just what he needed—getting intimate with a woman who might have betrayed him. If she hadn't, then *he* had betrayed *her,* unforgivably so.

Yes, it was exactly what he needed—and probably the last thing she wanted.

She laughed, enticing him to open his eyes and focus the binoculars. Even next to an exotically beautiful woman like Irina, Evie was an attention-grabber. She wore her usual gypsy getup, with her hair pulled back away from her face. Gold hoops and diamond studs caught and reflected the sunlight, and the gold bangles tinkled as she gestured along with her speech.

He could watch her for hours. When they were together, he'd often done just that, lying awake through many long nights, staring at her, marveling over his luck in finding her. She hadn't been the first beautiful woman in his life, but he'd thought she would be the last. He'd thought he was smart enough to grab hold of her with both hands and never let her go. But not only had he let her go, he'd shoved her away, fast and furious.

And now here he was, watching her again. Marveling over her again. Falling for her again.

Which was the mistake? Giving her up last year? Or wanting her back now?

He didn't know. These days, it seemed that was the only answer he had. For a man who'd been pretty damn sure of things all his life, it wasn't a comfortable answer to live with.

Suddenly Evie made a statement that caught his attention. "You're thinking about having a baby."

Pleasant surprise was evident in Irina's voice. "Yes. I haven't told anyone yet, but…yes. I've always wanted children."

"Yes, but you wanted them with Etienne."

He swung the binoculars across the table in time to see sadness cross Irina's face. "Yes," she acknowledged, more subdued this time. "But Etienne is gone. William is here. He's my husband."

"You're afraid that William doesn't want— No, you're afraid that he does want a child, that he would give you little input in how the boy is raised."

Though it was difficult to imagine MacDougal as a loving father, Jack had no problems seeing him as a controlling one. A child would be just one more possession—a living, breathing one to be molded into his own image. Pity the poor kid who would bear the brunt of MacDougal's demands and expectations.

"I could be a good mother," Irina said insistently.

"Of course you could. But William probably wouldn't let you. And if you protested, he would… He threatens to send you back to St. Thomas, doesn't he?"

The blush barely showed under the bronze of Irina's skin.

"He doesn't mean it. He—he's under a lot of pressure. He wouldn't send me back."

"The hell he wouldn't," Jack murmured aloud. The bastard had bought himself one pretty little wife. If she wasn't as malleable as he'd expected, how much trouble could it be to return her and buy another?

"You don't think I should get pregnant, do you?" Irina asked, disappointment evident in her face and voice.

"I would advise against it. You've only been married a few months. Having a baby is such an important decision. There's no rush."

He and Evie had been together exactly six weeks when she'd thought, for a brief time, that she was pregnant. He had decided instantly that he would marry her, watch her grow and be there at her side when their baby was born. Even though she'd discovered the very next morning that it was a false alarm, he'd still wanted to marry her and have kids—right up until the very moment Sonny had shown him the evidence that pointed to her involvement with MacDougal.

Legitimate evidence? Or planted by MacDougal himself?

The latter would explain why there'd been enough to suspect her but not enough to charge her. If they'd been able to put together enough evidence to take her to trial, they would have had enough to lead back to him. Instead, he'd merely given them enough to hang her, but not himself.

Just one more sin the bastard would have to pay for.

Jack was twisting his head to ease the tension in his neck when a car on the street out front caught his attention. The fact that there were tens of thousands of that particular model on the road was supposed to make it too commonplace to notice, but the nothing-special sedan was as out of place in this neighborhood as his Mustang or Evie's junker. It fit in just fine, though, in the government motor pool from which it'd been taken.

He fixed his binoculars on the driver, a fed by the name of

Browning, then his partner, Keith Stewart. It was easy enough to see that their interest at that moment was limited to Evie's car. They would run the tag, identify her, make her a part of their files. If she was lucky, they would quickly find out that her connection was to Irina, not MacDougal, and they would forget about her.

But had she been lucky even once since meeting *him?*

The sedan slowly drove past, then picked up speed and disappeared.

Another half hour passed before Evie finally took her leave. Jack watched her say goodbye to Irina, then walk to her car alone. He followed her car's progress down the drive, onto the street and out of sight, but didn't reach for his keys. Instead, he looked back at Irina. She remained at the patio table, her expression distant and thoughtful. When the servant approached her, she spoke in what appeared to be a sharp manner, and the older woman beat a hasty retreat.

What was on her mind? What made her look so...cold?

How about babies, a bad marriage and a husband as crooked as any Louisiana politician?

After a time, she left the table and moved to the middle terrace level. There she stepped out of her shoes, stripped off her clothes and stood for a moment at the edge of the pool. She wasn't the least bit modest or self-conscious. She was beautiful—perfect face, perfect body—and knew and accepted it.

As she dived cleanly into the water, he started the engine, backed between two tall sugar pines and headed for the Quarter. He parked near Jax Brewery and walked the rest of the way. Using the keys Evie had let him keep, he let himself into the courtyard, then the house.

She was standing at the dining table, removing her belt. The woven fabric was six inches wide and long enough to circle her waist three times. He'd watched her tie it earlier and imagined other, better ways to use it. One in particular, involving her delicate wrists and her bed, had made his temperature soar. Even now he felt himself growing hotter.

"I've got people waiting," she said, dropping the belt on the table, then pulling her top from her skirt. "I wasn't sure you were coming back."

He moved around behind her, slid his hands underneath the silky fabric and worked loose the tape that secured the transmitter. "Irina decided to go skinny-dipping after you left. I decided to watch."

She gave him a look over one shoulder. "Is she as beautiful naked as she is dressed?"

"More so."

"Did it turn you on?"

"No."

Her look turned disbelieving, then, as he reached around with both hands to loosen the microphone between her breasts, she faced the wall again. Her voice grew a bit huskier. "An incredibly beautiful woman takes off her clothes in front of you, and you don't get the least bit aroused? What does that say about you?"

His arms loosely circled her. His hands were underneath her blouse. He was hard and hotter than hell, and he couldn't remember ever being in more pain—or wanting it more.

He lowered his head until his mouth brushed her ear and lowered his voice so that it made her shiver. "It doesn't say a thing about me...but it says a hell of a lot about you."

Her breath came in short puffs. Her jaw worked convulsively, but no words came out. She raised both hands to his wrists, but she didn't pull his arms away. Instead, she simply clung to him.

He touched the tip of his tongue to her ear and made her shiver, made her fingers grip tighter around his wrists. The diamond studs, each a few points smaller than the one below it, were cool and solid. Her skin was damp and soft. Obligingly she bent her head to the right, giving him access to her jaw and the long line of her neck, and he took advantage of it, giving her small kisses and smaller bites. Tightening his embrace, he pulled her snug against his body—against his arousal—and let the wire slide to the tabletop, then slid his hands across her ribs, finding and cupping her breasts, rubbing his thumbs across her nipples.

With a groan, she sank against him. "Oh, please…"

Please stop? Please don't stop? He didn't know. He didn't care.

Twisting her head around, she took his mouth and thrust her tongue inside. She was passionate, greedy, hot. Just looking at her made him burn. Touching her like this just might kill him.

But what a way to die.

An instant too late, he became aware of footsteps in the hall. He tried to end the kiss, to push her away, but his body refused his brain's command. It was only when the steps came to a sudden stop behind them, when he heard Anna Maria's disgusted, "Oh, puh-leeze," that he was able to break the contact, to end the kiss, to slide his hands free and put a few inches between them. The distance left him with an empty ache that just might finish him off.

"Evie, you have seven people waiting out there," Anna Maria said, her voice muffled by the hands that covered her face.

He slid into a chair—not because he suddenly felt weak and needed the support, but only for the camouflage. "You can look now, Anna Maria," he said in his usual—with her—obnoxious voice. "We're decent."

She removed her hands from her eyes and glowered at him. "It would take a hell of a lot more than a few feet between the two of you to make *you* decent, Murphy. Getting out of here—and staying out—would be a good start."

"Sorry. I'm busy." He pulled the strips of tape from the transmitter, wire and mike, then used one to blot the adhesive left behind. While he worked, he glanced at Evie, whose eyes were closed. Her cheeks were flushed the most appealing shade of crimson, and her fingers were wrapped as tightly around the chair in front of her as they'd been around *him* a few short moments ago. "Give her a few minutes. She'll be in when she's ready."

Anna Maria looked as if she might protest, then thought better. Wordlessly, she did a one-eighty and returned to the shop.

Feeling Evie's gaze on him, Jack held the mike and transmitter together, then looped the wire neatly around both pieces. When he was finished, he stood up and moved indecently close to her. "I'll be back tonight."

Her only response was a dazed blink and a hard swallow.

He smoothed her top over the elastic waist of her skirt, wrapped the belt around her middle and tied it, then fingered the dangling ends for a moment, all the while holding her gaze. She looked aroused. Needy. Beautiful. She was the best part of his life, and the worst. The biggest right…and maybe the biggest wrong.

And he didn't care.

Picking up the equipment, he moved around her, then left the way he had come. He didn't want to go, but he would be back. Tonight.

And this time he might never leave again.

Evie closed up the shop at six, sent a worried Anna Maria on her way and went into the house, fully expecting to find Jack waiting. But the place was still, tightly locked up and empty but for her. She waited restlessly, watching as the sun crept down and the night turned darker, but he didn't appear. What if he didn't come, if he'd changed his mind or come to his senses? What if he'd decided that the very last thing he wanted was intimacy with a woman whom he had once suspected—in some ways still did suspect—in a murder?

Seven o'clock came. Seven-thirty. She showered and dressed in an outfit similar to the one she'd worn two days before—a full white skirt and matching top. Instead of the peasant look, though, this tank top was snug and clung everywhere it touched. It made her feel strong and sleek and feminine.

Fully dressed and with nothing else to distract her, she went to the phone, dialing his number from memory—funny the things she hadn't forgotten. She got his machine.

Her first impulse was to hang up. Her second was to leave the simplest of messages. "I'm going out. I'll be at Lou's."

Then she hung up, picked up her purse and made good on the message.

A few miles away, Jack lay on his bed in the dark, naked and damp from his shower, listening to her words for the second time. He'd spent the last hours trying to convince himself that he wasn't going back there, that he wasn't going to make love with her, that he wasn't going to make himself so damn vulnerable to her again. He'd offered up all his best arguments, but they'd been pointless and he'd known it from the start.

He was going. He was going to find some satisfaction for the first time in more than a year. He was going to lose himself inside her, and this time he didn't care if he ever found his way back.

I'm going out. I'll be at Lou's.

Lou's was the club where they'd met, where for three months they'd been regulars. He hadn't been back since their last time together. He would bet she hadn't either. But she would be there tonight. Waiting for him.

He rose from the bed and got dressed, then walked out the door.

Evie crossed the last street before Lou's, then paused on the curb to look back behind her. She had that funny feeling again, as if someone was watching her, but there was no one in sight. Any other summer evening, the sidewalks would be at least in use by, if not crowded with, tourists, but at this moment she seemed to be the only one about. Maybe it was the heat, remarkably oppressive even for New Orleans in July. Maybe it was the curious stillness in the air, as if something was merely waiting to happen. Maybe, through some odd circumstance, all the tourists had congregated on Bourbon Street, leaving the rest of the Quarter to the privacy of its residents.

And maybe she was just feeling antsy because Jack hadn't shown up.

Too aware of the prickling of hairs on the back of her neck, she took another long, fruitless look around, then headed for the club in the middle of the block. Six broad steps led to a patio with a low wrought iron railing, and double French doors with black-green shutters led inside.

Like any good French Quarter club, smoke filled the air inside Lou's, lazily circulated by ceiling fans and eventually drifting out open windows across the front. The bar stretched along one wall and was overseen by Lou herself. She drew a beer as Evie approached and set the stein on the scarred wood between them.

"You come alone?" she asked as if a year hadn't passed since the last time they'd spoken.

Evie shrugged. "That might change." Or Jack might have talked himself out of coming back. Under the circumstances, still being unsure of her guilt or innocence, that seemed likely.

"If you want company, you'll find it." Lou gave a graceful wave that encompassed the other customers.

Evie's glance skimmed across a dozen men, some attractive, some not, some looking her way, some caught up in the music or themselves. For a long time, she'd told herself that the day would come when she would look at a man and want to know him better—or, perhaps, merely to take him to bed. She'd insisted that someday she would stop comparing them all to

Jack and finding them lacking. Someday she would even fall in love with one of them.

She'd lied.

"I'm not looking for company." She paid for the beer, turned her back to the door and raised it for a sip. Suddenly, her hand trembled, spilling the cold liquid over her fingers, as the hairs on the back of her neck went on end again.

This time when she looked, she saw a man—tall, slender, blond. A stranger. There was nothing unusual about him— even with only a dozen men in the audience, he fit right in— and he was paying her no attention. So why did he set her nerves on alert?

A simple overreaction, she told herself as she made her way to the table in the farthest corner. She wanted Jack to show up more than she could bear to admit, and with each passing minute, she was more convinced that he wouldn't. She had felt the man's presence and had hoped...

The band finished their song, then went right into the next. She was listening, chin cupped in her hand, when the chair beside her scraped on the concrete floor. Straightening, she watched Jack sit down, then she smiled shyly. "You got my message."

"You didn't get mine this afternoon. I wanted you waiting at home, preferably naked, preferably in bed." He gave her a down and up look, his gaze lingering over her breasts, and the muscles in his jaw tightened. "This is good, though. Just don't ask me to dance."

That one look sent her temperature through the roof. When she wrapped her palm around her glass to lift it for a drink, she was half surprised that it didn't sizzle. She tried for a moment to pretend interest in the music, but the rushing in her ears muted it to a barely recognizable level. Everything was muted—except Jack and the way he was looking at her, the way he was making her ache. Such power, when he hadn't even touched her yet.

She shifted uncomfortably in the wooden chair, then gave him a sidelong look. "Want to go?"

"Not just yet." The answer came not from Jack but the blond man she'd noticed earlier. He was accompanied by another man, dressed similarly. Neither looked particularly friendly.

Neither, suddenly, did Jack. "What do you want, Stewart?"

"I want to talk to you for a minute, Murphy, while Ted keeps your…date…company." He said *date* in a way that made it sound like an insult—like a cash-paid-for-services-rendered arrangement—and accompanied it with a look of familiar hostility that Ted shared.

Cops, Evie thought with equal measures disdain and frustration. She'd never broken a law in her life, and yet every cop she met looked at her as if he'd like nothing better than to bury her under the jail, all because, with her less than respectable occupation, she'd dared to get involved with one of their own.

"You want to talk to me, Keith, call me at work."

"Five minutes of your time, Murphy, and then you can get back to whatever you were doing…if you still want to."

She felt Jack's gaze shift to her. He gave her hand a squeeze as he stood up. "I'll be back. Come on, Stewart, outside. You've got five minutes, and the clock is ticking."

Evie watched them walk out, then shifted her gaze as the other one, Ted, pulled out a chair on her left and sat down. A chill swept over her, leaving her hands unsteady, making her skin clammy.

"So you claim to be a psychic."

"What do you claim to be?" she asked stiffly.

He reached in his hip pocket and pulled out a black leather case, flipping it open long enough for her to read the agency name on his credentials. Federal Bureau of Investigation. She resisted the urge to dry her palms or try to clear the lump from her throat. She hadn't done anything wrong, she reminded herself. She was simply enjoying an evening out.

Ted put the case away, then extended his hand. "Why don't you read my palm while we wait?"

"I don't read palms."

"Then what do you do? Besides run cons on visitors to our fair city?" When she didn't answer, he leaned closer. "Would you prefer that I narrow the scope of that question? I'd be happy to."

She glanced at him and all her nerves went on alert again. Quickly she looked away.

"What do you do for William MacDougal? And what do you do for Detective Murphy?" His smile was smug and arrogant. "I think I can make a pretty good guess at the answer to the second question. Hell, you looked like you were about to crawl on top of him right here in public. Guess we all know how Murphy's spending his vacation, don't we? Are you providing the same services to MacDougal?"

Evie ached to slap that leering look from his face. She settled for spitting out, "Go to hell," as she stood up and shoved her chair back.

Then it happened. He grabbed her wrist and forced her back into the chair, and she saw images—dark, indistinct. She felt fear, frustration, a great, overwhelming dread. And she heard voices—clear, terrifying, deadly voices.

With a panicked cry, she wrenched free and scrambled to her feet, putting the table between them. Her heart pounding, her chest hurting, she stared at him with horror and whispered, accused, "You— Oh, God. Oh, my God."

Spinning around, she rushed across the room, neither noticing nor caring that people were staring. She had to get out, had to get away.

She had to get to Jack.

Chapter 9

Jack gave Keith Stewart a contemptuous look. "You interrupted my evening for this? To tell me that you saw Evie's car at MacDougal's house?" He muttered a curse. "Didn't you wonder even for a minute what she was doing at his house when he was at his office? Didn't it occur to you that if she was working for him, she would actually go where he was to meet him? Meetings work better that way, you know, when you're both in the same place."

Stewart looked and sounded like a petulant child. "And what explanation did she give you for being there?"

"She was seeing one of her regular clients—Irina Mac-Dougal."

"Irina?"

"His wife? You did know he was married, didn't you? Holy—" He rolled his eyes. "The *I* in FBI really does stand for 'incompetence,' doesn't it?"

"I knew he was married," Stewart said defensively.

"And did you also know that his wife is heavy into this

psychic stuff? She considers her spiritual advisor to be one of the most important people in her life.'' He considered her one of the most important people in his life, too. If these idiots hadn't interfered, he'd be that much closer to finding out all over again just how important.

''And you believe that's all it is?''

''Yes.''

Stewart stared at the street for a moment, then shrugged. ''Look, Murphy, no harm meant, okay? We just thought you ought to know.''

Before Jack could think of a suitable response that wasn't short on letters and long on vulgarity, Evie came flying out the door. Her face was pale, and her entire body was trembling when she grabbed his arm. ''We've got to go, Jack.''

Ted Browning was a few paces behind her, looking agitated and more than a little green. Jack looked from him to Evie, looking pretty sick herself, and let her pull him down the steps. ''What's wrong?'' he demanded as soon as they were out of earshot.

Her shudders increased, but she didn't slow her pace and didn't answer until he forced her to stop at the intersection. ''Evie, damn it, what's wrong?''

She clung tightly to him with one hand, touched him lightly, nervously, with the other, drew back, then clenched it into a fist. ''They knew, Jack. They knew that Celeste was going to be killed! They knew and they did nothing to stop it! They let her die, and they let me take the blame for it, and they let the people who killed her get away with it!''

Jack glanced back and saw the two men watching them. They stood unnaturally still, looked unnaturally wary.

He looked at Evie again. The nearby street lamp harshly illuminated her face, clearly showing her fear, her anger, her revulsion. ''What are you talking about?''

She drew a deep, ragged breath. It didn't calm her at all. ''He touched me. I tried to leave and he grabbed me, and I saw... I heard... They listened to those men plan Celeste's death, and they did nothing. They didn't warn her. They didn't stop them. They did *nothing,* because of their case, because it might jeopardize their damned case! They let her die, Jack! They *let* it happen!''

He stared at her, feeling a little sick himself. In his gut, he knew she was telling the truth—*knew* it, damn it—but he couldn't accept it, couldn't believe, couldn't quite... ''Do you realize what you're saying, Evie? These guys are feds—FBI agents, for God's sake! You think they stood by and watched a woman get killed for the sake of an investigation?''

''It's happened before!''

True again, and right here in New Orleans. Unaware that the FBI had them under surveillance, a couple of dirty cops had planned the murder of a woman who'd filed a complaint against one. The agents had chosen to not risk their case, and the woman had been killed as planned.

Those bastards had known that MacDougal intended to kill Celeste. They could have saved her, could have come up with any number of ways to warn her. Hell, they could have warned *him* and he would have gotten her out of there. Instead, they'd let her die.

She'd been betrayed by everyone she trusted.

And, God forgive him, so had Evie.

He glanced back at Lou's. Stewart and Browning were gone. Freeing his arm from Evie's grasp, he pulled her close to his side and started walking, turning the corner. This wasn't the most direct route to her house. He felt more comfortable with it for that reason.

She went quietly for two blocks, then dug in her heels, forcing him to stop. They were between streetlights, but he could see the beseeching look on her face. ''I had nothing to do with Celeste's death,'' she whispered tearfully. ''Can't you believe me now?''

He laid his hand against her cheek, opened his mouth—and

became distracted by movement down the street. A car turned onto the block, creeping down the middle of the street. Its interior was dark, and its headlights were off.

He had a really bad feeling about this.

He took a quick look around. There were no recessed doorways, no alleys, no shops open to duck into. The only cover was the parked car ahead—poor protection, but better than nothing.

The car accelerated with a squeal of rubber, and he grabbed Evie's arm, dragging her along as he sprinted for cover. As the first shot rang out, he shoved her to the ground. With the second shot, he covered her body with his. Muttering curses and prayers, he counted four more shots before the car raced away, leaving them in deathly silence.

He rolled to his side, then lifted her onto her side. The white of her outfit was soiled, but not with blood, thank God. She was pale, shaking, crying silent tears, but she was all right. He had to make sure she stayed that way.

Gently he got her to her feet, dusted her clothes, dried her tears. As he'd started to do before the car appeared, he cupped her face in his hands and answered her question with words that, he realized now, he'd wanted desperately to say—and mean—for more than a year.

"Yes, Evie. I believe you." Before she could do more than hiccup in response, he hustled her the remaining few blocks to her house. He stood close behind her on the stoop, watching warily over his shoulder while she fumbled with the lock. As soon as the door was open, he pushed her inside and locked it again behind him.

The hall lights were burning. He used the light to give her another quick exam. "You're not hurt?"

"No."

"Good. Go upstairs, get changed. Keep everything locked up tight. Don't answer the phone unless it's me. Don't—"

She caught his hands and squeezed them tightly, startling him into silence. "Where are you going?"

"I'm going to kill the bastards."

"Jack." Her tone was as chiding as her look.

"Okay. I'm going to find out everything they know, and then I'm going to kill them." His control snapped as the full impact of the last few minutes hit him. "My God, Evie, they shot at us!"

"Did you see them? Are you sure it was them?"

He breathed deeply. "No, I didn't see them. But what a hell of a coincidence if it wasn't them."

"Do you think they meant to kill us?"

A couple more deep breaths, and he was able to answer calmly, quietly. "No. They're both better shots than that. I think they meant to scare us."

She ventured a shaky smile. "Then they succeeded. I'm scared. Please don't go, Jack. Please don't leave me here alone." Her fingers flexed convulsively around his hand. "If they only wanted to frighten us, let them think they did. Let them think they're safe for the time being."

"That could be exactly what they're saying about us," he said with a scowl. It went against everything in him to sit tight and let Browning and Stewart walk away, even temporarily. He wanted the satisfaction of tracking them down like the cowards they were. He wanted to find out everything they knew, and then he wanted to punish them. For Celeste. For Evie. Damn it, for himself.

"What would they expect you to do?"

Exactly what he wanted—to go after them. To get her to relative safety, then leave her on her own while he went looking for them. And what if the shots hadn't been meant to frighten? What if they'd been meant to separate Jack from her? To leave her defenseless and at their mercy?

Freeing his hands from hers, he wrapped his arms around

her and held her close. "All right. I won't go anywhere. I'll stay here."

Somewhere inside herself, she found a small, amused laugh. "Don't sound so grudging. I'm sure we can think of something to occupy ourselves through the night."

Such an oblique reference to sex, and his body was responding as if she'd offered the bluntest, crudest of invitations. He held her a moment longer, then pushed her back. "Go upstairs and change. I've got to make a phone call."

More composed but still too pale, she nodded, then climbed the stairs with a slow, natural grace. He watched until she disappeared at the top, watched a moment longer, thinking about how desperately he wanted her, how badly he'd treated her, how little he deserved her. All these months he'd accused her of betraying him, when—just as she'd claimed—she was innocent. The betrayal was his, all his, and he didn't know how to make it right.

He wasn't sure it *could* be made right.

The sound of bathwater upstairs shook him out of his thoughts, and he went to the kitchen phone.

Bobby was home, watching TV. He agreed to Jack's request with no impatience and little curiosity. Less than fifteen minutes later, he was at the front door, a crumpled grocery bag in hand. "Is everything all right?"

Jack unrolled the bag from its contents, pulled out one holstered pistol and clipped it to his waistband in back. The other, a small five-shot .22, went into his pocket. He left the extra clips in the bag. "Yeah," he said grimly. "Everything's fine."

Bobby didn't look convinced, but he didn't argue. "If you need anything…"

"Thanks. I appreciate it." He locked the new lock, shut off all but the hall lights, then went upstairs. He did the same there, leaving only one bulb burning in the hall.

Evie was in her darkened bedroom, standing near one French door, gazing out. She wore a thin cotton robe that clung everywhere she was wet—and she was wet everywhere—and her hair was secured on top of her head with bright plastic clips. She looked vulnerable as well as strong, wholesome and at the same time sexy as hell. She was his past and his future. His greatest love and his most bitter hatred.

He let the bag slide to the floor beside the bed without breaking stride and walked right up to her. She backed away a few steps until the wall was behind her. He held her there with his body, held her hands against the wall at her sides with his.

That nervous smile came again, but where before it was fueled by fear, this time it was arousal. She moved fractionally, rubbing against him, then asked, "Is that a gun in your pocket or are you happy to see me?"

"Both."

"Oh. I didn't notice earlier..."

"I didn't have it. Bobby brought it."

"I thought you never left home without it."

"I rarely do, but tonight..." He tried to take a deep breath, but it caught in his chest when she moved again. "I got distracted." He closed his eyes for a moment, focusing on the ache, the need, that was about to destroy him, then looked at her again. "You don't have to do this, Evie. I'll stay, even if you don't let me..."

"Let you?" She tried to scoff but couldn't. "I want this—want you—more than I have words to express. I need... Please."

He searched her face and found the certainty he needed, and then he kissed her. It was as natural, as right, as it had always been, as if so many months and so much wrong hadn't come between them. He thrust his tongue into her mouth, and she accepted it with a little groan that sent heat flaming through him.

The kiss went on, moment after endless moment, feeding their hunger, stealing their strength. Her fingers tightened around his. Her moans—helpless little sounds of great torment and greater need—sliced through him, leaving raw, consuming arousal in their wake. His body grew impossibly hotter, impossibly harder.

Somehow she freed one hand and reached between them to caress him. He jerked his mouth free and swore aloud. "Damn, don't do that," he pleaded, but when he caught her wrist, he didn't pull her hand away. He pressed her palm harder against him, rubbed hard against it.

"Now," she whispered in a voice so thick and rough that he barely recognized it—a voice that he knew in his soul. "Help me…"

Her fingers fumbled over the button and zipper of his jeans. He didn't bother with the belt of her robe, but pushed the fabric to either side. She freed him from his jeans. He lifted her against the wall, sinking inside her with one long, hard, desperate thrust, and took her mouth with the same force, swallowing her gasp, sharing her moan.

This first time would be quick, hard, almost brutal. First times with Evie always were. He didn't try to hold back, didn't try to make it last, but let the climax come, driven by his own long-unsatisfied arousal, by the torment of her sweet body hot and tight around his, by the hunger and the need and the desperation. With a savage curse, he closed his eyes, held on tight and filled her, and felt her body shudder and tremble with its own completion.

First time, hard and fast, for the lust. Second time, slow and lazy and sweet enough to bring a strong man to his knees.

And that was where he belonged with Evie—on his knees. Begging for her forgiveness. Her understanding.

For her love.

Evie came awake with a sudden start. The first thing she noticed was the storm—brilliant lightning that split the night sky, followed almost instantly by thunder that reverberated through the old house, and both underscored by a relentless wind that rattled the windowpanes.

The second thing she noticed as she stretched was that she was naked except for a narrow strip of cloth knotted around her waist. She fingered it curiously, then recognized the nubby fabric as the belt that matched her bathrobe. Remembering, she slowly smiled. She'd put the robe on after her bath and Jack had frantically pulled it off in spite of the knotted belt. That had been somewhere between the wall, where they'd had wonderful hot sex, and the bed, where they'd made sweet love.

Jack. With her smile deepening, she turned toward him and reached a third realization: the bed was empty. He was gone. Not from the house—she was sure of that. He wouldn't leave her alone, not when he'd promised to stay. But he was gone from the bed, from the room. He was probably off somewhere, blaming himself for everything that had happened, whether he was responsible or not.

Sitting up, she worked the knot loose, then found her robe in the pile of clothes scattered across the floor. She pulled it on and tied the belt again, this time in a bow that could be undone with a single tug, and then she went looking for him.

The hallway was dark, and a press of the light switch outside her door accomplished nothing. The power was off—not an uncommon occurrence with a storm so violent. She kept a flashlight in her nightstand for just such times, but she didn't go back for it. She knew her way blindfolded, and the regular flashes of lighting provided some illumination.

She moved quietly down the stairs and turned toward the living room. Several of the French doors were open, filling the room with the sweet scent of impending rain and lowering the temperature a few refreshing degrees. Jack stood at one door, a shadow in a room filled with shadows, one shoulder against the jamb, the other hand on his hip. He wore jeans, a pistol, a bleak, guilt-induced expression, and nothing else.

She cleared her throat so she wouldn't startle him, but he

didn't look, didn't even, as far as she could tell in the lightning, twitch a muscle. He'd probably heard her leave her room, had probably been waiting for her to come down and hoping that she wouldn't.

She took up a similar position on the opposite side of the door, but instead of staring into the courtyard, she faced him. His gaze shifted her way, then darted off without making contact. When a moment passed in silence, he glanced at her again.

"Did the storm wake you?" His voice was low, husky, edged with wariness. He was uncomfortable—was blaming himself, surely, for distrusting her and believing the worst.

For that reason, she kept her own voice as calm and level as possible. "Yes, it did." She didn't have a clue if it was true. Maybe it'd been the thunder and lightning. Maybe it had been the incredible physical satisfaction—the first she'd experienced in more than a year. Maybe some part of her had realized he was gone and missed him. Maybe she'd realized something was wrong.

"The power's off."

"I noticed." A scraping sound drew her attention outside and she watched as the wind pushed one of her wicker chairs against the railing. It whipped through the live oak, thrashing the branches about, and ripped delicate blossoms from her flowers, sending them flying through the air. Still gazing out, she quietly asked, "Regrets?"

Finally Jack looked at her. She felt the connection. "Yeah."

Her breath caught in her chest, but she forced herself to ask the next obvious question. "About tonight?"

"Some."

"Oh." She managed a poor semblance of a laugh. "You should never ask a loaded question if you're not prepared for the answer. I wasn't prepared for that."

His gaze turned hard. "I regret damn near everything in my whole lousy life, Evie. You and Celeste are my two biggest regrets. I let you both down. She paid for it with her life. I don't want the same thing to happen to you."

Expecting a totally different answer than the one he'd given her, she breathed a little easier. "It won't."

"I promised her she would be safe, that I would protect her. I couldn't do it. I made the same promises to you, too, and I can't keep them. Hell, I can't even tell the good guys from the bad guys. I don't know who I'm after. I don't know who in hell I'm trying to protect you from."

"You'll find out."

"How?"

She shrugged. "You're a cop. You'll figure it out."

Slowly, grimly, he shook his head. "I'm a lousy cop. I trusted the cops and the evidence and the facts, and it was all wrong. The feds let Celeste die. They and who knows who the hell else manufactured evidence and manipulated the facts, and, like an idiot, I fell for it. I bought it all, even though I knew—I *knew*—you would never do what I accused you of doing. I've screwed up this case from the beginning, and now I've got you up to your neck in serious trouble." He made a derisive sound. "I'm a damn lousy cop, Evie. I can't figure this one out. I can't risk your life on my intuition or theories or hunches."

"So what are you going to do?" She deliberately, ruthlessly cut any hint of sympathy from her voice. "Are you going to give up, Jack? Are you going to let the FBI and MacDougal and whoever the hell else was involved get away with it? Celeste trusted you, and they murdered her. I trusted you, and they set me up for murder. Are you just going to ignore that? Are you going to simply walk away from it, because you might not be as much a hotshot cop as you thought?"

"Yeah. That's exactly what I'm going to do."

"You *owe* her, Jack. You owe *me*."

"I can't solve this case, Evie! Backing off is the only way I know to keep you safe!"

''Safe?'' she repeated. ''*Safe?* A few hours ago two FBI agents took shots at us on the street! They know that I know they stood back and let that woman be killed! You think I'm ever going to be *safe* as long as they're walking around free?''

He stared stubbornly outside, pretending to ignore her, but a flash of lightning showed the tightening of his jaw as she closed the distance between them, stopping in front of him. He still pretended, though, staring over her head into the night.

''You're not a lousy cop, Jack. You believed in the one thing you've believed in all your life—the evidence. The proof. The facts. All your life it's stood you in good stead—but this one time it let you down. The evidence wasn't the only thing manipulated in this case. You were, too, and those FBI agents know who did it. You can't let them get away with it, Jack—not the agents, not the killers, not MacDougal. You have to make them pay.''

Finally he dropped his gaze to her face. ''And what if *you* pay again? What if this time it's with your life?''

Her breath caught for a moment, then she blew it out. ''I don't want to die,'' she admitted. ''But it seems to me that the best way to make sure I don't is to put them in jail. To stop them, once and for all.''

''I don't know if I can.''

She laid her hand on his arm and found his skin unnaturally cool. ''Just last night you told me you would do it or die trying.''

''Last night I didn't know how wrong I had been. How easily I'd been fooled. How bad my mistakes had been.''

Last night he'd thought it might be possible that she was innocent. Tonight he knew he'd made some serious errors in judgment. He hadn't trusted her, and he should have. He had trusted the FBI agents, and he shouldn't have. And now tonight he was blaming himself, doubting himself, in every way possible.

''We're in trouble, Jack,'' she said quietly. ''We have to

find a way out of it. *You* have to find a way. I don't know
what to do. I don't know how to protect us. You do."

He stared at her a long time, then abruptly slid his hand
underneath her hair, grasped her neck and pulled her to him.
He held her tightly—as if he might never let go—and she
clung to him, the way she'd wanted to from the first night
they'd met. She felt the shudders that rocketed through him,
felt the helplessness and hopelessness. She knew from experience that he was feeling disillusioned, disappointed, frustrated and angry as hell, and she wished she could help him.
Maybe just being here *was* helping. It would have helped *her*
a year ago when she was disillusioned and disappointed.

"I don't know who to trust."

His whisper was barely audible and made her heart ache.
She raised her hands to his face and forced his head back so
she could see him. "Trust *me*," she said fiercely. "Trust me."

For a long moment, he stared, his gaze searching; then he
nodded. So simple this time, she thought with an ache. She
demanded, he acceded. How much sorrow could they have
avoided a year ago if he'd been so willing then?

No regrets, she reminded herself. He trusted her now. That
was enough.

Still holding her gaze, he slid one hand over her shoulder,
along the vee of the robe, underneath the fabric to her breast.
The pad of his thumb made slow, rough caresses across her
nipple, drawing her breath from her in a soft gasp, making her
entire body go weak with sensation. His movements were
careful, controlled, for her benefit, but she knew that wasn't
what he needed. He needed wild, intense, out of control.

So did she.

She pressed a kiss to his jaw, another to his throat, a dozen
more across his chest. Her fingers skimmed over taut skin and
hard muscle to faded denim. The snap was undone, and the
zipper slid soundlessly to its end. Easing her hand inside, she
found him, swollen, stiff, hot, and coaxed a teeth-gritted, mus-

cles-knotted groan from him. Rising onto her toes, she caught his earlobe between her teeth, then whispered an invitation— a demand—in his ear that made him groan again, that made his hips involuntarily pump against her hand.

Moving away from him, she gave her belt a tug and it fell away to the floor. Her robe was on its way off, too, sliding down her arms, when he grabbed her, twisted her around, claimed her mouth. He lowered her to the floor, her arms trapped inside the soft fabric, and filled her with one hard stroke. A few swift thrusts, and he emptied into her, but that was only the beginning. He played games with her, building within her a need to match the storm outside in intensity, made all the more tormenting by the fact that her arms were trapped at her sides by the tangled robe. She couldn't touch him, couldn't return his wicked caresses, couldn't do anything but feel, burn, throb, plead.

And she did plead. She begged him with bone-deep moans, ragged breaths, frantic little cries, until finally he could bear no more himself. Sliding his hands under her hips, he took her faster, harder, deeper, until she couldn't think, couldn't breathe, couldn't do anything but shatter into a million pieces around him. Even then, she was faintly aware of his guttural groan as his second climax exploded through them both. She felt the shudders, the rush of heat, the incredible satisfaction, as he filled her again, and then, for a time, she felt nothing.

Just *good.*

Gradually, awareness returned. She was lying on her back on the living room floor, about in the middle of the room. The rain had begun, a deluge that pounded and splashed and made itself heard above the thunder and wind. Her robe was underneath her, her arms caught in the sleeves, and Jack was still deep inside her. His jeans, soft against her legs, made her realize that twice tonight they'd done the deed with him more dressed than not. She liked such desperation in a man.

As if the same realization had just occurred to him, he

pulled away from her, wriggled out of his jeans, then lifted her on top of him, leaving her robe to fall to the floor. She took the still-rigid length of him inside her, then let him coax her down so that her head rested on his chest. Gently he stroked her—her hair, her back, her hip—and then he gave a great sigh that she felt intensely deep where her body sheltered his.

"Where did a lovely, delicate woman like you learn such words?"

There were a dozen ways she could have phrased the demand she'd whispered in his ear, and he would have responded to every one of them—but not quite the way he had responded to these particular words. She smiled primly. "Words are powerful. They can comfort, soothe, hurt, disappoint, arouse, satisfy."

"My words tend to hurt, don't they?"

She shrugged as if he hadn't broken her heart a dozen times over. "You believed what you were saying."

In the dim light she saw him shake his head. "I let the evidence convince me of something I knew in my heart couldn't be true. What does that make me?"

"Human," she murmured. "Not Supercop. Not even a superhero. Just a flesh-and-blood man who does the best he can and sometimes makes mistakes and has to set them right."

"This was a hell of a mistake." He hesitated, then asked, "Can it be set right?"

She pulled away from him and moved to lie beside him, settling on her stomach, supporting her weight on her arms. "That's up to you, Jack. Are you going to insist on taking responsibility for everything MacDougal and those agents and the other people involved did? Are you going to blame yourself for not magically knowing the truth, when everyone around you was doing their damnedest to hide it? Are you going to continue to hold yourself to a higher standard than everyone else? Or are you going to admit that you were wrong and get over it?''

He turned his head toward her. In the dim light, she could recognize his rueful expression. "You make it sound so easy."

"Forgiving is easy." She hesitated, then added, "Living alone is hard."

"Living with me can be harder. Believe me," he added dryly. "I have thirty-four years' experience."

"Yes, but I don't want as much from you as you demand of yourself. I just want a chance."

He held her gaze a long time before slowly, hesitantly nodding. As commitments went, it was pretty shaky.

But shaky with Jack was better than everything with someone else.

It was sure as hell better than nothing.

Thursday morning was bright, sunny, calm. The sky was a pale, thin blue and gave no hint of the storm that had finally moved on a few hours before dawn. The signs remained, though—the puddles that dotted the courtyard, the wicker chairs crammed together on the gallery, the flower petals that clung everywhere, it seemed, except to the flowers.

Jack was feeling pretty damn sunny and calm himself as he cooked breakfast for two. Though he'd gotten only a few hours' sleep last night, they'd been restful hours. He felt better than he had in a year—though he knew his activity while awake through the night had more to do with that than the sleep.

Evie had a hell of a lot more to do with it.

He wondered if she knew how badly he'd needed her tough talk last night. He'd lain in bed after they'd made love the first time, watching her sleep, and thought about all the months they'd been apart, about those bastards shooting at her and the danger he'd put her in, and he'd found himself on the verge of a full-fledged panic attack. He'd needed her anger, her arguments, her support.

He hadn't known until she offered how desperately he needed her forgiveness. Now he had it.

Now he had to keep her alive so he wouldn't lose it.

As he removed the skillet from the burner, she came down the stairs, dressed in her gypsy getup, looking exotic and beautiful. He felt a surge of pure, raw lust that was painful in intensity, but made no move toward her. There was time later for that. This morning they had plans to discuss.

"So the great Evangelina has decided at last to join us in the corporeal world."

She looked surprised—and why shouldn't she? Evangelina had never been a topic for teasing between them. Recovering, she came into the kitchen, squeezed past him a little closer than space limitations required and took a coffee cup from the cabinet. "You want to get physical, Murphy, I think I'm up for it. What about you?"

He deflected her hand when she would have given him a bold caress. "Later. We need to talk."

She filled her coffee cup while he divided breakfast— scrambled eggs, onions, fried potatoes and a healthy dose of pepper sauce—between two plates. They settled at the dining table, where his coffee was already cooling, and he gave her time to eat half her meal before he spoke. "Tell me everything Browning said to you last night."

"Brown— Oh. Ted." She took another bite before answering in a slow, deliberate manner. "He said it was obvious how Murphy was spending his vacation, and he wanted to know if I was providing the same services to MacDougal."

Browning was single and arrogant enough to think that every woman who saw him wanted him. Of course he would take one look at Evie and immediately think of sex—*vacation?*

Jack's gaze jerked to her face, and he saw that she was

looking back, her own gaze speculative. His face grew warm, and his throat tightened on the words he should say but couldn't think of.

"Are you on vacation, Jack?" she asked quietly.

He swallowed hard. "Y-yes."

"So this...investigation... It's all yours. It's not a departmental thing."

He shook his head.

"And there are no partners. No backup."

Again, he shook his head.

"It's just you and me."

"I'm sorry, Evie," he said at last. "The lieutenant made me take some time off. He thought I'd gotten too...involved with the MacDougal case."

"So he knows nothing about this. Sonny, the others—they know nothing."

Another negative shake.

"And if they find out?"

He rubbed his eyes with the heels of his hands before looking at her again. "Best case, they'll reassign me and probably send me to a shrink. That's what the lieutenant was threatening when he put me on leave. Worst case, I'll lose my job."

She watched him for a long time, then, with a grim smile, shook her head. "Damn, Jack. If I'd made that complaint to the city the day you were turning away my customers—"

"It probably would have ended my career. It definitely would've gotten me out of your hair."

"That was a hell of a bluff. Too bad you don't play poker."

"Look, if you want out, I understand. You didn't want to do it in the first place, but at least you thought you'd have backup."

"I *have* backup. I have you."

"But—"

"Frankly, Jack, I'm more comfortable with the idea of it being just you. Your partners never did like me. They never did approve of me. I'm not sure just how much they'd be willing to risk to protect me.''

''They wouldn't—'' He broke off. He couldn't say beyond a doubt that neither Sonny nor the others would let anything happen to her, regardless of their feelings for her, because he didn't know beyond a doubt that it was true. Not after last night.

He did know one thing for a stone-cold fact—*he* would die if it meant keeping her safe. And he would die if he didn't keep her safe. It would kill him.

''So…back to Ted.''

''Call him Browning,'' he said. ''Ted sounds just a little too chummy.''

The smile she gave him was womanly and sweet and purely sexual. ''Browning is an arrogant ass,'' she announced, then added, ''and he's scared to death that someone's going to find out what they did.''

And now someone *had* found out—Evie. Were there limits on Browning's fear? How far would he go to protect his secret?

He pushed the disquieting questions aside and concentrated on the discussion. ''He touched you, and you— What? Saw something?''

''It wasn't what I saw, but what I heard. All I saw was images in a dark place, a room or maybe a van or a truck. Two people, some kind of equipment. I heard voices—different voices, not the people in the dark. They were talking about Celeste. About…''

She made a nervous gesture, and her breathing became unsteady. Jack took her hand in his. Her fingers, icy cold, curled tightly around his as she drew a deep breath and forced out the rest. ''They were talking about killing her. About stopping her before she did any real harm. One of them asked, 'But what about Murphy?' And the other said, 'He's not a problem. I'll take care of him.'''

And he *had* been taken care of, Jack thought grimly. They—whoever the hell they were—had framed Evie and left him too distraught and hurt to figure out a damn thing.

"Then...then I heard the men from last night. Browning and—and—"

"Keith Stewart," he supplied quietly, and she nodded.

"They were arguing. One of them wanted to warn her, but the other was concerned about their case. One of them said, 'But they're going to kill her,' and the other said...'" She raised her gaze to his face. Her sorrow was exquisite as she whispered the final words. "'She's just a hooker. New Orleans is full of hookers.'"

After a long, still silence, Evie said simply, "Then I pulled away and I ran."

Minutes slid past. Slowly the warmth returned to her fingers. Jack felt as if it was draining out of him. Finally, he focused on one aspect he thought he might be able to deal with. "I thought visions were strictly that—seen. Not heard."

"That's clairvoyance. There's also clairaudience—hearing—and clairsentience. That involves smells. It's fairly uncommon."

"You have the first two." He noticed her quick, startled look at his apparent acknowledgment of her powers. *Was* he acknowledging them? Or was it merely easier—better—than saying, You claim to have...? He didn't know. "Do you also have the last?"

"On occasion. Do you remember I told Irina that I get these images of water when I'm with her?"

"She said it meant nothing to her."

"Every time I see her, especially when she touches me, I get this vision of a bayou. I see the trees, the vegetation. I hear the water lapping against the bank and the insects buzzing. I can smell the water, the mud, the lushness. It's...menacing. Frightening."

"What does it mean?"

Her shrug gave her a vulnerable air. "I don't know. Maybe nothing. Sometimes it's like the wires get crossed. Sometimes I have visions intended for clients whom I haven't yet met. Sometimes I get images or messages that have nothing to do with anything."

"You told her that you have an image—just an impression—of water. Why didn't you tell her what you just told me? Why were you holding back?"

She sat back and crossed her legs. Hidden in the fullness of her skirt was a slit that now fell open practically to her hip. Jack let the long, slender length of thigh distract him for a moment, let himself remember last night when she had straddled him, and earlier, when he'd been on top and she'd wrapped her legs around his waist, holding him deep within her. The memories were enough to make him hot, to stir the ache in his belly, to stir something more, so he forcefully pushed them to the back of his mind.

"I don't know," she replied. "I don't... I haven't given Irina a lot of thought when I'm not with her, for obvious reasons." She gave him a smile not intended to be sexually tormenting, but it was just the same. "Frankly, I'm not comfortable with our relationship. I know you think people like me don't have ethics, but some of us do, and what I'm doing with Irina violates them. You don't let someone else listen to a client's reading. You don't misrepresent yourself. You don't try to manipulate a client."

She fell silent for a moment, and her expression grew troubled. He suspected that she was putting some order to her thoughts and regrets for the first time. Plagued with enough troubles, thanks to him, she'd ignored these as long as she could.

Looking at him again, she went on. "Under normal circumstances, I never would have taken Irina on as a client. I wouldn't do business with a member of William MacDougal's family. I wouldn't take his money."

He believed that. She'd given away the first five thousand, and she genuinely hadn't wanted Irina's check.

"Also..." Raising one hand, she fingered the dime that hung from a chain around her neck. The odd charm had appeared after her first visit with Irina, and he hadn't seen her without it since. He'd figured it was some sort of good luck amulet and hardly worth asking about. Of course, he wore a good luck charm of his own. He just happened to keep his in a holster, with fourteen rounds in the clip and one up the pipe.

"Also?" he prompted.

Down the hall the door opened. Evie's gaze moved in that direction, and Jack turned to watch Anna Maria and Martine, the woman who'd been with them the night Slick had tried to pick up Evie, approach. Neither looked particularly happy to see him there. Well, the feeling was mutual.

"I see my charm didn't work," Martine said, giving him a disdainful look as she passed. "He's here."

"'Charm' and 'Murphy' are two words that are mutually exclusive," Anna Maria said. She stopped next to Evie's chair and subjected her to serious scrutiny. After a moment, she scowled at him—able to tell from one look what they'd done last night?—then took the nearest chair. "I was hoping you didn't suffer any damage from last night's storm."

The other woman picked up the thought. "Obviously the worst damage came before the storm."

Evie gave them both reproachful looks. "Jack, this is Martine Broussard. Martine, Jack Murphy."

"I hear your name often," Martine said. "From friends, from customers. Funny. No one ever has anything good to say about you."

"Martine—" Evie began, but Jack silenced her by doing something neither of her friends dared—touching her, claiming her hand possessively.

"If I didn't know you two were genuinely worried about her—and that you have good reason to worry—my feelings might get hurt,'' he said with a touch of sarcasm. Then he asked Evie, ''Do you feel comfortable talking in front of them?''

She smiled faintly at her friends, then him, and shrugged. ''We were just discussing why I haven't been honest with one of my clients.''

''The one with the evil house?'' Martine asked.

Jack looked at Evie. ''Evil house?''

''You heard us talk about it.''

''You said there was a negative energy. It's a long way from negative to evil.''

''I'd just met the woman. I couldn't very well tell her that her home is malevolent and evil and I won't set foot inside it if I can avoid it.'' She gave him a dry look. ''Why do you think we meet on the terrace in hundred-degree weather?''

Anna Maria leaned her arms on the tabletop. ''What have you been less than honest about—besides *him?*''

Evie told them the two versions of her vision. Both women listened with the avid interest of believers. When she was done, Martine spoke first. ''So instinct warned you not to tell her everything. Do you know why?''

After a long, uneasy silence, Evie sighed. ''I don't trust her. I like her. I feel sorry for her. I regret misleading her. But I don't trust her.''

''Why not?'' Anna Maria asked.

''This woman is a believer. I get within ten feet of her, and she zaps me. The first time she touched me, I thought I was going to run screaming in the opposite direction. The connection was so strong that I felt sick.''

''But?''

''But she's not that easy to read. There are things about her I can't see. Most of what I pick up is fairly unimportant to her in the present.''

''Having a baby is unimportant?'' Jack asked.

''It's something she wants,'' Evie explained hesitantly.

"But it's not a major focus. It should be. If she wants it as much as she says, I should have known before yesterday. I should have picked up on it sooner."

The other two women immediately responded. "She's blocking you."

"Projecting."

"Testing your powers."

"Maybe even reading you."

"Wait a minute. Wait." Jack raised one hand. "Blocking? Projecting? Testing?"

"Of course," Anna Maria said matter-of-factly. "If she's psychic herself, it would explain everything."

"Can't you recognize another psychic?"

Evie smiled. "We don't wear signs or have a secret handshake or anything like that. I can often tell that someone is sensitive, but all believers are sensitive or they wouldn't believe. They generally have some experience with ESP—"

"What you cop types call hunches," Anna Maria interjected.

"Or they see auras or have extraordinarily good instincts or whatever. But as far as recognizing a full-blown psychic simply from talking... I don't know if I can't do it or if it just hasn't happened yet."

"Why would a psychic want a psychic advisor of her own?" he asked.

"Because we often can't see our own lives. If I wanted to know what was in my future, I would have to find someone else to tell me."

"So...if she's also psychic...she might be able to read you?"

All three women answered in unison. "Yes."

"And what could she read?"

Martine and Anna Maria looked at Evie. *She* didn't look at anyone as she murmured her answer. "Everything."

The same bad feeling he'd had last night when the car without headlights turned the corner rushed through Jack now. While they'd been scamming Irina—sweet, lovely, vulnerable, lonely Irina—she might have been running her own scam. She could know all about him and his determination to bring her husband to justice. While Evie was trying to use her to get MacDougal, she could have been using Evie to protect him.

And the last woman MacDougal had needed protection from had wound up strangled and tossed into Lake Pontchartrain like so much garbage.

He'd gone into this—dragged Evie into this—without a clue in hell what he was doing. He'd brought her to MacDougal's attention, to the attention of two corrupt FBI agents, and he'd pretended to himself and to her that she was safe, while her cover might have been blown from the very first meeting.

God help him, he was a fool.

Damn.

He ran his fingers through his hair. "So we could be in more trouble than we thought."

She shrugged. "We may be all wrong here. I might not be as good as I think. Irina might not be as sensitive as I think. She might simply be testing me. Clients do that sometimes. It's their way of measuring whether we're worth their money."

"What is your gut instinct?"

She considered it a long time, then shrugged again. "I honestly don't know, Jack. Now that I know what to look for, now that I know to be on guard, give me more time with her. I may be able to figure it out."

"And what if she already knows what you're doing?"

"I don't think she does. If she knew I was working for the police, she would have to feel something—betrayal, anger, hostility. You know how those emotions feel, how they overwhelm you. They're difficult, if not impossible, to disguise. But I've never picked up anything even remotely negative from her.'' She squeezed his fingers tightly. ''Give me more time, Jack. We've come this far. Don't make me stop now.''

He should put an end to it now. Nothing they could accomplish was worth putting Evie in more danger than she was already in.

But her instincts said it was safe to continue. He put great faith in his instincts—except, unfortunately, when the evidence contradicted them. Was it right of him to trust hers, or was he simply justifying putting the case ahead of her safety?

From the opposite end of the table, Anna Maria was watching him with a hint of scorn in her blue eyes. ''One of these days you're going to have to trust her.''

It wasn't about trust. It was about Evie, safe or in danger, alive or dead.

But Evie thought she was safe, at least where Irina was concerned. He wanted to think so, too.

''When are you supposed to see her again?'' he asked, hearing the grim acceptance in his voice.

''Monday.''

''I want her to come here. I don't want you to go to the estate anymore. All right?''

Another nod.

''And you don't go out alone and you don't see anyone here unless Anna Maria's here, too.''

''That's the way we work anyway, except with my regulars.''

Leaving the table, he retrieved the small pistol he'd left under a chair cushion last night and offered it to her. ''Keep this with you.''

Evie stared at the .22 as if touching it might trigger those unsettling flashes she talked about. ''I don't know how to use a gun.''

''It's simple. You take off the safety—'' he demonstrated ''—point and pull the trigger. This one's most effective at close range. You can't miss.''

Still she refused to take it. "I don't know—"

"I do." Anna Maria took the pistol from him. She thumbed the safety back into the locked position, ejected the clip, ejected the round from the chamber, then efficiently reloaded. She did it all with a determination that gave a tremendous boost to his earlier opinion of her.

Though he'd rather have privacy for his next move, he pulled Evie to her feet, ignored the other women and kissed her hard, longer and more hungrily than he wanted, far less than he needed. "I'll be back."

She nodded, then sank into the chair. He was halfway to the back door when Anna Maria asked, "Where are you going?"

"To beat a confession out of a suspect." As he closed the French door behind him, he heard Martine's startled question.

"He's kidding, isn't he?"

Not by a long shot, he thought grimly. Stewart would be lucky if he didn't kill him. It would be a mercy the bastard didn't deserve.

Chapter 10

The day passed slowly with no word from Jack. Evie wondered where he was, what he'd learned, when he would come back. She'd endured Anna Maria's hovering and Martine's hourly phone calls and a day filled with customers who wanted their money's worth from the great Evangelina. Finally the end of her workday had arrived, and with it her last customer.

He was eighteen, maybe twenty, an arrogant young man in town with his wealthy parents and demanding the full parlor-games effect for his twenty bucks. Already short of patience, she'd known within two minutes that he wasn't going to be satisfied no matter what, and so she'd offered to return his money if he'd just leave. He'd refused and threatened to tell Daddy, a Shreveport lawyer, that she'd ripped him off, and so she'd agreed to perform.

She studied him across the table. He was handsome, but sullen, spoiled and used to getting his own way. He was also, for a cynic, more transparent than she ever would have expected.

"Come on, lady, I'm waiting," he demanded. "Tell me something about myself."

"You're rude and obnoxious—but a blind man could see that." She breathed evenly to calm her irritation. "You have a girlfriend in Baton Rouge."

"Like you couldn't tell that just by looking," he said scornfully. "Is this where I'm supposed to act surprised and say, 'Oh, my God, you know about Tiffany'?"

"Her name is Lisa." She smiled as a startled look crossed his face. "You think she loves you, but you're just amusing yourself with her until you graduate from college. From there, you plan to go on to law school, and then, after you settle into your career, you'll find a woman more suitable for an influential man like you." Another direct hit, judging from his sudden shifting in the chair. "Truth is, she's amusing herself with you...among others."

His expression turned dark. "You're lying."

"Ask Lisa. Ask..." Honing in on the name that popped instantly into his mind was like child's play. "Ask Matt."

"You're lying! You're making this up! She hasn't seen Matt in—" With great effort, he brought his temper under control and scowled at her. "Lucky guess. Do it again."

"You cheated on your history final last semester. You got caught driving drunk but used the influence of your family name to persuade the sheriff not to tell your parents. You stole money from your mother's purse and blamed it on a servant." She gave him a disgusted look. "You're not only rude and obnoxious, you're dishonest, selfish and spoiled, and your time is up. Get out." Surreptitiously she reached under the table and pressed the buzzer to signal Anna Maria.

He stood up, looming over her. "Listen, lady—"

At that instant, the door swung open and her cousin stepped inside. "Is there a problem here?" she asked innocently.

"No problem," the young man said sharply. "Get back out

there where you belong. We're not done here." He slapped another twenty dollars on the table.

Evie looked at the bill, then him. "I'm sorry. We close for the day at six o'clock. It's now six-oh-two."

"I'm not leaving. I've paid you. I want ten more minutes."

Before Evie could think of a response, Anna Maria spoke again, still calm, still using her show voice. "Evangelina, Detective Murphy, with the New Orleans Police Department, is here to see you."

It wasn't Jack who came through the door, though. It was Martine, looking pretty much like a B-movie gypsy herself but carrying herself with all the impressive authority of the real Detective Murphy. She gave the young man a coldly intimidating look as she asked, "You want me to run this guy in, Evangelina?"

Evie struggled to remain utterly serious. "I don't think it will be necessary. He was just leaving."

Looking frustrated at not getting his way, the kid reached for the money on the table, but Martine stopped him. "Leave it. Consider it a tip—and next time, try not to be so rude. It annoys people."

Muttering a curse, he left, slamming the outer door behind him. Anna Maria locked it, turned over the Closed sign, then returned to the reading room. After a moment's silence, all three of them burst into laughter. After the last twenty-four hours, it felt incredibly good to laugh.

"Don't you know that impersonating a police officer is a crime?" Evie asked.

Martine dropped into the chair the young man had vacated. "Impersonating a human being *should* be a crime. Why do jerks like that always find us?"

"Part of the price of doing our kind of business." Evie stood up and stretched, then began removing jewelry. "Thanks."

"Any time. But next time, Anna Maria, can't I be Detective

Broussard? Being Murphy is kind of creepy.'' Without waiting for a response, Martine shifted her attention back to Evie. ''Have you heard from him?''

She shook her head.

''What was he really going to do?''

Evie shrugged. She hadn't told them about the FBI agents, or finding out that they'd covered up Celeste's murder, or getting shot at. She hadn't wanted to worry them anymore than they already were, and frankly she hadn't wanted to think about it herself. She was edgy enough as it was without dwelling on new dangers and threats.

''He wouldn't really beat someone up, would he?'' Martine pressed.

''Why not?'' Anna Maria asked. ''Bad guys deserve to get beaten up. If a cop arrests somebody he *knows* is guilty and knocking him around a bit helps him to admit responsibility for his crime, why not?''

''Because sometimes the people the cops *know* are guilty aren't,'' Evie said quietly. ''Like me. Beating me wouldn't have changed that fact.''

''You're an exception, not the rule. This guy Murphy was going to see—*is* he guilty?''

For one awful instant, Evie felt again the fear, the horror, and shuddered. Oh, yes. Stewart and Browning were guilty as hell—and hell was where they belonged for what they'd done to Celeste.

''Let's change the subject here,'' she said, aware that her voice was none too steady. ''We're officially closed. Why don't you head on home, Anna Maria? And take Martine with you.''

''I'm not leaving until Murphy gets here. You got milk?''

Evie nodded.

''And almond mocha chip ice cream?''

She nodded.

''Then come on back, ladies.'' Her cousin circled the room,

blowing out candles, then opened the door into the house and grinned. "Mama Anna's gonna make you her special Kahlúa almond mocha chip shakes, worthy of drowning any sorrow and quenching any desire."

Not *her* desire, Evie thought as she obediently went along. Only one thing—one man—could do that, and he'd been out of touch most of the unbearably long day. She wondered what he'd found out from the two men, wondered what he'd done with the information. Would he turn them in to the authorities, or had he made some sort of deal with them—his silence for their information? Or, worse, his silence for her life?

Could he live with a deal like that? Could he let two federal agents get away with murder—or, more accurately, being accomplices to murder—simply to keep her safe? She hoped not, because *she* couldn't. She wanted them punished. She wanted justice.

Hell, she wanted revenge.

They ordered in pizza, then made their shakes while they waited. By the time Jack walked through the French door, looking weary and frustrated, the dining table was littered with napkins, pizza crusts, empty glasses and the last melted drops of Kahlúa almond mocha chip shakes.

Anna Maria and Martine took one look at him and immediately took their leave. Evie remained where she was, sitting cross-legged in the chair, one knee bent up to support her elbow, and watched as Jack slid into the nearest chair. She pushed one of the pizza boxes toward him, and he flipped open the lid.

"It's cold," she said unnecessarily. "You can heat it in the microwave."

He shook his head and took a bite.

She waited until he'd polished off two slices and was working on a third to ask, "Did you talk to them?"

Again, he shook his head. "I've been all over the damn parish trying to find them. Apparently, they don't want to be

found—at least, not by me. But Stewart has to be in court in
the morning. I'll catch him then.'' He smiled cynically and
asked, ''And how was your day?''

She thought of her last customer and shrugged. ''The usual.
Tourists and skeptics and true believers.''

''You haven't been out, have you?''

''I haven't set foot outside the house—though I was about
ready to go looking for you.''

His smile was thin, his amusement bitter. ''You wouldn't
like the places I've been.'' After wiping his hands on the last
clean napkin, he extended one to her. ''Come here.''

She went willingly, straddling his thighs, linking her hands
behind his neck.

''Why don't we run away?'' he asked, nuzzling the soft
spot behind her left ear and making her hot.

''Because this is our home. Because you can't walk away
from what's happened here. Because we may not even exist
away from here.''

Her last answer made him smile. He looked as if he'd
needed it as badly as she'd needed to laugh.

His hands made restless circles on her back, moving lower
until they brushed her bottom. ''You have anything on under
here?''

She stood up, wriggled out of her underwear, then sat down
on his lap again. ''Not now.''

''Then why don't you take me upstairs and—'' He finished
with the same words she'd whispered to him last night, words
that made her nipples tighten and made moisture collect between her thighs.

''Why don't I do it right here?'' she asked, moving sug-
gestively against him.

''Because once in a while, I do like to be naked and in
bed.''

Rising to her feet, she took his hand and led him upstairs
and into her room. She undressed herself slowly, undressed

him even more slowly, then drew him down onto the bed, took him inside her. For a moment, he remained still, eyes closed, muscles rigid. Then he fixed his gaze on her. "Are you on the Pill?"

"No."

"And we're not using condoms."

Once, twice, she slid against him, making his breath catch, his face pale. "No," she agreed quietly. "We're not." They'd already confirmed that there'd been no women for him since her, no men for her, so disease wasn't a problem. If pregnancy was...

For a moment, his hazel gaze locked with hers as he considered the implications. Then, just like that, he accepted them. He didn't pull out, didn't insist on using the condoms that he must know were in her nightstand. He simply nodded once, slid his hands to her hips and thrust deeply inside her.

An hour had passed, maybe two. Evie couldn't find the energy to lift her head and look at the clock on the nightstand. Darkness had settled over the room and silence had settled over the house, broken only by the sounds of breathing—Jack's deep and steady, as if he were asleep, and her own, softer, shallower. He wasn't asleep, though. She could tell by nothing more than the feel of his body against hers, than the very clear sense of awareness that emanated from him in the dark. He was wide-awake. Thinking. Worrying.

She wished he had come home with answers, but she wasn't surprised. Maybe she'd given him bad advice last night. Maybe she should have let him go looking for Stewart and Browning right away, when odds were good that he'd find them. *Maybe* she should have controlled her response to Browning's touch instead of all but screaming out her discovery to him. Then the bastards wouldn't have known they'd been found out and they wouldn't have made themselves scarce today.

"It's not your fault."

She drew back to look at Jack, but his face was in shadow. Rising on one arm, she turned on the bedside lamp and then stared. "How did you know ?"

He grinned charmingly. "Relax. I didn't read your mind or anything like that."

"Then how—?"

"Honey, you're looking at the master of self-recrimination. I know you well enough to know that at some point, you're going to start thinking, 'If only I hadn't let them know…'" His grin faded and his expression turned grim. "I've lived the entire past year thinking, 'If only I hadn't…' about damn near everything."

She plumped up a pillow, then leaned against the headboard. Blessed with an abundant lack of modesty, according to Jack—and plenty of privacy—she didn't bother with cover. "Well, *if* I hadn't reacted the way I did, they never would have guessed what I knew, they wouldn't have shot at us, and you wouldn't have wasted an entire day trying to find them."

"You had just discovered—rather graphically—that two federal agents let an innocent woman be murdered, then let the NOPD blame you for it, and did nothing. How do you think you should have reacted?"

"If I had walked out of there calmly and waited until we were out of sight to tell you…"

"If you *could* have walked out of there calmly, you would have. You had an honest reaction, Evie. Don't blame yourself for it. Stewart will be at the courthouse tomorrow, and so will I. I'll find out what I need to know then." He sat up, moved with his pillow to the opposite end of the bed and leaned against the footboard. The ceiling fan ruffled his hair where it wasn't damp from their recent exertion. Naked, his skin gleaming, his expression intense, he looked handsome enough to make her heart race—and dear enough to make it break.

She looked away, furtively wiped a tear from one eye and

cleared the lump from her throat. "I've been thinking about my—my vision. I take it those men—the FBI agents—had the other men under surveillance."

Jack nodded. "They probably had a wiretap. What you saw was probably them listening to and taping a phone call. I hope they didn't destroy the tape."

"They'd have to be fools not to."

"They had to be fools to do what they did." He made a dismissive gesture. "You'd be amazed at the evidence some criminals will keep."

"Did you know the FBI was also investigating MacDougal? Did they tell you?"

"The Bureau isn't known for its cooperation with local authorities," he said dryly. "Sharing is a concept they haven't quite learned. But, yeah, we knew they were interested. Racketeering is a federal crime."

"Did you have wiretaps?" When he nodded, she hesitantly asked, "Then why don't you have tapes of the calls I supposedly made to MacDougal?"

For a moment, the regret that crossed his face was intense. Then he pushed it away and bluntly answered, "We'd been having trouble with our equipment. Money's so damn tight in the department, and everyone's got priorities that don't quite match up with ours. We lost a number of calls where the equipment simply failed to operate. The calls from this house were among the ones we missed."

"And that didn't strike you as...convenient?"

"If it was the first time the equipment failed, or if it was the only evidence linking you to MacDougal, yeah, I would have wondered. But it wasn't, not in either case."

"Did you ask the FBI for their tapes?"

"Sonny did. They said they didn't have any. They said they weren't investigating MacDougal." His smile was tight and cold. "Obviously, they lied."

And with good reason, Evie thought. The New Orleans PD

went looking for evidence to make their case against her, and
the only evidence the FBI had to offer not only proved her
innocence but made a hell of a case against *them*. In their
place, she would have lied, too.

But then, *she* never would have been in their place.

"How could they do it?" she asked softly. "How could
they listen to two people plan a woman's murder and do nothing? How they could put *anything* ahead of her life?"

Jack reached for her, and she went into his arms, letting the
warmth of his body chase away her sudden chill. "I don't
know," he murmured. "You put a lot of time and energy and
money into an investigation—hell, you put a lot of *yourself*
into it—and you don't want to blow it before you make the
case. But you don't let someone die for it. There were a dozen
things they could have done. We could have taken Celeste
into protective custody. We could have made her disappear so
thoroughly no one would ever find her again. We could have
put her under twenty-four-hour guard and, when they tried to
take her out, we could have taken them out."

His arms tightened around her, and his voice dropped to
little more than a whisper. "We could have saved her."

Instead, Stewart and Browning had sacrificed her.

After a time, she tilted her head back to look at him.
"So...what's the plan?"

"I'm going to talk to Stewart tomorrow. I'll find out if they
kept the surveillance tapes and who the two men you heard
were. Then I'm going to track down the bastards and see what
they can tell me. I'm going to put together an airtight case
against MacDougal and—"

"And what am I going to do? Sit here and wait patiently?"

"Exactly. I'm glad you understand that."

She wanted to protest, but what could she say? She was a
psychic and a coward. There wasn't much she *could* do besides wait—but it wouldn't be patiently. "I wish this was already over and done with."

"It will be soon." He gazed down at her, his expression inscrutable. "Eager to see the last of me?"

Would closing the case mean the end of their relationship? she wondered with a flare of panic. After last night's conversation and tonight's brief discussion about birth control, she had assumed that, with MacDougal out of the way, their lives would go back to the way they were a year ago. He would move back in, and they would pick up where they'd broken off and put into motion plans for a future, a marriage, a family. Had she assumed too much?

"No," she said quietly, then asked, "Are you eager to be rid of me?"

His answer was just as simple, just as quiet. "No."

Her *no* meant, No, I love you and I want to spend the rest of my life with you. What did his mean? Love forever? Or just sex for a while?

He slid down on the bed, then turned onto his side to face her. They were indecently close—but not close enough. "Did I tell you how sorry I am for not believing you?"

Though he hadn't said the exact words, she bobbed her head.

"I am sorrier than I have words to express."

"You expressed it just fine."

"Did I beg your forgiveness?"

She smiled as she stroked a strand of dark hair from his temple. "You begged for a number of things, though I don't believe forgiveness was one of them. You begged for relief, for mercy, for my body—"

He silenced her with a kiss designed to make *her* beg. Before long, she did just that with words, with frantic caresses and helpless pleas. Before long he gave her exactly what she begged for. Pure pleasure. Sweet satisfaction. Merciful relief.

Quiet settled over the room once again. The day's weariness overtook Jack, dragging him into a badly needed rest. She watched him in the dim light, stroking his beard-roughened jaw, easing the lines of tension that etched his forehead, feeling the strong, steady beat of his heart, and in a soundless whisper, she begged one last favor of him.

"Please don't break my heart again, Jack."

This time, she surely couldn't bear it.

When Keith Stewart came out of the courtroom Friday morning, another agent was with him—and Jack was waiting. Making an effort to appear nonthreatening, he pushed away from the wall and approached the two men. "Stewart. Sinclair."

Stewart paled. Sinclair closed the file he'd been flipping through, took note of Jack's jeans and polo shirt and remarked, "Hanging around the courthouse on your day off? You really need a vacation, Murphy."

Jack shifted his gaze to him. Remy Sinclair was the Assistant Special Agent in Charge of the New Orleans FBI office and was in line to be the next SAC when his boss retired at the end of the year. Like Stewart, he'd earned his reputation working organized crime. Unlike Stewart, he'd done it without compromising himself or anyone else. Jack liked him, as much as he liked any fed.

Once he got what he wanted from Stewart and Browning, he would probably turn them over to Sinclair.

"I'm *on* vacation," he said in response to Sinclair's comment. "I just wanted to talk to Keith for a minute. I had trouble catching him yesterday."

"Yeah, I'd heard you came by the office," Sinclair said. "Keith, I'm late for an appointment. I'll see you later. Murphy."

Jack hadn't thought it possible, but Stewart turned even whiter as Sinclair took his leave, and he broke out in a cold sweat. "Look, Murphy—"

Jack took his arm in a brutal grip and pushed him toward the nearest fire stairs. There, in relative privacy, he shoved him against the wall and quietly said, "I want to know everything."

"I—I—" Stewart's gaze darted toward the door, up one flight of stairs, down the other. Apparently seeing that escape wasn't an option, he decided to bluff. He straightened his jacket, combed a hand through his hair, squared his shoulders and tried to look as if he weren't the least bit concerned. "I don't know what you're talking about."

"I'm talking about you and Ted Browning and the role you played in the murder of Celeste Dardanelle."

Stewart tried to pretend ignorance, but the sweat that popped out on his forehead and the nervous movement of his eyes made the attempt pathetic. "Who? Celeste— Oh, yeah, your informant that got killed. You tried to pin it on MacDougal but couldn't. You even tried to pin it on your own girlfriend, but couldn't pull that off, either. Now you're blaming us? You'd do anything to avoid accepting responsibility yourself, wouldn't you?"

Jack leaned a few inches closer. The son of a bitch would have crawled into the wall behind him if he could have. "Don't screw with me, Stewart. I'd just as soon kill you as talk to you. Tell me what I want to know, and maybe I *won't* kill you."

"I—I don't know wh-what you're talking about."

"While tapping MacDougal's phones, you got surveillance tapes of two men planning Celeste Dardanelle's murder." His voice grew quieter, colder, more menacing. "I want those tapes."

"I—I don't know— I never had a wiretap on MacDougal's lines. I've never worked a case on him." When Jack made a derisive sound, Stewart quickly insisted, "It's true. Ask Remy. He's overseen every case I've done since coming here. He'll tell you."

Jack stared at him. Maybe it *was* true. But the nervous twitch in Stewart's cheek and the convulsive bobbing of his

Adam's apple suggested that it wasn't the entire truth. Evie's vision *proved* it wasn't the entire truth. "Then where'd you get the tapes?"

"I'm telling you, there aren't any—"

"You had the killers under surveillance for some other reason, didn't you? And you heard them planning Celeste's murder, and you thought—what? What goes through a cop's mind that convinces him to let a woman die? Were you worried about blowing your case? Afraid that if you warned her, they would know you were watching them? Did you think it might not look good on your record to risk an expensive, time-consuming investigation just to save one woman's life? After all, she was just a hooker. New Orleans is full of hookers."

At the echo of familiar words, Stewart stopped breathing, and Jack honestly thought he was going to pass out right there on the concrete floor. Then he drew in a noisy, hiccuping breath, his shoulders sagged, and he ducked his head in shame. "We'd spent months, hundreds of hours, thousands of dollars trying to nail these guys. If she suddenly disappeared, they would have been suspicious. Hell, they would've *known* they were being watched. They would have... We never would have got them after that."

"So you let her die."

"There wasn't any other way."

"There were a hundred other ways!" Jack's shout echoed through the stairwell and made Stewart flinch. Struggling to regain some measure of control, he asked, "Why didn't you tell me? I could have handled it."

Stewart gave him a look that, in spite of the fear and the guilt, was pure disdain. "*You* were the last person we would have told."

Jack opened his mouth to demand an explanation just as the door was shoved open. People streamed into the stairwell, complaining about an elevator stuck between floors. They pushed Jack to one side, Stewart to the other. A woman in three-inch heels stumbled against Jack, smiling warmly when he steadied her, murmuring her gratitude in a syrupy Southern voice. By the time he turned his attention back to Stewart, he was gone.

Jack swore viciously enough to make several people stare, then give him a wide berth. Pushing past them, he made it into the corridor, but there was no sign of Keith Stewart. Swearing again, he reentered the stairwell and went downstairs, then outside.

You were the last person we would have told, the bastard had said. Why? Because he would have taken a plan to kill *his* informant very personally? Because he would have insisted on doing whatever was necessary to protect her?

Maybe they hadn't trusted him. After all, he had been mentioned by name by one of the killers.

But what about Murphy?

He's not a problem. I'll take care of him.

Why *had* they named him? Of all the people involved in the MacDougal investigation, why had he been their only concern? And why had they been so sure he wouldn't be a problem?

He'd started out this case thinking he had all the answers and needed only the proof. Now he knew he had no answers at all. Only questions.

Fortunately, he knew where to go for help in finding answers.

He located a pay phone, made one call to arrange a meeting, then headed for the location at the foot of Poydras. He parked in a nearby garage and walked to the Riverwalk. Sonny was already waiting at the water's edge.

"Maybe the lieutenant was right about you needing a couple weeks off," Sonny said. "You don't look like the walking dead anymore."

"I've been sleeping better." Amazing what taking the edge off a lifetime of unsatisfied lust could do for a body.

Even more amazing what Evie could do for a man's spirit.

"You getting that sleep with someone? I only ask because I've been by your place a number of times and you're never there."

Jack shrugged. Even when he was a teenager beginning what just barely qualified as a sex life, he'd never discussed it with anyone. Considering who he was sleeping with now, even if he was inclined to confide in his partner, he couldn't. Sonny would think he'd gone over the edge—and maybe he had. Not fifteen minutes ago, hadn't he stood back there at the courthouse and thought to himself that Evie's vision proved Keith Stewart was being less than honest?

But if this was over the edge, he liked it. In fact, he might try for stone-cold insane. He'd probably be really happy there.

"Okay," Sonny said, good-naturedly accepting that he wasn't going to get an answer. "You called, I came. What's up?"

Jack gazed out at the river traffic—a barge, a paddle wheeler, a cruise ship docking upriver. He deliberately avoided looking at Sonny as he began. "I've been working the last couple of weeks. On the MacDougal case."

"Yeah, like that's a surprise. Not even the lieutenant thought you would leave it alone for two whole weeks."

"I've also been talking to Evie."

Beside him Sonny went still. "Evie—DesJardien? The lying bitch that had you so—" He managed to stop the obscenity he'd been about to use. "So she's still alive. I was hoping someone had done her in."

"She was set up, Sonny." Jack felt his partner's stare, and finally he turned to meet it. There was surprise, dismay, but mostly scorn in his expression.

"That explains why you're sleeping better," he said derisively. "She's doing it to you again, J.D. She's got you so twisted that you don't know up from down or truth from lies. Didn't you learn anything last time?"

"Sonny—"

"Is she that good? I know she's a pretty little thing—kinda exotic looking and all—but is she worth screwing up your life over? Is she that hot? Does she like weird, kinky stuff? Because if that's the attraction, hell, J.D., you can get that—"

Jack interrupted, his voice flat and cold. "The FBI has tapes of MacDougal's people planning Celeste's murder."

Just as he'd expected, that shut Sonny up. He closed his mouth, opened it, then closed it again. He paced away a dozen feet, then came back and gripped the railing with both hands until his knuckles turned white. "How did you find that out?"

"You want the truth? Because it deals with Evie, and I'm not ready for another lecture about her."

His jaw tight, his gaze locked on the west bank, Sonny nodded.

"She had a vision."

The tension eased enough to allow him to scoff. "When did you become a believer, J.D.?"

"Maybe I should have been one all along, because about five minutes after Stewart and Browning found out that she'd had this vision, someone took a half-dozen shots at us. I just came from talking to Stewart. He admitted that she's right. They've got tapes."

Sonny was silent a long time—but not still. He leaned on the railing. He paced. He shoved his hands in his pockets, then pulled them out again and cracked his knuckles all at once. He did his best thinking in motion, expending nervous energy.

Jack remained still, where he did *his* best thinking.

"You're saying that Keith Stewart and Ted Browning— *Special Agents* Stewart and Browning of the *Federal Bureau of Investigation* taped a conversation in which persons unknown—to us, at least—planned to kill our informant, and they just sat on it? It never occurred to them to warn Celeste? They never thought to call us?"

Jack shrugged.

"*Why?* What the hell were they thinking?"

"They were thinking about their case and all the ways coming forward could screw it up."

Sonny dragged his hand through his hair, then made an effort to calm down. "So...you haven't heard these tapes. You don't know who the men were."

Jack shook his head. "Our conversation got interrupted. He took off before I could stop him. I'll have to find him again."

"We need the tapes. If we can prove who killed Celeste, then we stand a good chance of making a deal that will give us MacDougal." Then his expression turned sarcastic. "And as a bonus, that'll prove sweet little Evie wasn't involved and you can spend the rest of your life scr—" At Jack's sharp look, he dropped that line of thought. "You want my help in finding Stewart?"

"No. He's edgy enough as it is. Right now he thinks only Evie and I know. If he finds out I've told you—"

"He may disappear or destroy the tapes. Okay. You find him. I'll tell the others." Suddenly, Sonny grinned and slapped him on the back. "Damn, J.D. You did it. You're gonna clear this case."

Two weeks ago the possibility would have left Jack damn near paralyzed with fear. It was only his obsession with this case that had gotten him through the past year. How would he survive without it?

Today the answer was simple—with Evie. Whatever happened, whatever the future held, he would survive it with Evie.

Evie was awakened early Saturday morning by a kiss and the familiar scent of aftershave that tickled her nose and made her smile. Blindly she wrapped her arms around Jack's neck, pulled him closer and breathed deeply. Then she realized that his jaw was clean-shaven and that her arms rested on fabric, not bare skin. Opening her eyes, she saw that he was wide-awake, dressed and apparently kissing her goodbye. "Where are you going?" she asked petulantly.

"To work."

"You're on vacation, Jack."

"Yeah, right. I'm still looking for Stewart."

"You spent the better part of two days looking for him." Last night's weekly girls' night out had become a sitting-and-waiting-for-word-from-Jack. It'd been nearly midnight when he'd walked in the back door and Anna Maria and Martine had walked out the front. All that time gone, and he'd had no luck beyond the brief conversation with the agent at the courthouse.

"Yeah, well, today I'm going to find him. Remember—"

She rolled her eyes. "Don't go out alone, and don't see anyone here without Anna Maria in the next room with her trusty—*your* trusty—little pistol."

"Don't be a smart-ass, Evie. If anything happened to you..."

It would be more than he could bear. She knew that. Serious now, she pressed a kiss to his jaw. "I swear, I'll be careful." Then she added, "You promise, too."

"I'll be back, don't worry. I'll keep coming back until you don't want me."

"Always," she murmured. "Forever."

For a moment he gazed at her as if there was something he wanted to say. The moment passed, though, and he smiled faintly. "I'll see you later." He made it to the door before she stopped him.

"Jack? Promise."

"I'll be careful. I'll come back to you. I swear."

She listened to the sound of his footsteps in the hall, on the stairs. A moment later she thought she heard the distant click of the back door. Another moment, and she imagined the creak of the courtyard gate.

He was gone.

For a time she lay there, wishing she could sleep again, knowing she couldn't. Finally she got up and made the bed. She did housework and laundry, then showered and dressed, and it wasn't even nine o'clock yet. She took a cup of coffee onto the gallery, but being even just barely outside alone seemed to violate Jack's orders and made her feel guilty. Besides, she felt creepy out there—as if someone was watching her. The first two times she'd felt that way, she'd written it off as an overactive imagination. This time she suspected there might really be someone out there. An FBI agent? One of MacDougal's men? A cop friend of Jack's, there to look out for her?

She was retreating back into the relative safety of the house when the phone rang. She started to grab it up, then remembered Jack's directive—*Don't answer the phone unless it's me*—and waited impatiently beside the answering machine for the incoming message tape to start.

"Hi, Evie, it's me," Martine said. "I just wanted—"

Evie grabbed the receiver. "Hey. I'm here."

"Oh, Gypsy, I knew you were there," Martine said with a laugh. "I just thought you might be…ah, otherwise occupied."

"No such luck this morning. How about you?"

"I was at your house until eleven-forty-seven, remember? Not much sense in going out that late. It leaves so few hours to enjoy the nightly catch."

"Six or seven hours aren't enough for you?" Evie asked dryly.

Martine's laugh was husky. "Six or seven hours is my idea of foreplay, honey. Want some breakfast?"

"I have nothing in the house."

"I thought we could play tourist and have beignets and café au lait at Café du Monde."

"Jack said—"

"Don't go out alone. But you wouldn't be alone, Gypsy,

you'd be with me. But if you prefer, I can pick up a to-go order and bring it to your place.''

"Beignets aren't as good unless they're fresh and hot." Evie glanced outside. It was a bright, sunny Saturday—typical of a New Orleans July. There would be tourists every step of the way from here to the other side of Jackson Square. And Jack had said she could go out with Martine or Anna Maria, and it wasn't likely the FBI agents would come within a mile of her when they knew he was looking for them, and... Darn it, she wanted to go. "Okay. Why don't you come on over here? I'll get ready."

"I'll be there in five minutes."

Getting ready consisted of putting on her shoes, emptying her coffee in the sink and leaving a note for Anna Maria. She had just finished propping it on the bar when the doorbell rang.

"It's a beautiful day in the neighborhood," Martine greeted her in a singsong voice. "And something's going on. The tourists are so thick you have to beat 'em off with a stick. Is there some sort of festival today?"

Evie shrugged as she locked up. "I haven't read the newspaper or turned on the television since—"

"Since *he* walked back into your life." Martine gave her a sidelong look. "How's it going?"

"He said he would come back to me for as long as I wanted him."

"Well, it's not 'I love you, please forgive me, please marry me and let me spend the rest of my life groveling at your feet to make up for my behavior,' but it's a start."

Evie smiled at the impossible image of Jack groveling as she followed Martine down the steps and onto the sidewalk. It wasn't Mardi-Gras bad, but there were far more people on the streets than she'd expected for a regular old Saturday. She didn't like crowds as a rule, and this one was no exception. She walked next to the curb, leaving herself an escape route in case anyone got too close, and Martine stayed near her side as a buffer.

As they approached Jackson Square, a group of young men came around the Presbytére, laughing, in high spirits, enjoying their time in the Big Easy. One of them bumped into Martine, then stepped to the same side she did, then to the opposite side when she did.

"Wouldn't you know?" she murmured to Evie. "And I left my beating-off-tourists stick at home." She took hold of his arms, turned in a half circle with him, then started to pull away, but he caught her hands and held on.

"Do you know you're the most beautiful woman I've seen since I got to New Orleans?" he asked with a seriousness that only a very young man—or a drunk—could pull off.

"I bet I am. And how many of me do you see?"

"No, really. You really are. You're beautiful."

"Thank you." She tried again to free herself, but he refused to release her. "Sweetheart, you're handsome and sweet, but it's too early in the morning for games."

"It's never too early for games," he protested. "Want to join us for drinks? For breakfast? For a good time?"

Evie caught Martine's attention, rolled her eyes, then gestured ahead. Heading for a less congested area to wait, she stepped into the street, passed the boy's friends, then stepped onto the sidewalk again. Turning back, she watched Martine deflecting the kid's passes. Evie didn't worry about her for an instant. If there was one thing Martine Broussard knew, it was how to handle the opposite sex. With a few well-chosen words and the same seductive smile, she could make a man feel like the most important man in the world or cut him off at the knees and make him grateful to be there. Her ex-husband seemed to be the only man immune to her charms—and, of course—

"Detective Murphy."

The voice was so soft, the answer so on target, that it took

Evie a moment to realize that it was real and not in her mind. Recognizing it in the next instant, she slowly turned and found Irina MacDougal standing a few short feet away.

Swallowing hard, she looked back at Martine. Her friend was surrounded by the boys now, her dark hair barely visible in their midst. Evie counted six around her, all of them young, strong, built like linebackers. Suddenly their teasing didn't seem quite so friendly, quite so innocent.

When her gaze returned to Irina, the woman shrugged, her dark curls swaying with the movement. "I paid them. You leave with me, without creating a scene, and in another few minutes, they'll let her go. She'll never know there was a threat."

"Leave and go where?"

"For a drive. I want to talk to you."

"And if I refuse to go?"

"Look at your friend. Look at my friends. Imagine the harm they could do a slender young woman without even trying."

As Irina had directed, Evie looked back once more. Martine, normally so capable and self-sufficient, looked vulnerable, defenseless. Innocent games—what the boys probably thought they were playing—could so easily get out of control. Menacing games—which they might know they were playing—could turn to tragedy.

For one frantic moment, Evie considered screaming. She and Martine were both well-known on these blocks. Surely someone who knew them would come to their aid or her screams would attract the attention of one of the police officers assigned to foot patrol in this area or some courageous tourist would step in—

"All these tourists out this morning," Irina said softly. "One got mugged just a few minutes ago on the other side of the square. She's giving a rather hysterical report to the police officers who patrol here. With this crowd, it's doubtful they would even hear a scream. Let's go, Evangelina—before things get out of control and your friend suffers for it.''

She gestured to a car parked illegally nearby. With great reluctance, Evie walked the few yards with her and slid into the front seat. Irina instructed her to fasten the seat belt, then bent in to secure a handcuff around her left wrist. The other half was already locked around something underneath the seat.

Moving quickly, Irina got into the driver's seat, secured her own seat belt and pulled away from the curb. Evie twisted around to watch as Martine finally managed to free herself from the young men; then the car turned the corner and she could see nothing. She faced forward again, folded her hands tightly in her lap, then asked, "We're going to the bayou, aren't we?"

Irina glanced at her. "'An impression of water.' You knew it was a bayou from our very first meeting. You lied to me. Why?''

"You lied about its significance.'' Evie shrugged. "That makes us even.''

"Except I was paying for your services. I was under no obligation to be truthful with you. *You* did have such an obligation.''

It was foolish to feel bad because she'd behaved unethically with a client. Irina was hardly the typical client. They'd both gone into the relationship with ulterior motives, of which Evie's was the more acceptable. Still, she did feel a faint sense of guilt. She'd never betrayed a client before.

Stubbornly pushing away the guilt, she asked, "How good are you?''

Irina stopped at an intersection, motioned a group of tourists to cross the street, then fixed her dark gaze on Evie and replied simply, "I'm the best.''

Evie didn't doubt the truth of her reply. She'd met a number of genuine psychics, but Irina could dance circles around them all. She'd been out of her league from the beginning. Too bad she'd found out too late.

And it *was* too late. She'd known from the start that someone was going to die before this all played out. She'd even suspected that it might be her.

Now she knew.

Irina picked up speed once they got out of Quarter traffic and headed out of the city. Evie closed her eyes, breathed deeply to control her regrets and concentrated on the woman beside her. She was easy enough to read now. Obviously, with Evie's death imminent, she felt no need to protect her thoughts. "Your husband didn't order his accountant's murder. He doesn't have any idea what happened to him. *You* killed him. Why?"

"He was betraying William with your Detective Murphy. All those years William had trusted him, had given him a good job, with security, benefits, a salary commensurate with his responsibilities, and the man repaid him by funneling information on the business to the authorities." She shrugged. Though her eyes remained closed, Evie felt the slight shifting in the air. "He was disloyal. He threatened William's livelihood. He threatened my security." Another shrug. "He had to die."

"You tricked him into coming to the house. You waited until your husband was out of the office and away from the house, and you called the office and told the accountant that William wanted to see him at the estate. Then you took him to the bayou."

"I didn't want his body found. They were careless when they killed that woman—Celeste. They should have made her disappear, the way I made Mr. Greenley disappear."

When she said *they,* images exploded into Evie's mind. They made her breath catch in her lungs, made her heart stop beating for one painful moment, then begin again in a rhythm that made her tremble. Her eyes jerked open, and she stared at Irina in shock. In panic. In fear.

Irina smiled serenely. "Yes. You thought your Detective Murphy might be safe, but he's not. You don't have to worry about leaving him behind, Evangelina. He'll be joining you shortly. *They'll* see to it."

Chapter 11

Jack rubbed his eyes with the heels of his hands. A few more hours of fruitless searching and watching had left him edgy and frustrated as hell. He was about to give up and head for Remy Sinclair's house to tell the ASAC everything when his pager went off. Turning into a convenience store lot, he jerked the pager from his belt, expecting to see Evie's or Sonny's number displayed. The number wasn't familiar, but he dialed it anyway.

It was the emergency room at Tulane. His hand shaking, his voice barely working, he identified himself and told the clerk he'd been paged.

A moment later Remy Sinclair came on the line. He sounded grim. "I don't know what's up between you and Stewart, but you'd better get over here right away."

"What's happened?"

"Some kids found him and Ted Browning in their car this morning. They'd both been shot. Browning's dead, and Stewart's hurt pretty bad. They're getting ready to take him to surgery, but he's insisting on talking to you first."

"I'll be there in five." Dropping the phone, Jack raced back to his car. Within minutes, he was walking through the ER doors. Sinclair met him near the nurses' station and took him to the cubicle where Keith Stewart lay on a gurney, surrounded by a medical team impatient to take him away. He looked more dead than alive, Jack thought with a shudder, and his voice was so weak that he had to lean close to hear.

"Safe-deposit box," he whispered, the words thready. "My bank... Tapes..."

Jack nodded once. "Who was it, Keith?"

He opened his mouth, grimaced, drew in an achingly loud breath, then whispered, "Cops, Murphy. It was..."

Leaning closer, Jack read his lips as much as listened to the names, and he went cold inside. Cold fury, cold rage—and a hurt so hot that it burned. He stared at Stewart for a moment—for a lifetime—then took a step back. A nurse moved him another step back as, on a signal from the doctor, they pushed the carrier from the cubicle and toward the waiting elevator.

Once they were gone, Sinclair came toward him. "What was he talking about?"

Feeling desperately sick, Jack shifted his gaze to him. "Find out where he banks. There are tapes in his safety-deposit box there that will tell who murdered Celeste Dardanelle and Ted Browning. Then get a warrant—and pray you find them before I kill them."

When he started to leave, Sinclair grabbed his arm. "Who?" he demanded. "A warrant for who? What is this about?"

Jack answered with one cold, bitter word.

"Betrayal."

Though they were still miles from their destination, Evie smelled the bayou as soon as they turned off the paved road onto a dirt lane. On a hot summer's day like today, the smell should evoke pleasant memories of lazy days, splashing in the water, afternoon swims. For a moment, she entertained the pointless regret that she didn't have such memories—no lazy summer days, no splashing. Hell, she'd never even learned to swim.

Irina, in an oddly sympathetic voice, demonstrated *how* pointless the regret was. "It wouldn't make a difference. I'm not going to drown you."

No, she was going to shoot her—and that bit of news didn't come from the great psychic unknown. Evie had seen the pistol tucked in the map pocket on the driver's door.

With a forlorn sigh, she raised her fingers to cover her nose, trying to filter the bayou smell with the scents of her own skin, hand lotion, perfume. Instead, the strongest fragrance on her hand was Jack's aftershave. Sorrowfully, she let it fall again. Better to think of what lay ahead instead of what was lost behind. "Why are you doing this?"

"You tell me. I'm being as open as I can."

A dozen or more images assailed her—dark images. Frightening ones. Pain and heartache, evil and selfishness. Betrayal, revenge, malice. "The malevolence in that house comes from you, not your husband," Evie said softly. "Does he have any idea what you are?"

"He knows what he needs to know—that I make him happy. That I'd do anything for him. That I am the most beautiful, the most valuable, of his possessions. I can keep him safe. I can watch over him in ways that no one else can."

"You knew from the beginning the real reason I came to you."

Irina's smile was lovely. "I knew everything—and you knew nothing, except what I chose to show you."

"Why didn't you send me away?"

"Because that wouldn't have stopped Detective Murphy. They killed Celeste, and he convinced Mr. Greenley to take her place. I killed Mr. Greenley, and he sent you. By keeping you around, I had perfect insight into what progress he was making and what he had planned. I could stop him before he got too dangerous." She made a graceful, dismissive gesture.

"He's obsessed with ruining my husband, and the only way to stop him is to kill him. And this *will* kill him. He's an honorable man. The whore's death almost destroyed him. Now, knowing that he's brought about the death of the only woman he's ever loved will finish the job. I have no doubt of that."

"How can you possibly be so greedy?" Because that was what this was all about—money. MacDougal had it, he gave it to Irina, and she liked it. She liked the life-style he provided her, liked the great house and the servants and the shopping and the attention. She liked being married to a rich and powerful man, and she was willing to kill—had already killed—to keep him in that position.

"We all have our passions. Yours is Detective Murphy. You love him more than life itself. You would kill to protect him, to keep him safe. My passion is wealth. I worked all my life to get it. Now that I have it, yes, I will kill to keep it. It's what matters to me."

"Then I feel sorry for you."

Irina gazed at her so long that the car veered off the road. Gently guiding it back, she smiled. "Yes, I believe you do. And I feel sorry for you, because I'm going to live a long and prosperous life, and you... You're going to die."

The sandy road rounded a bend, then ended abruptly. The bayou lay ahead, exactly as Evie had envisioned it. The water was dark and murky. Logs rotting at the water's edge contributed to scents so overrich and heavy that her stomach shifted uneasily.

Like the big, beautiful house, Irina had made this place evil. She'd brought death here.

Irina shut off the engine, and for a moment the silence echoed in Evie's ears. Then the bayou sounds became obvious—the soft lapping of water against the bank. The buzz of mosquitoes searching for a meal. The call of birds in the tall trees.

She wondered exactly where they were. If her body would

ever be found. If Jack would know what had happened. But what did any of that matter? She would be beyond knowing anything. She would be dead.

Holding the gun in one hand, Irina unfastened the handcuff from Evie's wrist. She resisted the urge to rub it and instead opened the door and climbed out. For an instant, her legs didn't want to support her, and she held onto the door until she felt steadier. Then, at Irina's command, she moved away from and in front of the car.

The sun shone hot and bright on her there in the clearing. She appreciated that. She didn't want to die in darkness, in the gloomy shadows that surrounded them.

Though the grim acceptance that had settled over her told her escape was impossible, she couldn't resist looking around. The water was behind her, and not an option. The road lay in front, one narrow lane that ran through the woods. Its unobstructed path would allow for the easiest progress, but it would also make stopping her pathetically easy. On either side of the clearing were tall trees, with heavy undergrowth that would tangle her feet or no undergrowth—no cover—at all.

"I'm sorry to do this to you."

She looked at Irina again. "No, you're not."

The woman considered her disagreement for a moment, then nodded. "You're right. I'm not particularly sorry. It's just something that's got to be done."

She was raising the pistol from her side when the sounds of an engine became audible. Swiftly, Irina lowered the gun again, then turned to watch the car come around the curve.

Taking advantage of her distraction, Evie bolted out of the clearing and into the shadows. The thin soles of her sandals offered little protection from the rough ground, but she paid no attention. The full folds of her skirt snagged on branches and bushes, but she ran on.

"You fool!" Irina screamed behind her. "She's getting away! Stop her!"

A bullet splintered a branch three feet to her right, forcing her to dart to the left. The second shot kicked up a spray of dirt only inches away, but still she ran. Driven by panic, by fear, by a desperate need to survive, she crashed through the undergrowth, zigzagged around trees, splashed through water.

She ran for her life.

Shoving the door open with enough force to make it bounce on its hinges, Jack stalked into the bar that was a second home to the detectives in his division. The man he was looking for sat at a table in the corner with a beer untouched in front of him, and a handheld radio and a cellular phone beside it. Drumming his fingers nervously on the tabletop, he looked like a man with trouble—but he didn't yet know what trouble was.

Jack stopped across from him, and he slowly looked up. When his gaze connected with Jack's face, he started sweating and he moved one hand reflexively to his belt and the pistol he wore there. He stopped when he saw that Jack's pistol was already drawn.

"You bastard."

Sonny drew a shaky breath. "J.D., buddy, you don't understand."

"You killed Celeste and framed Evie. You killed Greenley. You killed Browning, and you damn near killed Stewart." Jack felt sick just saying it aloud. "You're right. I don't understand. I don't want to. I just want to see that you pay for it."

"It wasn't me, J.D. I didn't kill anyone, I swear. It was Haskins and Gomez. Things just got out of control. It was never supposed to go this far. No one was supposed to die. We were just watching out for MacDougal—messing with the case a bit. Then you put Celeste in, and she was getting too close, and Haskins... The rest just happened. You gotta believe me, J.D." He brushed his hand over his face, then looked up again with an expression of utter misery. "God, I'm glad it's over. I've wanted out from the beginning, but I was afraid.

I knew too much. I thought they would kill me—Haskins and Gomez—if I tried. Oh, God, I'm glad.''

Jack stared at him—at his partner and best friend—and knew he was lying. Haskins and Gomez didn't have the smarts—or the guts—to put together a scam like this. They didn't come up with ideas. They followed orders.

Sonny's orders.

"You gotta believe me, J.D.,'' Sonny said frantically. "You gotta know I would never—''

"I don't know a damn thing about you.''

Sonny took a breath, studied him for a moment, then turned off the panicked act. "Hey, it was worth a try.'' He gave a careless shrug. "You know a few things about me, J.D. You know I always look out for number one. You know I'm always looking to make a deal if it gets me what I want.''

Jack shook his head slowly. "We've got enough evidence to make a case against you, Haskins and Gomez. I don't need your deal.''

"What about Evie?''

"What about her?''

He gestured to the radio. "Irina's got her. We didn't kill Greenley, J.D. Irina did. She's some sort of hotshot mind-reader. She knows stuff. She knows you were still after her old man. She knows you sent Evie in to try to scam her. I've had Haskins watching her, while she's been watching Evie. He just called in a while ago. She picked Evie up off the street this morning, and she's going to kill her.''

A sudden, icy dread gripped Jack, even as he shook his head, even as he denied Sonny's words. "Evie's at her shop. She's safe.''

Sonny slid the cell phone across the table. "Prove it. Call her.''

Shifting the pistol to his left hand, Jack punched in the number. Anna Maria snatched up the phone before the first ring ended. "Anna Ma—''

"My God, Murphy, Evie's gone! She and Martine went for

breakfast and she just disappeared! One minute she was there and the next she was gone and we can't find her anywhere! Murphy, what are we going—''

Moving with great care, as if something inside him just might shatter, he disconnected the call and laid the phone on the table. ''Where are they?'' he asked, as calm and cold as the man who faced him.

''Haskins followed them to some bayou out in the sticks. I'll have to show you. And when we get her away from Irina, I walk away too, right?''

The chances that Sonny was lying were pretty damn good. Jack knew that. But what if he was telling the truth? What if he really did know where Evie was? Trusting him might get Jack killed. Not trusting him might get Evie killed.

It was no contest.

Jack nodded in agreement, though he had no intention of letting anyone walk away, least of all Sonny. Backing away from the table, he gestured with the gun. ''Let's go.'' And, please, God, he added silently. *Don't let us be too late.*

Her ears were ringing, her chest aching, her side throbbing. Evie lay flat on the ground, wriggled into the space underneath a downed tree, and tried to concentrate on both keeping her mind blank and planning her next move. It was hard to concentrate, though, when every breath was agony, when her eyes stung from the sweat, when her legs were so shaky that she doubted she could stand to save her life.

Thank God, right now the best way to save her life was lying still and silent. She didn't know how far she had come from the clearing—miles, judging from her body's desperate demands for rest. In reality, probably not even half a mile. She didn't have a clue how far she would have to travel to be safe, not that it mattered. Ten yards was too far. She would never make it.

A spider crawled across her trembling hand. She flicked it away, took a deep breath and held it, then listened. There were sounds off to the right—footsteps crackling and scuffing. Her hunter, Danny Haskins, was making no effort to silence his movements, which meant they were pretty damn sure she could never escape. They thought her situation was hopeless.

But they were wrong. She was still alive, and as long as there was life, there was hope.

Lowering her head, she rested her forehead on her hands. Her clothes clung heavily to her. Her hair was damp where it brushed her skin. Her skirt was ripped in a half-dozen places, her arms marked with scratches, and she'd lost a sandal somewhere on the run. She'd never been so miserable or so scared in her life.

Correction—in the next instant, she became tremendously more scared. Moving with such grace and ease, Irina approached the log. At first all Evie could see was her feet, in sandals as delicate as her own; then the bright colors of her dress; then, as she knelt in the dirt and ducked low, her face— and her gun.

She smiled sweetly, as if greeting an old friend whom she hadn't seen in a while. For one moment, Evie wondered if the woman was insane, then immediately decided that wasn't the case. Irina was simply evil. She could treat Evie as a friend one moment, put a bullet in her brain the next, and then go about her life as if nothing had happened. Pure, soulless evil.

"She's over here, Detective Haskins," she called, and immediately the lumbering sounds shifted in their direction.

Before Evie could find the strength to scoot out, Haskins reached under the log, grasped her belt and hauled her to her feet. When she swayed unsteadily—due as much to physical exhaustion as to the images that his touch generated—he shifted his grip to her arm. "Why don't you just kill her here instead of making me drag her all the way back to the clearing?"

"My husband pays you well for taking care of his garbage," Irina said firmly. "We'll go back to the cars. That's the spot I've chosen. That's the place where she'll die."

Haskins gave her a shove. "Come on, let's go," he grumbled.

Evie stumbled along, alternately pushed ahead of and pulled behind Haskins. She was too tired to put up a fight and too realistic to try to reason with him. He had sold himself and his badge to the highest bidder, had betrayed the people who trusted him. He had killed Celeste Dardanelle, had strangled the life from her before tossing her body into the lake, and he had taken perverse pleasure in doing so. There was nothing she could say that might persuade him to help her, nothing that might turn him back from the path he'd chosen, and so she said nothing at all.

By the time they reached the clearing, she didn't even have the energy to raise her head. She stood, limp and weary, relying on Haskins for support, until Irina spoke delightedly. "Look, Evangelina, you wished for your Detective Murphy, and here he is. Detective Roberts has brought him to watch you die."

Evie jerked her gaze up. Indeed, there was a third car parked on the road, and Jack and Sonny were walking toward them. Jack looked colder, angrier, more dangerous, than she'd ever seen him. Had Sonny brought him here to kill him? But if that was the case, why did Jack have his gun? Surely Sonny would have disarmed him unless…unless Jack didn't know. Somehow his partner and friend whom he trusted had lured him out here—on the pretext of rescuing her?—and Jack didn't have a clue that he was meant to die here with her.

She opened her mouth to warn him, but Haskins jerked her up hard against him, then clamped his hand over her mouth, forcing her lips cruelly against her teeth, drawing blood.

"How nice of you to bring him, Detective Roberts," Irina said as if welcoming guests to her home. She took a few steps in their direction, then suddenly froze as Sonny brought his gun up in one swift, smooth movement and pulled the trigger. A small, neat hole appeared in the middle of her forehead, with an uglier, bigger exit wound in the back of her head.

She was dead before her body hit the ground. Evie could feel it—could feel all that power and strength and evil snuffed out.

"Well, that takes care of one problem." Sonny swung the gun around toward Jack. "Throw your weapon in the water." When he hesitated, Sonny gestured toward Evie and Haskins. "Throw it in the water, Jack, or we'll give Evie a hole to match."

Until the instant the shot had been fired, Jack had harbored some small hope that Sonny had told the truth in the bar— that he hadn't killed anyone, that the deaths were all Haskins's and Gomez's doing. He'd wanted to believe that the man he'd worked with and trusted and considered his best friend for twelve long years wasn't capable of cold-blooded murder. He'd needed that hope for Evie, for himself.

The hope had died with Irina.

Now he took a few steps toward the water's edge, then tossed the pistol. It landed with a splash before sinking out of sight. "You screwed up this time, Sonny. You think your boss is going to overlook the fact that you killed his wife?"

"I screwed up two years ago when I accepted the first pay-off from MacDougal. I've just been trying to keep from going under ever since."

"How many people do you plan to kill?"

"As many as I have to, to get out of this alive."

Jack slowly shook his head. "By now Sinclair knows everything. He's got the surveillance tapes. He's got people out looking for you."

"But they won't find me." Sonny waved the gun. "Get over there."

Circling Irina's body, Jack stopped a half-dozen feet from Evie. She'd tried to warn him that people were going to die before this case was finished—had tried to warn him that *she* might die—but he'd refused to listen. God, he wished he'd never gotten her involved with this. He wished he'd had time to make up to her for the past year.

He wished he'd gone ahead this morning at her house and said what he'd wanted to say. *I love you.* It wasn't much, but he wouldn't mind dying quite so much if he'd said it one more time.

Haskins joined Sonny on the opposite side of the clearing, leaving Evie to stand on her own. She swayed unsteadily, but Jack resisted the urge to move to her side. Distance between them might not help, but in case he had some great flash of inspiration, it certainly wouldn't hurt.

At just that second, he did get a flash, but it wasn't inspiration. It was the sun glinting on a chrome-plated pistol, fallen half out of Irina's pocket. He wondered how long it would take him to reach it, free it from the fabric and squeeze off two shots. Too long, without some sort of distraction. If only Evie were farther away... If only he could keep both men's attention on him, she could ease closer to the water, could dive in and take cover at its edge while he made a dive for the gun. It might work—*might*—and any chance was better than dying without a fight. If he could just somehow signal her...

Abruptly she looked at him, her expression utterly blank. Then her gaze shifted the slightest bit toward the water and she gave an almost imperceptible nod.

For an instant he was too startled to move; then he swung his gaze back to Sonny. "Your only chance to get out of this alive, Sonny, is to turn yourself in. For God's sake, you killed an FBI agent and a mobster's wife! You think there's anyplace on earth where you can hide from that?"

"I'd rather take my chances running than prison. I put a lot of people in Angola. You think they wouldn't be happy to see me there? You think MacDougal doesn't have connections there?" He shook his head determinedly. "I'll be out of the country before your bodies grow cold. I'm sorry, J.D. You're the last person in the world I wanted to hurt. I just don't see any other way." He steadied the pistol, sighted in on Jack. Beside him Haskins did the same with Evie.

"Now!" Jack shouted, lunging toward Irina, landing hard and coming up with the gun as Sonny's first shot tore into the woman's lifeless body. He fired once, rolled away toward the cover of the nearest car and fired again. Haskins went down.

Jack shifted his aim to Sonny. His partner—his friend—hadn't sought cover. He was standing straight and tall, as calm as if this were just another summer day, wearing a look of sick satisfaction as he took aim on Evie and squeezed the trigger.

The shot sounded like an explosion, and, for a moment, time stopped. She stood on the bank's edge, a startled look on her face as if she couldn't quite understand where the blood staining her blouse had come from. Then, in slow motion, as gracefully and elegantly as she did everything, she tumbled backward into the water and disappeared beneath the surface.

Jack surged to his feet, and a scream reverberated through his body, burst through his head and rushed in his ears, drowning out the pops as he emptied his clip into Sonny. Satisfied that his partner—his friend—was dead, he dropped the gun and dived into the water, and he prayed.

Vehicles lined the narrow road, parked half on the shoulder, half in the dirt. Besides the original three, there were cars belonging to the sheriff's department, the NOPD, the FBI. There were two cars from the medical examiner's office, waiting to claim the bodies, and an ambulance. Back closer to the road were the reporters, all wanting details and grisly shots of the scene.

Evie stood beside the ambulance, ignoring the paramedics' attempts to coax her onto the gurney. They'd cleaned and bandaged her shoulder, front and back, and had tried to start an IV, but she'd refused. She'd accepted the blanket they offered, though, and wrapped it around her sodden, torn and now cut clothes, and she'd stood in the sun, giving it a chance to warm her from the outside in.

So far she was still feeling pretty cold.

Jack sat at the edge of the bayou a dozen yards away. He'd told their story to the first officers on the scene, repeated it for virtually everyone who followed and then had gone to sit alone. His head was bent, his shoulders rounded. He looked so forlorn. So lost.

Leaning against the ambulance, she managed with some effort to unfasten her one remaining shoe, then made her way to him. The weeds pricked at her tender feet, but she had enough discomfort in her shoulder—and in her heart—to make such minor irritation meaningless.

Stopping behind him, she rested her good hand on his shoulder. He didn't react in any way. "It wasn't your choice, Jack. You did what Sonny forced you to do."

"I trusted him." His voice was raw, thick with anger. "I trusted him with my life—with *your* life."

"That proves how good he was at his lies." She moved to his side, started to sit and winced at the stab of pain that shot from her shoulder out. "Can you help me down?"

Quickly, carefully, he lifted her into his arms, then settled her on the ground beside him. "You should be at the hospital."

"I'm not going without you."

He settled his haunted gaze on the water. "I almost got you killed."

"There's a lot of blame to go around for what happened here. I'd say the least of it belongs to you and me."

That made him look at her—really look at her—for the first time since he'd pulled her, waterlogged and sputtering, out of the bayou. "Not you. You aren't responsible for any of this."

"We all made decisions, Jack, and the results of all those decisions converged here today. Sonny and Danny Haskins decided to sell their honor to the devil for a bigger paycheck. Irina decided that power and wealth were more valuable to her than anything, even life. The FBI agents decided to protect their investigation at all costs. You decided to trust men you believed to be as good and honorable as you."

"I decided to force you to help—to risk your life."

"You didn't make that decision for me," she said gently. "I could have afforded to be shut down long enough to take legal action against you. I could have made some effort to refuse you. Even the smaller decisions... I could have refused to leave the house for breakfast this morning, and when those boys surrounded Martine so Irina could get me into her car, I could have refused. I could have stood my ground and screamed. I could have run, gotten help, fought. Instead, I decided to go with Irina—to come here with her. I think..."

When she didn't continue, he prompted her. "You think what?"

"I think...maybe I didn't want to refuse you. Maybe I wanted to be coerced into helping you, because..." A blush warmed her cheeks as she touched his cheek. "I'd never stopped loving you, Jack, and I missed you so desperately. Maybe, deep down inside, I decided that having you in my life that way was better than not having you there at all."

Giving her a look that started the warming inside that the sun hadn't managed, he brushed his hand over her hair. "You know what my biggest regret was?"

"That we were both going to die?"

"Well, yeah. But my second biggest regret was that we were going to die without me telling you that I love you."

She swallowed over the lump in her throat. "You've told me before."

"But I hadn't told you this time, and I said a lot of things before that kind of negated that one." He gently tucked a clump of wet, matted hair behind her ear. "I love you, Evie."

"I love you, too."

"I'm going to marry you."

"I'm going to let you."

Satisfied with her response, he lifted her into his lap, settling her so that her injured shoulder was away from him, and for a time they sat quietly. She rested her head on his shoulder, listened to the steady beat of his heart, and knew in her own heart that they were going to be all right. They would deal with all the betrayals, all the hurts and shocks, and they would come out of it stronger than ever, with their love stronger than ever.

After a while, he looked down at her. "Do I smell as bad as you do?"

Evie's laughter burst out, then ended quickly in a grimace of pain. "Yes, you do."

"Do I look as ragged as you?"

She touched his face, smoothed her fingers across his jaw, brushed them over his mouth. He automatically kissed them. "More so."

"Let's get back into town, where we can clean up and the doctors can do whatever they need for your shoulder." Holding her carefully, he got to his knees, then to his feet and started toward the ambulance. She knew she should tell him to put her down, that she could manage the short distance under her own power, but she liked being in his arms too much.

"Does this mean you can read me now?" he asked conversationally as he lowered her to the gurney in the back of the ambulance.

"What are you talking about?"

"Back there. You knew I wanted you to dive into the water. Even though you can't swim, you were going to do it."

"Of course I was going to do it. I trust you."

The paramedics settled her in, then closed the doors, giving them some measure of privacy. A moment later the front doors closed, and they began the slow journey back to the road.

Jack slid from the bench to his knees beside her, smoothed the blanket over her, then leaned close. "So...can you read me now?"

"I don't know. Maybe. You're not so close-minded anymore."

"Do you know what I'm thinking now?"

Laughing, she slid her good arm around his neck and pulled

him closer. "I don't need to be a psychic to know that," she murmured. "Any woman could tell…"

"Not any woman. Just you." And then he kissed her, a lovely, claiming kiss that made her heart ache and made her long for home and their bed and a body that didn't hurt with every breath.

When he drew back to catch his breath, she caught her own breath, then laced her fingers with his. "Do *you* know what *I'm* thinking now?"

Solemnly he shook his head.

"I've found someone safe, and I'm holding on tight, and I'm never, ever letting go."

* * * * *

Look for the exciting debut of
Marilyn Pappano's new series,
THE COWBOY CODE.
Don't miss CATTLEMAN'S PROMISE,
available in May
from Silhouette Intimate Moments.

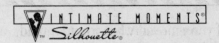

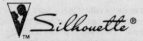